CIRCLES
OF
DECEIT

PAUL CW BEATTY

Circles of Deceit

Published by The Conrad Press in the United Kingdom 2020

Tel: +44(0)1227 472 874
www.theconradpress.com
info@theconradpress.com

ISBN 978-1-913567-36-1

Copyright © Paul Beatty, 2020

The moral right of Paul Beatty to be identified as author of this work has been asserted in accordance with the Copyright, Designs and Patents Act 1988.

Typesetting and Cover Design by:
Charlotte Mouncey, www.bookstyle.co.uk

The Conrad Press logo was designed by Maria Priestley.

Printed and bound in Great Britain by Clays Ltd, Elcograf S.p.A.

To Willow and Dylan,
the next generation of our better selves.

CHAPTER I

The National Petition

Dr Kay stood and listened as the bells of Ludworth's mills sounded. It was time for most of the workers to drag themselves home to eat whatever the day had put on their tables if indeed, they were lucky enough to have tables at which to eat.

Ludworth's mills, unlike the better paying or more prosperous, larger mills of Stockport, eked out a living in these days of poor trade. They were small but they endured, and though the wages were low, wages were still to be earned.

It would have been natural to think that all the piecers and weavers, carders and warehousemen would have gladly gone home for rest, but Dr Kay knew better. Though they were leaving the mills in small groups, in a few minutes, streams of fustian jackets, woollen shawls and children's caps would converge on where he stood, at the door of the Primitive Methodist chapel.

Made of serviceable stone, the chapel had a double row of arched windows on two floors, with a side door which opened into a small tiled hall and a staircase that could be followed up to the sanctuary. On Sundays, the members, many of whom would also attend this evening, made their way to sing their praises to God in that sanctuary, but tonight, the meeting would be in the Sunday School hall on the ground floor. This evening was about business, politics and change.

Kay went in and joined Mr Bracegirdle, a middle-aged man 15 years Kay's senior, one of the stewards of the chapel, who was already seated at a trestle table. Dr Kay went over and, ignoring the ledgers and minute book, took a copy of a four-square printed sheet off a large pile. He held it up, read it, and put it back in its place.

It was only a few minutes when he heard the door open and the first worker came in. The room filled with people. Some sat on the small benches used by the Sunday School, while the children sat on the floor at the front. Soon the hall was full, but still, they came. Doors were propped open so those outside in the entrance hall could hear. Eventually, there were groups of people gathered outside the hall, looking in through open windows. Mr Bracegirdle glanced at his watch and stood.

'Welcome, Brothers and Sisters. Thank you for coming to this extraordinary meeting of the Ludworth and District Society of Chartists. Our first piece of business is to elect a chair for these proceedings.'

'If I can be so bold, there's no need for that Mr Bracegirdle. You've never done 'owt to offend, and we trust ye. In any case, we know where ye live if we've got a bone to pick with ye!' Laughter followed.

'Are we in agreement Brothers and Sisters?' Everyone in the room shouted, 'Aye!' at the tops of their voices and started to clap. Mr Bracegirdle looked embarrassed, 'Thank you for your confidence.'

His proposer interrupted him, 'Alright, alright, we don't need a sermon squire! What's next?'

'I think Dr Kay is in the best place to address that. I'll hand over to him.'

Kay held up the sheet of paper from the pile, the one that he had already read. 'Brothers and sisters these are the details of the new National Petition approved by the Chartist Conference.'

'Bloody sight longer than the last one!' shouted someone at the back to general laughter.

'Hush yer swearing, Jo Briggins,' chided a grey-haired woman. 'This is a Sunday School and I'm still fit enough to box yer ears like I used to when I was teaching thee.'

'Jo, I think you're right in essence,' said Dr Kay, 'It's definitely longer.'

'God bless him, but that's what happens when you get an Irishman like O'Connor to draft it,' shouted another voice.

'Whatever we think about the document, the law is clear, we have to know what the petition says. Then we must adopt it as a statement we agree with before we can sign it ourselves or ask others to sign.'

A hand went up somewhere near the back. An old man got up, cap in his hands. 'Do it say anything different from our six principles?' Muttering started as they said their well-honed catechism.

'A vote for every man over twenty-one.'

'Secret ballot so no bugger can tell 'ow I vote.'

'Tory, in yon Jo's case, no doubt!'

'No property qualification to be Member of Parliament, so any of us can stand!'

'Except if you're a woman!'

'Don't worry about that Mary. First job for a Chartist parliament.'

'Payment for Members so they can do their jobs in London.'

'Equal constituency sizes so small constituencies can't outvote big uns.'

'Annual parliaments to stop fraud and bribery.'

Dr Kay raised his hand. 'Yes, Brothers and Sisters, all our principles are still here.'

'Then what more is there to say? Let us vote!'

'Are you all so moved?' asked Mr Bracegirdle.

'We are!'

'Then all those in favour?' Every hand in the room was raised.

What came next was a storm of activity. People started signing on the spot. There was much back-slapping, congratulations and hugging.

Hands were steadied by friends so that older Chartists might sign for themselves. Those who could only make their mark had them attested by others, who initialled the petition forms.

For those intending to approach their neighbours, the terms of the petition were given out, along with blank forms.

Gradually the happy storm passed, and people drifted away. Dr Kay and Mr Bracegirdle were the last. The evening light had faded and there was only the glow of the sun left in the autumn sky. Mr Bracegirdle locked the chapel door and shook hands with his friend.

'A fine meeting Leslie.'

'Indeed. They are certainly stalwart.'

'I noticed you did not tell them about the national target for the number of signatures?'

'No, I thought best to avoid that. Four million signatures is a terribly high bar to jump, but that is what the national leadership believe is required to be sure that Parliament will debate the issue: there or thereabout.'

'Will we make it?'

'That entirely depends on the enthusiasm, efforts of the members, and whether there is significant intimidation or violence as signatures are collected. Regrettably, these are times when the possibility of that sort of interference cannot be dismissed.'

CHAPTER 2

An evening excursion

Men of Manchester, Feargus O'Connor Esq. will deliver three lectures, in The Hall of Science, Campfield, on Monday, Tuesday and Wednesday the 7th, 8th and 9th March. The lecture on Monday will be on the Use of Land in Ireland, that on Tuesday will be on Repeal of the Legislative Union between England and Ireland, and that on Wednesday 9th will be on Class Legislation and Government.

John Murray, Secretary, National Charter Association

'Slow down you brutes!' came the voice of the coachman, struggling with the horses.

'I'll wedge the wheels, Fred,' shouted the footman. There was a pause as the four-wheeler came to a stop, then the footman opened the door. 'The Hall of Science, Ladies and Gentlemen.' He tipped his cap.

'So, this is it?' said Elizabeth.

'Yes, this is it indeed,' said Mr Cooksley.

'Well Thomas,' said Mr Hopgood, 'Are you ready to run the gauntlet of this cathedral of atheism? Are you not worried that there will be inscribed over the door, Abandon hope all ye who enter here?'

'Even if I had never been in this building before, I would not be afeared of entering as a pilgrim.'

'What, would you not even be afeared of the giant of a man who inspired it and its counterparts up and down the country?'

'Robert Owen, you mean. No, he would not fright me. In fact, I should like to shake his hand. He should stand as a reminder to all us church folk that when the Church fails, God uses others to bring hope and vision to the people.'

The ladies took the arms of their husbands. Constable Josiah Ainscough was surprised when Rosemary, the Hopgood's daughter, slipped her hand into the crook of his arm.

'It is a fine building is it not Josiah?' she remarked.

'It is indeed,' he replied, wondering what Rosemary's intimate little gesture might mean.

Of late, Constable Josiah Ainscough's duties had been exhausting. The cotton industry was in one of its periodic downturns and everyone in Stockport was poorer as a result. There had been more petty crime, more domestic violence, and more trade disputes. The worst thing was the number of people beaten up for being, or not being, Chartists, League-men, Irish, or some other section of the community.

Coming off duty earlier that day, he had found a folded note on his doorstep.

Dear Josiah,

It has come to my attention that Feargus O'Connor, the famous Chartist leader, is to speak this evening at the Hall of Science in Manchester. His subject will be the Use of Land in Ireland. It's a topic of interest to our Catholic

neighbours and a rare opportunity to hear a real expert
on the matter. If you are free, your presence would be very
welcome. We will meet at the Tiviot Dale Manse at six
o'clock. I have engaged a coach to take us into Manchester,

Yours affectionately,
Thomas Cooksley

Josiah smiled to himself. As ever his estimable guardian was right. Hearing Feargus O'Connor on his expert subject of land reform in Ireland was an opportunity not to be missed. He would make the effort – there was also the interest of seeing the man who was leading the fight for the adoption of the Second Chartist Petition speak.

*

The Tiviot Dale party consisted of six. As well as Josiah himself, and his guardians, Martha and Thomas, there were Elizabeth and Richard Hopgood, and their daughter Rosemary.

Richard Hopgood was one of the growing band of Methodists making a mark in the town's business. He had worked his way up from an office boy to chief clerk in a medium-sized cotton mill. There he would have stayed, except that he inherited a financial stake in a rather rundown calico dyeing works in the town. Given this opportunity, he had decided to take control of the firm and run it himself, a determination that had been rewarded. Despite the state of the cotton trade, Hopgood and Co. were now stable and profitable.

There was a queue at the Hall's main door. 'Penny to get in the body of the Hall, tuppence for the gallery, sixpence to sit with Mr O'Connor on the stage. All proceeds to the cause of the Charter.'

The man gathering the fees looked at them, took off his cap and, with an impudent grin, bowed. 'Are you Ladies and Gentlemen bound for the stage?' He was short and fair-haired, about Josiah's age but more muscular across the shoulders.

'They'll not be welcomed up there, especially with that peeler bastard with them!' shouted one of his companions.

'Hold your tongue, there are ladies present! Anyhow, you might get more than you bargain for. I reckon the Reverend Gentleman could preach longer than you'd be prepared to listen, even with a pint pot in your hand!"

Mr Cooksley paid, and they went up the gallery stairs. The Hall of Science had a three-sided steeply raked balcony, with blocks of seats divided by gangways. On the ground floor below was an open stage with an impressive brass lectern. The seats on the stage were starting to fill with dignitaries.

'I see some of the choir are already in their places,' quipped Mr Hopgood.

'Personally, it is not the choir that would worry me if I were taking this service.'

Josiah could see what he meant. It was standing room only in front of the stage. Just below the lectern, there was a group of about fifteen well-built men. A small family of mill workers and their children tried to make their way to the front for a better view and immediately the men formed an outer line facing away from the stage, folding their arms. A particularly burly man stepped forward from their ranks holding a heavy walking stick, with which he patted his hand. When the grand-father of the children spoke to him, the walking stick was used to prod the older man in the chest for his impertinence. The family group retreated.

People were filling up the balcony as well. Three well-dressed middle-aged men came and sat across the gangway from the Tiviot Dale party.

'I hope he's fierier than he was last night,' said one.

'Bound to be. Land reform is one thing, but Home Rule for Ireland is certain to produce much more fireworks than the price of potatoes in Connemara,' said another.

Josiah looked towards Mr Cooksley, who had blenched. 'Josiah if last night was land reform, then tonight will be Repeal of the Legislative Union between England and Ireland or Home Rule for Ireland for short. When O'Connor tried to make that lecture in Birmingham there was a brawl. Oh my, what a terrible mistake! We must get the ladies away from here before the meeting starts!'

A door at the back of the stage opened and the platform party, including Feargus O'Connor, took their places at the front of the stage. Immediately the men who had prevented the family group getting near the front of the stage unfurled and waved banners. These were not Chartist banners. They were green, and those who raised them were shaking their fists at O'Connor.

Josiah had never seen any banners used by the people opposed to the Chartists, but there had been violence in other places where people purporting to be supporters of the Anti-Corn Law League had confronted them. His suspicion was confirmed as a chant started. 'No Charter before Free Trade. No Charter before Free Trade.'

The gentleman who had led in the platform party stood

14

behind the lectern and raised his hands for order.

'Please, Gentlemen. Please, let us proceed in a dignified way.'

'Josiah what is happening?' asked Martha Cooksley.

'There's going to be a riot,' he said quietly, without adornment, but Rosemary Hopgood heard what he had said.

'A riot! Oh, Josiah save us!' She seized his arm so tightly, he thought she might be going to faint at any moment.

'Hush child,' said Martha, taking Rosemary's hands firmly in hers. 'Josiah is a better judge of such matters, and we will be safe if we take his advice. Mr Hopgood, please calm your daughter. What shall we do Josiah?'

'Get up slowly and go now. Go quickly but don't rush, especially on the stairs. You don't want to fall if there's a crush. I will bring up the rear.'

'Good,' said Martha, 'Follow me.' Impelled by his mother's resolve, the group moved to the stairs. Josiah saw them start down. He was about to make his escape when he turned his attention to what was happening on the platform.

The man at the lectern was still trying to start the meeting in good order. 'I wish to propose the Rev. Mr Schofield should take the chair this evening.' But the League-men had lifted someone and pushed him onto the platform. He barged the man who was proposing Mr Schofield out of the way. At the top of his voice, he shouted, 'We'll have no Chartist placeman. Doyle! Doyle! Doyle!'

Two large Chartists came from the wings and, none too ceremoniously threw Doyle's proposer off the stage. Josiah started to make good his escape, while below the Chartists started to chant, 'Schofield! Schofield!'

Mr Schofield came forward to the lectern.

'There's going to be a vote,' said one of the Chartists across the gangway. A forest of hands shot up and the volume of cries of 'Schofield! Schofield!' doubled.

On the platform, a man stood up. He put a bugle to his lips and blew. The note echoed around the hall, a rallying signal for every fit Chartist to look to his fists. With a terrible cry, they fell on the League-men.

CHAPTER 3

Mêlée and relief

Every respectable citizen started to run for any safe way out. It was clear that the League-men had come prepared with staves of wood, metal bars and even the occasional cudgel, as well as stones to throw. The people on the stage were taking cover behind their chairs as best they could. Only Mr O'Connor seemed undaunted, coming to the front of the stage, to cheer on his Chartist boys.

Rapidly the fighting broke down into small groups; two or three Chartists onto a couple of League-men, or vice versa. In one mêlée, three Chartists were beating seven bells out of Mr Doyle.

Suddenly, a small boy emerged, running from the crowd. He was going as fast as his legs would carry him away from the fighting. Still, on the balcony, Josiah wondered where all the children were who had come into the hall with family groups. Then he saw that in one corner there was a growing collection of children. They were being protected from being trapped in the brawl by some of the older men and women, but their escape route was cut off.

The three men from across the gangway were still there, watching what was happening, bouncing on the balls of their feet and throwing shadow punches in solidarity with the real punches being landed below.

'Oh yes, take that sir, take that,' said one of the gentlemen, almost jumping into the air.

'Uff, that must have hurt. Come on, get up, give as good as you get.'

Josiah thought they must be old soldiers. Better to think of them as Three Musketeers: Athos, Porthos and Aramis. Up for the fight but just too far away, and perhaps a bit too sore in the joints to get involved.

One glanced over towards Josiah, followed the direction in which of Josiah was looking and saw the children. He tapped one of the friends on the shoulder and soon all of them were looking at the children's situation.

Josiah looked across to them. 'If I could get down there, I'd have to see what a uniform might manage.'

'Good for you,' said Porthos.

'Seems we might be able to lend a hand here lads,' said Athos.

Josiah started to pay them more attention.

'There is another way down,' said Aramis, 'Follow us.'

The Musketeers led Josiah to the far end of the balcony, where it met the wall next to the stage. On the right, half-hidden by the rake of the balcony floor, was a low doorway that led to an iron, spiral staircase to the ground floor.

'Thank you, gentlemen, I'll do my best,' said Josiah. But the three were taking off their coats and smart clothes.

'We're going to make sure you do, we're coming with you,' said Aramis.

Once they emerged onto the ground floor the problem of getting to the children was clear, they were on the other side of the stage, in front of which was the fiercest fighting.

'We could go across the stage,' suggested Josiah, 'and bring them back to this door.'

'I don't think even Dianne Burrell could get them, children, up the spiral stair. They must be frightened to death,' said Athos.

'Who is Dianne Burrell?' asked Josiah.

'She's the black-haired beauty who was organising them,' said Porthos.

'So, it will have to be a relief column then,' said Josiah. 'We'll have to skirt around the front of the stage and push in from the far side. With a bit of luck, we'll be able to open a corridor up for them to escape.'

'Good plan,' said Athos. 'Everyone ready?'

'For Dianne and the Charter!' shouted Porthos.

'Charge!' yelled Aramis. It was all Josiah could do to resist shouting, 'All for one and one for all!'

The outflanking manoeuvre worked well, but as soon as they tried to push into the crowd towards the children, the world disintegrated into a fury of ducking blows, landing punches and acquiring bruises. Looking back later, Josiah didn't remember much of the next few minutes. Unconscious to his own pain, he surrendered to the business of inflicting pain on others. He seized an arm here, dislocating it with ease and returned punches with his fists. At one point he smashed someone's nose with the ball of his hand, hearing the bone crack and grind as he did it.

Dianne Burrell, whoever she might be, must have seen what they were trying to do because after a little time they were joined by a wedge of men and mill women who had pushed out to help them.

The older men could be quite handy, but the mature mill women, most of them mothers with children trapped in the enclave, were in a league of their own in terms of viciousness and want of fair play. They did a good line in kicking shins with their clogs, removing the courage of younger opponents with names and curses that would have made a sailor blush – but their most fearsome tactic was gouging at faces and eyes.

Finally, the siege was relieved, and the children streamed out and away. A woman, who Josiah realized must be Dianne Burrell, turned to the Musketeers.

'Thank you, brothers,' she said.

Athos blushed like a boy of twelve. 'It was nothing,' he said, though the blood from a gash across his forehead and the way he was holding his shoulder spoke differently. 'Anything for you Dianne.'

Josiah could see why Dianne was so idolised. The black hair, the pale complexion, her general bearing: upright, assured. She was well named after the goddess of hunting – fierce and courageous.

CHAPTER 4

A blade in the moonlight

Josiah's consideration of Dianne Burrell's merits was interrupted by a tap on the shoulder. 'Constable, I was wondering if you could help in a delicate matter?' It was the Rev. Schofield.

'Of course, Sir.'

'I wondered if you might try to persuade Mr O'Connor to quit the field. I am greatly feared that he is placing himself in danger and that his presence is encouraging the fighting.'

It seemed to Josiah that very little encouragement was needed to fight, but duty was duty. 'I will do my best,' he said.

Feargus O'Connor was a "big" man: an important politician and a fiery public orator whose words could reach the intellectual or common person, whether he spoke in the House of Commons or to a Chartist meeting. But as Josiah approached O'Connor only one meaning of the word big had any real importance. O'Connor was over six feet tall, muscular and a daunting physical presence. Josiah wondered if saying yes to this diplomatic mission had been a bigger mistake than coming to the wrong lecture.

The League-men had run out of stones, and the Chartists were driving them back. The fighting was now in the middle of the hall, and though still fierce in places, as the noise of battle made clear, it would not be long before the Chartists were victorious.

In the meantime, the stage had become a safe refuge and the platform party no longer needed to cower. Other Chartist supporters, still unable to escape from the hall, were drifting onto the stage. O'Connor had his back towards Josiah and was remonstrating with his aides and various others.

'No, I will not go. I will be damned if I'll be driven from this platform by Cobden's lickspittles!'

As Josiah and the Reverend approached, O'Connor turned. 'Good God Schofield, what sort of little rat have you dared to drag up here to talk to me! Get that Constable out of my sight!'

'Please Feargus,' said Schofield. 'Listen to what he has to say.'

'What he has to say! God's Bones! I thought I had an agreement with the Manchester Police that they would not send officers to this meeting! Why is this scalpeen disobeying the orders of the Superintendent of Police! Get him out of here!'

Josiah swallowed hard. 'Mr O'Connor, I am not from the Manchester Police, I am a member of the Stockport force.'

'Then you have no right at all to be here. You're outside your jurisdiction!'

In for a penny in for a pound, thought Josiah. 'I am not here in any official capacity, Sir. I am here as an ordinary citizen.'

'Then why are you in uniform?'

'In obedience to Mr Peel's guidelines for the conduct of all police officers; that we should always be in uniform in public so that we can be identified and therefore not be accused of spying on the populace, Sir!'

A slight smile passed across O'Connor's lips. 'I had forgotten that particular piece of guidance, and I should not wish to deny any citizen the privilege of hearing my magnificent oratory,' he said, raising a laugh from the onlookers. 'But you picked to attend a lecture with a rare controversial topic Constable.'

'That's because he's here on the wrong night!' said Athos from behind to more laughter.

'I asked the constable to talk to you Feargus,' said The Rev. Schofield, 'He agrees with me that your continued presence here is making the fighting worse and that you may be personally in danger.'

Athos chipped in again, 'Mr O'Connor, the constable has already played a gallant part in helping my friends to get the children trapped by the fighting to safety. I think you should listen to him, at least in recognition of that service.'

'Very well. What have you to say, Constable?'

'That violence of this nature is no substitute for reasoned argument, and that you, above all, Sir, should prize reasoned argument, since your effective wielding of that weapon in court is the reason, you're here at all.'

'Hm. Not only a citizen but a man who knows his own mind.' This remark is greeted with more laughter. 'Have you any more gems of wisdom to share with us?'

'Yes, Sir. There is no doubt that you are a man of courage as well as conviction. I saw you come down to the front of the stage when the stones were being thrown thick and fast. But I judge you to have a foolhardy streak when goaded, as I have myself. Mr Schofield is worried that real harm may come to you if you do not withdraw. He speaks out of affection for you, I with the dispassionate eye of a policeman. I think you should heed his counsel.'

The crowd of Chartists that had come up to the stage for safety had grown, and many of them were rather excited to be so close to their hero. One person was not agitated though, and that was what drew Josiah's attention to him. This man was small, light framed. His coat and general appearance were the same as dozens of others who had come to the lecture. His cap had a broad peak, pulled down low so that his face was in shade. Josiah could not get a clear idea of what he looked like, but he moved smoothly, threading his way purposefully towards Feargus O'Connor; a cat stalking a bird.

Instinctively, Josiah sidestepped an astonished O'Connor and threw himself at the man. The gun Josiah had glimpsed was knocked clear and rattled harmlessly away across the platform. A woman screamed, O'Connor saw the gun, the would-be assassin darting away.

O'Connor looked at Josiah. 'It seems you have a valid point Constable.'

Josiah was already chasing the man, who made it to the main doors, turning sharp left outside. He ran across the main road, dodging a horse and cart, and fled down a narrow street. Josiah was close behind and managed to see his quarry take a sharp turn into a narrow lane. Josiah was still with him but after two more quick turns, lost him and had to stop.

There was a small square just ahead from which led four alleyways. Two seemed to head back towards the Liverpool Road, the other two continuing down towards a canal basin. Josiah's luck had run out. There was a faint rustle to his left and he felt a moment's panic that he had been outmanoeuvred.

From a deep shadow, a voice whispered, 'Don't move your head or even breathe deeply Constable. Trust me, I'm a Manchester officer. Keep looking straight ahead. He went first left. Beware, he'll wait for you at the next turn. He'll try to stop you there before he has to run away across the open land beyond. Go left slowly. I'll go around the other side of the building and take him by surprise. One of my officers is watching on the open side; he'll have seen him. With a bit of luck, there'll be three of us to take him. Nod your head if you agree.'

Josiah nodded. He turned into the nearest and narrowest of the alleys and walked down it with as much nerve as he could muster, his heart pounding. He could see the end of the alley outlined by moonlight. He tried not to hesitate, feeling that any pause might indicate to his quarry that he knew that the man was hiding.

Then there were voices shouting; someone had been discovered. Josiah ran forward. Ten yards beyond the buildings a uniformed policeman was fighting desperately with Josiah's quarry. The policeman had his truncheon out, but the man was elusive as a snake. A second figure came around the farther side of the building, but the assassin had the advantage. He raised his hand, and Josiah saw the pale flash of a knife as it stabbed downwards, and the officer fell.

The quarry was away again, Josiah hard on his heels, running along the backs of buildings and down a slope towards a group of barges. The assassin ran straight over the moored barges, using them as a makeshift bridge. Uncertain, Josiah chose the prudent route around the basin, losing ground as a result.

About a hundred yards ahead, on the other side of a warehouse, was a carriage with its door open. The assassin threw himself in and the horses were whipped to life. Hands pulled him to safety and the carriage door closed. All Josiah could do was stand uselessly in the road watching Feargus O'Connor's attacker escape.

CHAPTER 5

A well-appointed Station House

Pursuit over, Josiah was aware of the bruises he had acquired in the riot. His ribs hurt, and once he started to cough, he was soon bent double gasping for breath. When, at last, he could breathe with confidence, he walked back to where a group of men, none of them in uniform, were surrounding the officer who had been struck down.

The owner of the voice he had heard out of the darkness was talking to the officer, 'You were very lucky not to have been killed.'

'Yes, Inspector.'

'I told everyone that they were not to approach the bastard alone. If you had waited, he'd have been outnumbered three to one.'

'Due respect Sir, how was I to know that you and that other officer were about to appear from around the corner? Not that I had any choice; as soon as he saw me, he flew at me.'

'Constable Tyler, you just don't have enough faith in the genius that comes with rank, and that's all there is to it. But seriously Bob can you walk?'

'I think so, Sir.'

'Good.' The Inspector turned to one of the men who were not in uniform, that Josiah had thought was an ordinary

26

passer-by. 'Hudd, go with him to make sure he gets home safely.' Josiah realised that these men were in fact policemen.

The Inspector addressed the others, 'Very well gentlemen. My thanks for your efforts this evening. If tonight's your normal duty night then please get along to your beats, the rest of you get some rest.' Then, speaking directly to one of the officers, before nodding towards Josiah, he said, 'Rogers, and you too. I'll need you back at the station house before you go home.'

*

The Central Manchester station house was not far. Over the main entrance, there was an oil lamp shrouded in a square blue glass lantern with Police inscribed on the front. The station house itself had a front desk manned by an officer with the most impressive mustachio Josiah had ever seen.

'Anything to report, Sandiway?'

'Nothing Sir. It's been a very quiet night. People shut their doors and stayed in. I dare say they were worried about trouble at the meeting.'

The door from the street creaked open, and four young officers, all like Rogers, dressed in ordinary working clothes, came in. The last was a young man carrying Josiah's hat: it was the man who had taken the money at the door of the Hall of Science from the Tiviot Dale party. He offered Josiah the hat. 'Your party got away without mishap and should be well on their way back to Stockport by now, he whispered.

'At last, I thought you five would never get here. The sooner we get on, the quicker we'll be away to our beds,' said the Inspector

Josiah now understood. He had misjudged the number of

officers who had been policing the meeting. Uniformed officers had provided a perimeter out of sight of the hall, inside had been the incognito officers. The officer with the hat passed it to him. 'Handed in by three friends of yours. They thought you'd need it back.'

The inspector led the way to an office at the back of the station. Josiah and the other officers followed. There were no other chairs in the office, so all they could do was prop themselves up on any bit of furniture they could find if they didn't wish to stand.

'So, let's see what you lot have learned about basic detection. What can you tell me about the stranger within our midst?'

Rogers was the first to speak. 'Well, from his uniform I know he's part of the Stockport force, but that's all I can tell.'

There was a silence in which feet were shuffled.

The officer who had retrieved the hat spoke up. 'I think I can add a few facts from my observations. He is from Stockport and off duty. Second, he has very good taste in companions, especially female companions, judging by the girl on his arm when he arrived, though I deduce he's likely to be a man of serious mind. Not surprising that it appears he's a son of a Methodist manse, and only a young lady of the Methody persuasion would think that a lecture at the Hall of Science was an ideal good time.' There was a chuckle around the room.

The Inspector smiled. 'That's very good Ingliss if it's right. Anyone anything else to add?'

'Well actually Inspector, I think I've still not completely shot my bolt. I think this officer's name is Ainscough, Josiah Ainscough. The tyro who was involved in the Children of Fire case in the Furness Vale last year. But the best part of all is that he was only present this evening by mistake. He intended to be at last night's meeting. He fished up this evening in error.' This time Ingliss was greeted not by a polite chuckle but a full round of laughter, including from the Inspector.

'Well, how this Constable Ainscough got here this evening is our good luck. Constable, my Chosen Men you see before you, and the Manchester police force in general, owe you a debt of thanks. While we were watching for an attack on Phillip Burrell, Constable Ainscough was saving our bacon and the life of Feargus O'Connor to boot. I am Inspector Markus Fidel,' the Inspector said, standing to shake Josiah by the hand.

'Ingliss, after Mr Ainscough you were closest to the action. Did you see anything?'

'Not much Sir. Nothing at all before Constable Ainscough knocked the pistol out of the assassin's hand. I managed to get a grip on his coat as he rushed past me at the main door, but he shook me off.'

'So that leaves Constable Ainscough here as the only one likely to be able to recognise him if he saw him again?'

'Sorry Inspector, though I was closest, his cap put his face in shadow. He was small and rather lightly built, but the only distinctive feature was the way he moved: he was very calm, no panic or even urgency. I think I'd say he had a very great nerve, as cool as anyone we've ever encountered.'

'And he had help, organised in advance,' added Josiah.

'How so?' said Inspector Fidel.

'There was a carriage waiting for him the other side of a transhipment wharf. Someone inside helped him in.'

'I don't suppose you saw anything of that cove?'

'Only hands grabbing at our assailant's clothes. The coach

was a four-wheeler with a pair of horses capable of making a quick exit. But it was well placed in deep shadow. I wouldn't even recognise the coach if I saw it again. May I ask a question Inspector?'

'Of course.'

'You said you had your eyes on the wrong target. Did you expect someone to be attacked at the meeting?'

'Fair question. We got a tip-off that there might be an attack on Phillip Burrell, the Chartist.'

'Is he connected to Dianne Burrell?'

'He's her father. It wasn't just that we had a tip-off that put us on our guard. We believe, but can't prove, that there have been two similar attacks in crowds at political meetings in the last few months.

'The first was in Birmingham during a meeting addressed by Feargus O'Connor on the same subject as tonight's. The victim was an organiser of the Anti-Corn Law League boyo's, like the ones involved in this evening's shindig. He was found after the meeting away from the main hall, stabbed and left to bleed to death.

'The second one was nearer to home. It left a trade union leader from near Oldham in a bad way, with two stab wounds in the back after a strike meeting. He's alive but only just. Now it looks to me as though our information was wrong and Feargus O'Connor was the real target.'

'I don't think so,' said Ingliss. 'I never saw Phillip Burrell at all, and so I asked around. He wasn't there tonight. He should have been, but the word was he'd been called away on union matters.'

'So, our assailant saw his chance to have a go at the biggest fish of the lot and chanced his arm?'

'It's possible. But just as before, there's no proof. So we're none the wiser really.'

'Except of course you now know that there is a professional assassin abroad showing interest in killing radicals in crowds. Though that's not proof, your assumptions about the previous incidents are made much more plausible,' said Josiah.

'That's true, but why go to that amount of trouble is still a mystery,' said the Inspector. 'In the meantime, all we can do is be vigilant. Constable Ainscough, if you get wind of anything in the Stockport area that's relevant, I'd be obliged if you send word to me. You'll have a more sympathetic audience than you're likely to get from that idiot Prestbury.' The Inspector looked at his watch. 'Ingliss, take Mr Ainscough to Travis Street Station and make sure he gets a friendly engine driver to take him back to Heaton Norris. It's far too late for a regular train now.'

*

The streets towards the station were dark and rather foreboding, though the clear night sky afforded a brilliant view of the moon as it began to set, as well as the stars that shone out brightly. As they walked to the railway they started to chat.

'How long you been in the Manchester's?'

'Right from the start. I thought it might offer an interesting life and I wanted to avoid joining the family trade.'

'What trade was that?'

'Burglary.'

'Hmm. Couldn't have been a firmer break really.'

Ingliss laughed. 'Not really. They put me on a beat well away

31

from my old haunts and I was happy enough. Then Inspector Fidel arrived, and he brought me into the group he calls his Chosen Men. Rogers, McLeish, Hudd and Woolley are all part of the group. We do "unusual" jobs.'

'Like working in ordinary clothes?'

'And undercover when needed.'

They were approaching the railway station. Ingliss led Josiah round to a gate that led to a warehouse near the marshalling yards. 'Enough of shop-talk. The young lady who was with your party, what's her name?'

'Rosemary Hopgood,' said Josiah, surprised at the turn of the conversation.

'I don't want to put my foot in it, but anything between you and her?'

Josiah thought how Rosemary had been keen to hold his arm, so he supposed that she might like to think there was, but if he were honest, he found her rather silly.

'No, nothing. May I ask why?'

'Well you will probably be surprised, but where young ladies are concerned, I'm a bit bashful.'

He was right, Josiah was surprised, if he'd been asked to guess, he would have thought Constable Ingliss a pretty fair ladies' man.

'I don't often notice young ladies,' Ingliss continued, 'but I liked her look. Best to know a bit more of her in case I ever meet her again. After all, you never can tell.'

Ingliss led Josiah over to an engine that was being coupled to a line of goods' trucks. There were two men on the footplate. One was checking the controls and gauges mounted at the back of the engine's copper dome. What each control did was a mystery to Josiah, but he looked forward, on the journey back to Stockport, to observing how the driver used them.

'Bert!' shouted Ingliss. The driver jumped down from the footplate and came over to them. He was much the same age as Ingliss and himself.

'You always pop up at the strangest times Ned,' and he gave Ingliss a huge hug.

'Bert, can you do me a favour?'

'Of course. Name it.'

'Can you give Mr Ainscough here a lift back to Stockport? He's from their police and he's been very helpful to us this evening.'

Bert shook Josiah's hand. 'It will be a pleasure. We'll be off when I've checked the couplings.'

Josiah turned to Ingliss. 'Thank you, and in the same spirit as you're asking for Rosmary's name, in case we meet again, call me Josiah.'

'And you must call me Ned.'

They shook hands, and there was a *whoosh* of steam from the engine.

'If you want that lift, Mr Ainscough, you better come,' shouted Bert, from the footplate.

The fireman helped Josiah up. Bert let the steam into the main cylinders and the coupling to the wagons tightened, creaked and clanged. Slowly the sound of wheels grinding on iron rails filled Josiah's ears and the taste of coal smoke was on his lips.

The train moved forward onto the mainline and Ned Ingliss waved farewell.

CHAPTER 6

The letters of Rosemary Hopgood

Wednesday 9th March 1842

Dear Cynthia,

I'm writing this by candlelight, just after midnight. I just had to write to you since I'm far too excited to wait until tomorrow morning.

You will never, never believe it. I have been to the most exciting occasion of my life and in the company of such a handsome, charming, brave young man. To think, with all those young men in London, I have to come back here to smoky, stinking and ridiculous Manchester to meet with such an Adonis.

It fell out like this. Pappa and Mamma thought it would be a good thing for my education to go along to a big meeting in Manchester. What a bore, but I don't argue about such things; it upsets Pappa but since he buys me all those pretty essentials of life, I make it a rule to play the dutiful daughter.

We went by coach, which Pappa and Mamma seem to think is very swanky, though those of us who have lived, even a minute, in the glory of the Metropolis, know better.

We met the minister and his frumpy wife at the chapel manse. I was wondering just how I was going to tolerate an evening of speeches and the like when there HE was.

Of all things, he's a Policeman, even though he went to grammar school. It's a very common sort of profession if you can call it a profession; even lower than being a manufacturer like Pappa. But I couldn't help myself; he looked so very handsome in his uniform.

I just about remember him from before I came to London, but he went off somewhere romantic on the Continent and has only recently come home. What's even more romantic than his uniform is that he's an orphan. He's an orphan who was brought up by the stuffy old minister!

The meeting we went to was in the biggest Hall in the whole of Manchester. That was exciting, but I could tell it was going to be a dreadful bore when I looked at the platform. Rows of serious people dressed in black, looking stern, and not one of them smiling. At least we sat in the balcony since the ground floor was full of the hoi polloi, the rude mechanicals as it says somewhere in Shakespeare. The smell from downstairs was revolting.

I was settling down and hoping for some opportunity for flirting with Josiah that's his name when that old fool of a minister realized he's got us there on a wrong night. Jo, that's what I'm going to call him in my most secret thoughts, was magnificent. He immediately took control and got us all away, safe and sound. I'd have been lost without him. Apparently, it's a good thing he did, there was a riot or some such after we had got down the stairs and left.

I shouldn't write it, but I will: I'm in LOVE! I WILL become Mrs Josiah Ainscough, come what may!

Your perpetual friend and cousin,
   Rosemary

CHAPTER 7

La Haye Sainte

So now I know you, in your black and silver uniform. You who have only your fists and your pathetic stick with which to demand obedience. No rifle nor musket. No sharp sword or dagger. Nothing to protect you but the respect of the people. You are a servant, a humble servant, not a soldier, not a man of honour. You know nothing of true honour, nothing of true respect.

Grand-père meant everything to me. He was tall, grand, and honourable: a high bear-skin hat, white crossed bands over his white vest, trousers beneath his black coat — scarlet flashes at the collar and cuffs. When he passed, people in the street doffed their hats, called him *Mon Brave* and always gave him space to pass: an Imperial Guard.

I loved him when he was not away with the Emperor. I would climb up on his chest and pull at his long mustachios, and he would laugh and hug me. I thought he was invincible. When the Emperor came back from Russia without his army, we waited and prayed. We need not have worried. He got back, still in uniform, with his pride intact. Unlike the day he came home without his uniform, bareheaded, without even his hat.

That day he looked old and beaten. The Emperor was defeated, and his enemies had imprisoned him, then they carved up the spoils. Grand-père mourned. But as quickly as the news of Napoleon's fall was confirmed, a new rumour started, people muttered, 'The Little Corporal has escaped.'

'Napoleon is free.'

'He marches from the south.'

Paris held its breath.

An officer visited Grand-père. 'Will you return to colours Sergeant?'

We were not surprised. His reputation was great, he would return? but Grand-père refused him.

The next day a Capitaine called. He was carrying a new sword, a sword from the King. Grand-père took the sword and examined it. He appraised the steel and the sharpness of the blade. He studied the grip and swirled it round to test its balance. Then he looked at the Bourbon coat of arms on the hilt. 'He asks you to return,' said the Capitaine 'You will have nos sous-equipe, Monsieur.'

'I will come mon Capitaine.' The Capitaine was relieved. 'Provided I can take mon petit fils with me as my drummer boy.' The Capitaine agreed.

I was given a uniform and a drum. I was ten years old.

*

We marched out in column order, with Marshall Ney on a chestnut stallion at our head, waving his cockaded hat. The crowd cheered. Did they expect what was to happen? I marched and drummed and marched again. It was all I could do, and when I was tired the guards took turns in carrying me and my drum.

Outside Auxerre, we stopped. There was a cloud of dust on

the ridge in the distance: the dust of a marching army.

'That's not a large force,' said Grand-père.

'Certainly not as large as us,' said a compatriot.

Ney came forward. We stopped short of the road. We could see the column coming towards us. Then their ranks opened and a figure stepped into view.

'The Emperor,' said someone, 'Mon Dieu he is here!'

He was taller than people said, taller and leaner. The angles of his face sharp. As he surveyed our lines his eyes sparkled with a strange ferocity.

On our side muskets were levelled. The first rank of the Imperial army imitated us.

Napoleon advanced and spoke. 'If there is any man among you who would kill his Emperor, here I stand.'

There were scattered shouts of Vive Napoleon!

Grand-père threw down his musket and surged forward to offer Napoleon the King's sword.

The march north was triumphal. Every village cheered, flowers were thrown — not that royalists were likely to show their faces. But we marched, not a forced march but quick enough.

The word was that the Emperor was intending on bringing the battle to the enemy before they were prepared. As more regiments joined us it looked as if we would have enough numbers.

But the journey was not without opposition. There were skirmishes but only one serious engagement. We ran into a force of some 500 royalist troops. They were mostly infantry, accompanied by a detachment of cavalry and a battery of cannon. They had no hope against us, but they were clever. Their purpose was a delay. They found a position on a ridge in a wood and dug in. They could not stop us, but they could tell the Royalists how far we had come. They could warn the enemy and limit our hope of giving surprise.

It was the guns that had to be silenced. Our cavalry would deal with the rest. But the guns were hidden in the trees. Napoleon was impatient. Who would volunteer to turn skirmisher?

Grand-père was the first. Rifles were issued.

'How will we know where we are to attack?' asked one of the men.

'We will need drum signals,' said another.

They both looked at me.

'He's small, they'll not see him.'

'He can also shoot said another voice.' This was true because I had been taught using a small hunting rifle.

I stood up before anyone could stop me. 'Mon Capitaine, I will serve the Emperor,' I said and saluted.

There was laughter but they saw my resolve, and laughter faded.

'Are you sure?' asked Grand-père.

I nodded.

The men were in pairs, one to load and one to shoot. The Capitaine, Grand-père and I held to the rear. We crept slowly through the undergrowth. We could tell where our skirmishers were by the movement of the bracken as they moved forward.

Then the first shot was fired. I heard screaming. More shots. The squad to our left was in trouble.

'Call group three back,' shouted the Capitaine.

Three strokes on my drum, then the signal for withdrawing.

They moved back towards us. But there was a cavalryman in the wood. He saw us and, sabre drawn, charged. I picked up my rifle. It was already loaded. I levelled and fired. He fell from his horse. He was the first man I killed. We spiked the guns and killed the crews.

From then on, they took more care of me. I was no longer a mascot or a manikin, at best a good luck charm. They tutored me in shooting, they showed me how to hide.

*

Day by day we went north, and much of the time it rained. We named the march 'The Flight of the Eagle'. As we got closer to Brussels there was a rumour that the army would rest and then march at night, but the Prussians were seen gathering. The Emperor fought them at Ligny and won, though it was bloody. Ney had to retreat from engaging Wellington's troops. A day later we were near Mont Saint Jean ridge, where the British were in the defensive file.

From where I was, I could see more men, more horses, more cannon, more engines of war than I had thought the world could hold. The rain of the previous days had made the ground sticky with mud. Moving, even for someone as light as me, was toilsome. I wondered how hard it must be to move a canon.

Grand-père patted me on the back. 'Do not be afraid mon brave. We will be victorious.'

The Old Guard was held behind the lines. Towards our left was a fortified farm, Hougemont.

At first, the men looked to their equipment. They checked the cartridges for their muskets, the sharpness of their bayonets. All the time we listened for the sounds of battle, but the morning was nearly passed before we heard the first shot.

'Look', shouted someone, 'look.'

'We are attacking the farm,' said another.

'That's an easy target.'

There were puffs of smoke, and then a roll of a cannonade across the whole battlefield. The Grande Battery had opened fire, bombarding Wellington's line on the crest of the ridge.

'Up and at them,' we cried, waving our hats.

The canons went quiet and our infantry advanced. The faint sound of pipes and drums coming to us on the wind.

'They'll be fixing bayonets lads.'

Our infantry climbed the face of the ridge and were nearly at the enemy lines when there was the smoke from a disciplined volley. Our advance faltered.

Then from behind the ridge came a surge of grey horses: the British heavy cavalry. They were like a wave in water, breaking onto a beach. They swept the infantry away, drowned them, submerged them, engulfed them.

A collective groan rose from us.

'Wait,' shouted Grand-père.' The British cavalry was out of control.

'A counterattack, a counterattack!' Our Lancers were out, faster, lighter, with fresh horses.

The British retreated.

The battle went to and fro. But still that 'easy target' of Hougemont had not fallen. Then from our left, Ney led a charge. Avoiding the farm, he attacked Wellington's flank, but Wellington was prepared, his infantry in hollow squares. Ney's cavalry were useless against them. He retreated with fewer troops than when he charged, and fewer horses, dead before English bayonets.

Late in the afternoon, news came that a second fortified farmhouse, and the closest to Wellington's lines, La Haye

Sainte, had fallen to us. Canons were rushed into the farm-house's shadow. There, at close range, they started to bombard the squares that had foiled Ney.

A rider came down the lines. 'Capitaine, Capitaine. The Old Guard is to advance as quickly as possible.'

We formed up a block of soldiers twenty wide. I was next to Grand-père on the left. The drums rattled and the fifes squealed, and we marched across the open ground and through the rest of our army. We passed the guns at La Haye Sainte and advanced up the ridge towards the broken British troops. Our bayonets flashed and on we marched, up to the crest, on to certain victory.

As we came over the crest, a long file of infantry rose from the grass. They fired a united volley. Then another rose in front of them and fired a second volley, then a third file, which dropped down to reveal the first file ready with a fourth volley...

We hesitated. Balls shredded flesh and bone. Men who had carried me and taught me to shoot had their faces obliterated. I saw throats tattered; arms smashed. Grand-père was the last to fall, taken in the chest by two musket balls. I tried to support him, but I could not. He slid down to the muddy ground and I was buried under him. The last thing I saw was the British advance past where he had fallen.

*

I did not remember how I was saved. At first, all I knew was someone forcing me to drink. Then the jolting of a wagon and rough sections of bread between my lips.

There was a woman, she sat me up and I saw mountains and smelled flowers. Later I could sit outside. It took days – or was it weeks? – before I could speak. By then they had given me the book that they said I had been clutching when they took me from the battlefield. It was small, dirty with a cracked cover: *The Sayings of Maximilien Robespierre.*

I had been given a new world, one that Grand-père had embraced. In my heart, I resolved to be like him.

CHAPTER 8

The letters of Rosemary Hopgood

29th March 1842

Dear Cynthia,

I have to confess that I'm not making much headway with furthering my affection for Josiah Ainscough. In fact, I think he is pretty much oblivious to my approaches to him. Of course, there is the problem that the only place I really have any chance to talk to him is before or after chapel. At all other times, he is about his Police duties while I run errands for Mamma or while the days away in other ways like assisting cook, embroidering or visiting the sick.

I have tried some tactics to attract his attention. I engaged him one Sunday on the subject of what he thought of the latest Manchester fashion in bonnets. But he does not seem to have much of an opinion about fashion. On the following Sunday, I tried to engage him after the service on the meaning of his fellow local preacher's sermon. He explained in attentive detail, but I must confess I did not have much more of a clue as to what it all meant than I had when I'd listened to the original. I'd be very grateful

for any suggestions on topics of conversation from you.
    *But even with his resistance, I'm not finished yet. Watch
out Josiah Ainscough, I'm on your trail.*

Your perpetual friend and cousin,
    Rosemary

CHAPTER 9

Mr Prestbury at bay

Letter to The Manchester Trumpeter, 14th April 1842

Sir,

Despite the plethora of comment in the pages of your journal and other organs of the press, concerning the disgraceful rioting between Anti-Corn Law League supporters and Chartists at a recent public meeting at the Hall of Science, one significant detail of that night's events has not, in our view, been subject to enough comment. I refer, of course, to the Mystery of the Lone Policeman.

A riot was provoked by Mr Feargus O'Connor's planned lecture on the subject of the Repeal of the Legislative Union between England and Ireland. A group of Anti-Corn Law League supporters tried to prevent Mr O'Connor speaking. When this group was opposed by Chartists present, a pitched battle broke out, which some now call the Battle of Campfield. This altercation caused many individual injuries and considerable damage to the Hall of Science.

Mr O'Connor has flatly denied that there were any Policemen present at the event in his article in the Chartist newspaper The Northern Star. He has repeatedly and often declared that he would never accept protection of the police wherever he might speak. However, there are many reports from independent witnesses that at the height of the fighting one lone police constable, in uniform, could be seen attempting to do his duty in the face of both mobs.

It does not seem he was a constable from the Manchester force. Since no-one reports seeing any Manchester police in the vicinity of the Hall of Science, combined with other reports that this constable was off-duty, it appears he was there, quite properly, in an individual's most important office, that of a citizen. Whoever he was, or which force he came from, many witnesses attest that he led efforts, with other level heads from both sides, to protect children caught up in the mêlée.

Since that night, this officer has remained commendably silent. However, it seems to us that, while we respect his decision to remain anonymous, some public acknowledgement of gratitude for his sense of duty should be made. Thus, we have started a public petition commending his action.

Those wishing to sign it will find copies at the Hall of Science itself, and in other places of meeting and worship in the Campfield area.

Signed

Joseph Archibald   Michael Jenkins
Arthur Longstaff   Dennis O'Conner
Elizabeth Spilling   Peter Richer

'Mr Cooksley! This is intolerable Sir. Quite intolerable!'

Josiah had never seen Mr Prestbury so angry, then again, he had never seen his guardian in such high dudgeon either. If they had been lesser gentlemen, then they might well have settled the matter with their fists.

'But Mr Prestbury I am sure you can see...'

'I can see nothing Sir. You have invaded my office with the sole purpose of interfering with my official right to discipline Constable Ainscough. I insist you leave immediately, Sir. And shut the door behind you!'

'I will not, Mr Prestbury. It was entirely my fault that Josiah was at the meeting at The Hall of Science. I made a stupid mistake that put him in an awkward situation at the wrong meeting.'

'What pray, would have been the right meeting?'

Mr Cooksley looked slightly embarrassed. 'The one the previous evening.'

'And why pray do you think that would have been a proper meeting for one of my officers to attend? O'Connor and his Chartists are as pernicious members of the school of agitation as our MP Cobden and his Anti-Corn Law League.'

This scene had been precipitated the previous evening when Mr Prestbury heard a rumour that the anonymous Lone Policeman, the hero of the Battle of Campfield, was named Ainscough. He had been so incensed he immediately sent round a note to the manse at Tiviot Dale, assuming that Josiah still lived there, and summoning him to a meeting at the Magistrate's Court before roll call. This mistake delivered the note into Mr Cooksley's hands. He appeared at Josiah's door early enough to ensure that Josiah met with Mr Prestbury at the requested time, but he also insisted that he went with his former charge. 'At least I can offer my mistake in mitigation of any sentence Prestbury feels he has to impose,' he had said.

Josiah did not like the sound of *mitigation of sentence* but there was no stopping Mr Cooksley. The fact was that Prestbury's note had immediately resurrected all Josiah's doubts as to his suitability as a policeman. His future looked less than secure.

'I must protest Mr Prestbury. To lump the Chartists and the Anti-Cornlaw League together as mere agitators is both to misjudge the differences in their positions and the common cause they make on the need for social reform.'

'I was under the impression that all you Methody did not engage in party politics?'

'That is true. But though we may feel that our primary calling by God is to perfect our conduct and personal holiness as citizens of the New Jerusalem, we remain citizens in our community on earth and neighbours to other people.

'We also read our Bible where we find the witness of the Prophets in which we see that God is not disinterested in how a country governs itself. Therefore, there may be a justice God is concerned with that inspires both Chartist and Leaguer alike, in which Methodists too have a part.'

'And pray what possible common cause can be made between Chartist and the Anti-Corn Law League save their desire for the tearing down of the legally constituted government? They are mere Jacobins Sir, Jacobins!'

Mr Cooksley looked truly shocked at this last remark. 'Mr Prestbury, you surely do not think that either group desire an equivalent of a French Revolution?'

'That, Sir, is exactly what I think. I will go further and say, so that you know my mind clearly, that I and others believe that shortly, in concert or separately, these sons of agitation will try to engineer a revolution that will have to be opposed with force.'

'You wish another Peterloo?'

'I consider Peterloo unfinished business Sir.' Mr Prestbury strode over to the door, swung it open and held it with a clear indication that the discussion was at an end. 'Now Sir, Good Day!'

Mr Cooksley picked up his hat, and with a sympathetic glance to his son, left. Mr Prestbury slammed the door and returned to his desk. Josiah drew himself to attention and awaited the judgement that was coming.

*

Josiah had often heard it said that good news travels fast, but his own experience was that good news did not often travel faster than bad news. In the case of the result of his interview with Mr Prestbury, it was almost exactly two days before a knock at Josiah's front door presented Ned Ingliss', complete with an ironic smile. 'It has come to Inspector Fidel's attention that you have had a little local difficulty with that dammed stupid man who passes himself off as the leader of the police in this small out of the way place.'

Josiah grinned. 'Come in Ned, would you like some tea?'

'Well actually, even though it is early in the morning, I'd probably prefer something with a bit more of a bite and made from barleycorn. But bearing in mind Methody scruples, tea will be acceptable.'

Ned sat by the range and Josiah made the tea. 'What happened?' he said as Josiah passed him a cup.

'Someone told Prestbury I was the Lone Policeman. He exploded. He made it clear he'd never been happy with me in the police. He said he thought I was a hopeless officer and he was suspending me without pay until the full Watch Committee meets at the end of May.'

'And then?'

'He'll recommend my dismissal, but I may leave the force before that,' Josiah pointed to some papers on the kitchen table, 'I'm already drafting a letter to that effect.'

'That's pretty much what Inspector Fidel thought. Now, though I would have come around to sympathise in any case, I'm here today at the behest of said Inspector. If you've not got anything better to do, he wants to meet you in the Good Hope Inn, just on God's own side of the Stockport-Manchester border.'

'What does he want to see me about?'

'He wants to talk to you about a couple of things, but I've been specifically ordered not to say anything to you about them before he speaks to you. The sky is blue Brother, and it's a nice day for a stroll, so I suggest when we've finished our tea we go for a constitutional.'

*

As soon as Josiah and Ned got to the Good Hope Inn, the land-lady nodded them through to a back room, where Inspector Fidel, with a pint of ale at his elbow, was already tucking into what looked and smelled like a good steak and kidney pie. Constable Rogers was there but not eating. As Ned and Josiah entered Rogers positioned himself at the door, to prevent any interruption. Fidel got up and shook Josiah's hand. 'Nice to see you again Constable.'

'Not constable at the moment, Sir.'

'That does not surprise me, though it's a damn shame. Let us see what we can do about that.' The Inspector sat down and put his meal to one side.

'First things first,' he tapped the breast pocket of his jacket. 'In here I've got a letter of appointment in your name signed by my superintendent. All I have to do is put a date of appointment into space he has so kindly left and you'll be a constable of the Manchester police force. Your beat will start at the station house in Central Manchester, but it will concentrate on Travis Street Station. You will be responsible for protecting the passengers and detecting any crime involving the transportation of goods and people by rail between Manchester, Stockport and beyond.

'At this moment, you may be a constable looked down on in Stockport by your commander, but you can walk out of here a respected member of the Manchesters and, it goes without saying, one of my Chosen Men. What do you say?'

Josiah paused and thought hard. It was a great compliment. 'It is a very tempting offer Sir and I greatly appreciate the confidence you show in me, but I came into the police force partly because through it I could serve my hometown. I'd like to try to maintain that commitment if Mr Prestbury gives me the opportunity.'

Fidel felt in his waistcoat pocket, took out a half-crown and tossed it over to Ned.

'That was the stake, was it not Constable?'

'It was indeed, Sir.'

'You bet Ned I would take the offer and he said I wouldn't?'

Josiah didn't know whether to be affronted or flattered.

'Exactly and though I'm not pleased to lose a half-crown, I am pleased that you hold to your principles even under pressure. The letter can be honoured at any time in the next three months. So, if you are dismissed in the near future the offer will still be open. All you will have to do is say the word.

'Had you said yes just then, I'd be ordering you to do the next thing we need to discuss. As it is, I'll now be asking for your voluntary help. Give him the background, Ned, while I finish my pie and ale.' Fidel dragged his plate back in front of him and, after a good swallow of the ale, continued to eat.

'Josiah, things have moved on a bit since the night at the Hall of Science. Phillip Burrell was away advising about a dispute in one of the Ashton mills. So we went back to our informant who said they only had the name, Burrell.'

'But there was a Burrell present, Dianne Burrell,' said Josiah.

'Precisely,' chipped in Fidel. 'She is a prominent Chartist and could have been a target on that account; but she has an equal, if not more important reputation, as a union organiser of women weavers. In that capacity, she's taken employment, not far from here, at Leavington's Mill.'

'That's a woman only mill.'

'Yes. Paid less and thought of as being less likely to strike,' said Ingliss.

'We want you to keep an eye on Dianne Burrell in case she's still on the Sneaker's list, that's what we're calling our assassin, and conveniently a clerk's job in the offices of Leavington and Co. is about to become vacant.'

'How can you know?'

'Because we are going to create it. One of the clerks at

Leavington's fancies himself as a bit of a fence so we turned him informant, but the superintendent thinks that having a reliable man keeping an eye on Dianne Burrell for the next few weeks is more important. We'll arrest him tomorrow and by Friday morning they will be well behind with getting the pay organised, so if an experienced young man turns up out of the blue, looking for a clerk's position, I'd expect him to be hired on the spot. Are you interested in the appointment?'

CHAPTER 10

The letters of Rosemary Hopgood

29ᵗʰ April 1842

Dear Cynthia,

   My efforts to become close to Josiah are becoming harder and harder. His visits to chapel are rarer and so I have been trying to make the most of his presence when I can.

   Last Sunday I tried to hint that I knew he was doing something very important. At first, he pretended he had no idea what I was talking about. It took an extended bout of hints, and pretence, that I knew much more than I do, to get any sort of reaction, but it didn't have the effect I desired. I think he suddenly thought I knew something important, which apparently, I didn't.

   Anyway, he became very defensive and told me in so many terms that I should not gossip about such matters, that these are difficult times for people, including many of our neighbours, as well as people in the chapel. Then he stalked off, leaving me to regret what I'd said without my being clear as to what I'd done that was so wrong.

   I found out a little later that he is, it appears, to be in bad odour with the Stockport police and has been suspended by Mr Prestbury, the Chair of the Watch Committee. But there is also a rumour that he is working for the Manchester force undercover. If that is the case, then it is just so romantic.

Men, what a strange and inconsiderate group! How can they make romance, affection, yes even LOVE, so difficult! Where are the heroes of the romantic novels I read? Oh Josiah, how sad I feel that you cannot see what a good a catch I would be for an ambitious young police officer.

Your perpetual friend and cousin,
  Rosemary

1st May 1842

Dear Cynthia,

My feelings for Josiah are at an end! I find him impossible to speak to. He considers himself so high and mighty, way above me in so many ways that I can hardly believe I ever gave him a second look. Conceited, stuck up, foolish and generally so inconsiderate as to be a complete waste of time.

When I spoke to him last, he seemed totally unaware of what I had been trying to show to him, what I can offer him. Finally, I made him see what I thought of him. I held him in my gaze and told him how I really felt. He looked astonished. Then he said, after he had apologised profusely for giving me the wrong impression, that he could never feel the way I did. I was, according to him, too young, too immature and too gauche. He said that I had matured in many ways, but he did not feel that he could or ever would love me in the way I so earnestly desired.

Earnestly desired! I have finished with him. I shall cut him on all occasions in the future. I will find another lover to push in front of his face and he will rue the day he ever jilted Rosemary Hopgood!

Your perpetual friend and cousin,
Rosemary

Chapter 11

Junior Clerk Breakspeare

Josiah was on the doorstep of the mill offices of Leavington's early on Friday morning. He was dressed reasonably smartly, he was after all an experienced clerk who'd fallen on hard times and he was hoping for the best.

The door opened and a stooped, wrinkled man of about sixty looked out. 'God lad ye'r 'er early.'

'Haven't you heard, it's the early bird that catches the worm?'

'Sometimes early birds get shot for their pains. What ye' after?'

'A job. I heard you might be short of a clerk and I'm a clerk in need of a job.'

'God almighty, bad news travels fast!'

'So, it's true?'

'Day before yesterday, but that's about the size of it. Peelers turned up and off he went. He was a...' the man mimed some passes of swordplay, then tapped his nose with his left forefinger, 'If you take my meaning.'

'You mean he was a fence?'

The old man grinned. 'I can see you're a man of distinction and discernment. The name's Angel, Wilfred Angel. You can come and sit in the waiting room until 'is Nibs arrives. Seeing as I like you, I'll even share my tea with ye.'

Josiah reasoned His Nibs must be the mill manager. 'Won't he be cross if he catches you?'

'Worse than a hurricano in the Jamaican sea, but he never gets up early enough to be 'ere before half eight, so he'll never know.' Wilfred made a drinking motion with his hand and tapped his nose again, 'If you follows my drift.'

The waiting room was sparse: bare boards, a simple trestle on one side next to a white-washed wall. Most mill waiting rooms were reasonably comfortable. Even in the establishments of the meanest of owners, there was some attempt to make a positive impression. It was, after all, the first part of the mill that potential customers saw. People with cloth to procure had the whip hand in times like these and usually needed impressing if they weren't to take their custom elsewhere. But the owner of this waiting room was saying *I don't care what you think. If you don't like my terms, get out.*

Angel came back with tea which was brackish and cheap, in a cracked and battered cup. A picture of dust gleaned from the bottom of several tea chests came to mind. Josiah endeavoured to look pleased.

'Thank you, Mr Angel, I am in need of this.'

The latch on the door to the yard rattled and a thin tall youth came in. He eyed Josiah with caution. 'Pray introduce us,' he said to Angel in a rather haughty way.

'Clerk Morison, this is Mr…' said Angel.

'Breakspeare, Josiah Breakspeare,' Josiah stood. 'At your service.'

'Chief Clerk Morison,' emphasis was laid on the chief. 'Pleased to meet you I'm sure,' but at least he offered his hand to shake. 'May I be of assistance?'

'I am here enquiring if there are any vacancies in the mill office.'

Morison pouted childishly, though he was attempting to look disdainful. 'I don't know what gave you such an outlandish idea,' he said. 'As Chief Clerk,' again the emphasis was placed on *Chief*, 'I can assure you that there are no vacancies in this establishment. I will not delay you in your quest for employment elsewhere. Good day.'

Josiah tried to look astonished. 'But Mr Angel said there was a vacancy. I've heard all the talk in the town about the previous incumbent.'

Morison shifted from foot to foot. 'That position is filled.' The façade of importance was beginning to crack.

'Oh aye?' said Angel. 'That's the first I've 'eard of it.'

'You don't know everything, you old blighter!' Morison's house of polite manners and cultivated accent had crashed in pieces. 'My cousin's coming to see His Nibs this morning, so it's good as taken!'

The latch rattled again, and another young man came in. 'Angel do tell me I can smell tea. I got up late, had no time for any sort of bite, and my stomach will grumble all morning if there's no tea either.'

'Comin' right up, Mr Hugh.' The young man saw Josiah and immediately offered a smile and an open palm.

'Hello, Hugh Sidcup at your service,' he said. 'Who might you be?'

Josiah took Sidcup's hand. 'Josiah Breakspeare.'

'You here for the job?'

'I had hoped so, but Mr Morison says it's filled.'

Sidcup turned to Morison. 'Oh, Aristotle; you really are a

foolish man.'

'I am Chief Clerk you know Hugh.'

'That's because His Nibs told you, you were?'

'Yes. So, I must be.'

'No more than I am. He told me the same.'

'What!'

'You are very naïve Aristotle. You should know by now His Nibs just likes to set us against each other for sport. He told you not to say, didn't he?'

'Yes.'

'And you just could not keep your trap shut, could you?' said a deeper voice. Another man was standing in the doorway from the yard. Even Josiah had not heard the latch so much as click. Thickset, large moustache, a good quality gold watch and chain suspended from the waistcoat that covered his ample belly, this had to be His Nibs.

'Mr Tate' said a surprised but not a very disturbed Sidcup. 'Good morning, Sir.'

In contrast to Sidcup, Morison had gone as white as a sheet. 'Good morning Mr Tate,' he barely managed to say.

'I'll put this to you two very simply. Neither you Sidcup nor you Morison are the chief clerk until you get a letter from Mr Leavington himself. That letter won't be signed by the Master until I suggest to him it is appropriate to do so, is that clear?' They both nodded. 'In the meantime, I'll be looking at both of you to show me which, if either of you, should be made chief clerk. Do you understand?'

'Yes,' said Sidcup, who still did not look too incommoded.

'Yes,' said Morison, with a hangdog expression.

'Now get about your work. We are short of one clerk and

we have to put up the wages for two hundred workers before midday tomorrow. Angel, throw that slop you made out into the yard and make me some tea from my caddy in the safe.'

Apart from the door to the yard, there were two doors at the end of the room. Sidcup and Morison went through the one on the left into an inner office. Then Angel went through the second door, presumably to make Mr Tate's tea.

Tate turned to Josiah. 'Who might you be, Sir!'

'Josiah Breakspeare, Mr Tate.'

'And your business here?'

'I am an experienced clerk and I had heard that Leavington's were in urgent need of someone with my experience.'

'Normally I'd deny anything of the sort and throw you out the door without explanation just for your cheek. I still might mind, but you already know we require a new clerk. Where have you been working?'

Josiah eased into the story that he had cooked up with Ingliss and Inspector Fidel, 'St Mungo's Mill in Huddersfield.'

'St Mungo's has a good reputation. Why did you leave? In trouble, were you?'

'No. I'm originally from Stockport. My mother is ill and I'm her only support, so I've come home to take care of her.'

'Sentimental fool,' said Tate. 'You should have let her go to the workhouse rather than give up a good berth at St Mungo's. Still, their loss and yours maybe my gain. Without a letter of recommendation, you could be spinning me a tale and the door still beckons.'

Tate looked slightly crestfallen when Josiah produced his letter. It had been provided by a friend of the Inspector's at St Mungo's, and as a result, looked very official. Its author indicated that Josiah Breakspeare was a good and reliable worker and went as far as to promise to Mr Breakspeare instant reinstatement if his personal position enabled him to return to Yorkshire.

'Where did you learn to clerk?'

'In the dying works in Edgeley, then Mellor Mill and then in a couple of the silk mills in Macclesfield.'

Tate folded the recommendation up but didn't give it back to Josiah. 'I'll take you on for two months at two-thirds the normal pay of a junior clerk. At the end of that period, if I decide to take you on permanently, I'll pay you full pay from then. That do you?'

Josiah doubted that any of the savings from employing him at such a low rate would go anywhere other than into Tate's pocket. Something had paid for that gold watch and continued to pay for the love of spirits which tainted Tate's breath even this early in the morning, but Fidel's gambit had worked, and Josiah was in. He nodded his assent.

'Good,' said Tate, and they shook hands on the agreement. 'Who knows, I might make you chief clerk if it suits me. Your letter would warrant it.'

The latch on the door to the yard rattled again and a young man who bore some resemblance to Morison came in. 'Excuse me,' he said, 'But my cousin said that there was a position going as a clerk here.'

'Oh, he did, did he?' said Tate. 'Well, your cousin was wrong. I've got a new clerk, so be off!'

Aristotle's cousin looked puzzled, hesitated and opened his mouth to speak, but Tate would have none of it. He took the youth by his shoulders, turned him around and kicked him through the open door out into the yard, where he tripped and fell into a pile of horse muck. Three passing mill girls laughed heartily at his misfortune, one stepping on him before he had time to get up.

CHAPTER 12

The receipt of custom

Josiah read the name of the next person from the wages' ledger. Running his finger along the line, he checked the number of days and shifts they had worked that week. Then he noted their weekly wage and their number, which was in the column just after their name. He took from a frame to his right a metal tag bearing the worker's number and clipped it to the rim of a metal pot, something like an egg cup but smaller. Finally, he counted the money to be paid into the cup and put the cup, with its wages, into a snug circular hole in a wooden tray.

Hugh Sidcup looked over his shoulder. 'I can see you've done this before.'

'Not this system, but it's straightforward.'

'Don't forget you'll need the cups in numerical order. There are plenty of trays, so I usually make a separate tray for each half-score as I go along.'

Josiah looked puzzled.

'Ten to twenty in the first tray, twenty to thirty in the next tray and so on. It saves having to put them all out in numerical order after they are all done.'

'Thanks, I'll remember.'

'There's not much time when they come to the window,' he

indicated the foot-square hatch in the wall, on the far side of which was the waiting room. 'They are keen to get their money, and with His Nibs breathing over your shoulder it helps to be able to find the right number quickly.'

'Get on with your work Sidcup, I'm sure Mr Breakspeare can work things out for himself. He knows if he can't that we'll think less of him.'

If Tate expected laughter, he was disappointed: his sarcasm was regular, and time had worn such jokes very thin.

'Right you are Mr Tate,' said Hugh. He went back to his seat on the other side of the room. The bell on the weaving shed began to ring, signifying the end of the working day.

Provided there was enough work to do, Leavington's ran a single fourteen-hour shift, from 5 am to 7 pm, except Saturday and all of Sunday. Mr Leavington was a churchgoer and kept Sunday sacred.

Josiah watched as the girls filed past his window, knocking the cotton dust from their hair and clothes as best they could. They stretched aching shoulders. They were mostly quiet, and some were stooped in tiredness, either from the day's exertions or possibly from years of backbreaking work.

One, though, walked taller than the rest. She took off the scarf she had round her head and fluffed out her black hair. Dianne Burrell still looked as indomitable as she had at The Hall of Science. Josiah felt a very incongruous protector; thinking she looked more fitted to be his. But the Sneaker was real, and Josiah had seen how calm he had been creeping up on O'Connor, so if Dianne was the assassin's target then he hoped he was equal to the task of protecting her.

*

Saturday morning: fifteen trays of pots, correctly labelled, were ranged next to the payment hatch. Wages would be exchanged on the presentation of the worker's tally disc, which was probably the most precious thing any worker at Leavington's possessed. Without the discs, there was no pay.

The factory bell rang. Then the noise of the transmission shafts that ran the length of each shop, driving the clatter of the looms and the rumble of the carding and spinning frames, subsided. The drone of machinery that insinuated itself through every timber and stone of the mill, that in just over a day had become so much part of Josiah's world he had forgotten it, was replaced by the drumming of wooden clogs on floorboards and stone steps, and by the giggling and chatter of female voices.

'Here they come,' said Mr Tate. 'Stand to it Mr Breakspeare. I'll be watching you. No mistakes now.'

Josiah soon got into the swing of the matter. A hand would come through the hatch with a disc. He took the disc, found the cup, emptied it and placed the disc back on the pile of coins in the person's palm.

There was no real contact between him and the workers. To see the face belonging to the hand would have meant bending and peering through the hatch. He'd often heard workers referred to as hands and had always thought that it simply indicated that they lived by their practical skills. This ritual reminded him most of receiving the bread and wine at communion, though at the altar rail a complete person was present, whose humanity was acknowledged in the sacrament. These hands were detached from the person to which they belonged. That there was a real person attached was irrelevant and of no importance to the mill.

Once satisfied, a given hand was quickly removed to be replaced by another. In what seemed very little time, nearly all the pots were empty. Hugh had warned Josiah that not all the pots would be collected.

'Some will be away on Saturday because of illness and the like,' he had said.

'What happens then?' Josiah asked.

Hugh had shrugged. 'His Nibs does his level best to hold on to at least some money as a sort of fine, but if it's pressed then they get their money; unless they're dead of course.' Josiah wondered how often that occurred.

Now there were only five or six cups left. Was this one the last? No, there was another. Josiah decanted the money into the palm and returned the tally. Then, for the first time, there was a pause and a sign of individuality. The hand shook the money, weighing it, before closing on the pay and retracting.

Josiah was just collecting the next pot in response to the proffered hand when there was a knock on the door to the waiting room. Angel went to answer it.

'Mr Angel,' said the knocker.

'Miss Burrell,' said, Angel. Josiah nearly dropped the last pot. 'What can I do for you?'

'I want to see Tate. Effie Wheeldon's wages are short a day's pay.'

'I'll see if Mr Tate is available.'

'I am,' shouted Tate from inside his office,' He had given up watching Josiah a little while before, but he had left the door to his inner office open, presumably to be the first to know if anything went wrong. He came out smoking a cigar.

'Have you forgotten your manners, Angel? Let the lady in.'

He looked around for some reaction to his sarcasm, but though Hugh tried to smile the only one who joined in by laughing was Morison.

When Dianne Burrell was over the threshold Tate made a great show of sticking his head out of the doorway and looking up and down the waiting room. Then he shut the door behind himself. He looked at Josiah.

'That's the lot Mr Breakspeare.' Josiah shut the hatch in the door and started to tidy up the pots and trays. Tate turned to Dianne Burrell.

'If Effie Wheeldon wishes to dispute her pay, then she'll have to do it in person. Assure her I'll give her my full attention.'

'I am afraid that won't do Mr Tate. She's not here because her brother is sick.'

'What's that to me?'

'I would have thought you should be asking what's that to Mr Leavington?'

Tate ground his teeth. 'If she's not here, then she can't collect her pay, that's the rule.' He pointed at her with the spittle-covered end of his cigar. 'So, I'd be obliged if you'll return the cash you collected just now to Mr Breakspeare here so he can put it back in the safe, and I'll take Effie's tally into safekeeping.' Tate held out his hand.

'If that's the rule it's the first I've heard of it,' said Dianne. 'Effie and her family need the money badly. At the very least I'll take what I hold for her, but I'd prefer to take everything she's owed.'

Tate pulled on his cigar and blew the exhaled smoke into Dianne Burrell's face. 'I'm a man of Christian charity Miss Burrell. I'll let you keep the money for Effie as a kindly act but extra money's another matter.'

'Why? After all, I'm sure you'll agree that right is right and wrong is wrong,' said Dianne. 'All you have to do is show me what it says in the ledger and we'll be able to settle it here and now. That way you'll not be put to any inconvenience later.'

'Now lass,' said Tate, 'ledgers and accounts are complicated things. I'm sure pretty lassies like you don't understand them.'

'Better than you probably. But there's one way to find out. Show me the ledger.'

'Of course,' beamed Tate. 'Mr Breakespeare, get the ledger down.'

Josiah walked over and took down the wages ledger and opened it on the desk. 'Please Miss Burrell, what is Effie Wheeldon's tally number?'

'One hundred and fifty-three,' she replied.

Josiah looked up the record. 'There should have been 2s 4d in her pot. Is that correct?'

'Yes, that is correct.'

'So why would there be any question that it's not the correct sum?' asked Josiah.

'Effie thinks she was marked out of work on Tuesday last when she was only late. She agrees she should have been fined for the lateness, but she did a full shift otherwise, as her overseer will confirm.'

Josiah looked for the record for Tuesday. 'She is marked out of work, but there is a small question mark next to the entry.'

Dianne Burrell came over and looked to where he was pointing. He was standing close to her and he could smell the cotton dust on her plain dress and the sweat of her day's labour, but under the smell were notes of fresh soap and a scent of violets.

'I can help there,' said Hugh. 'Miss Burrell, Mr Breakespeare would not know since he only just joined us yesterday, but that question mark means the overseer was not sure. In normal circumstances, it would have been checked.'

Josiah saw an opportunity. 'Mr Tate, may I suggest we pay Miss Wheeldon's wages as if this is an error, and that in the coming week I check with her overseer to see that this is the case? The deduction can be made next week as easily as now if she was absent.'

Tate looked angry, but he paused to think before answering. After another draw on the cigar, he nodded. 'Very well, we will do what Mr Breakspeare suggests.' Josiah did a quick calculation of the extra money and gave it to Dianne.

'Thank you, Mr Tate, and you Mr Breakspeare for your sensible suggestion.'

She made to leave, but at last Tate's irritation in not having put her in her place, together with anger at being bested, got the better of him. 'All well and good Burrell, but I could sack you for having used Effie Wheeldon's tally to take money that wasn't owed personally to you.'

Dianne Burrell looked Tate in the eye, Josiah thought that she looked almost pleased with Tate's threat. 'I think, Mr Tate, that in the current state of dissatisfaction in mills in general, and this one in particular, that sacking me for sticking up for Effie might be a very unwise move. Very unwise indeed.' She held his gaze for a split second and Tate looked away. Then she left, leaving a lingering scent of violets in the air.

CHAPTER 13

Warp and weft

'Breakspeare!' shouted His Nibs.

Josiah left the ledger he was correcting and went into Tate's office where his boss had his feet up on the desk. He'd just come back from what must have been a very disagreeable meeting.

'Breakspeare, go across to the spinning shed, find Hostler and tell him that Cairncross is demanding delivery of his thread by the end of the week, and I've told him he'll have it. Put the fear of God in him if he hums-and-hahs.'

Josiah walked over to the spinning shed wondering exactly how he was going to put the fear of God into the sort of overseer who worked for Tate. The noise of the spinning room hit him when he opened the door, an amalgam of thunderous rumblings interspersed by clangs and bangs of wood on metal or metal on wood produced by the room's three forty-foot-long spinning mules.

Everywhere he looked the air was a snowstorm of cotton dust which muted all colours, even the vivid scarves worn by some of the younger women. Surveying the scene was Dianne Burrell; aware of him she turned.

'You look as though you've never seen this before, Mr Breakspeare.'

'Not as bad as this at least,' he replied.

Dianne Burrell frowned and sighed. 'I suppose Leavington's is one of the worst mills. I should not let familiarity make me forget that.'

Josiah changed the subject. 'His Nibs has sent me with a message for Mr Hostler.'

'I'll take you to him. I've been sent over to see him about some linen thread we need for some heavy-duty warps.'

Hostler surveyed the spinning shed from a raised dais. As they came up to him, he looked carefully from one to the other. When Josiah told him what Mr Tate had said, all he did was grin. 'Tell him we'll do it, but if you can ask him next time he's showing off to his drinking cronies, not to make good his boasts by breaking our backs.'

Josiah wondered if the presence of Dianne had moderated his reply. In any case, Hostler also found the three large bobbins of the thread Dianne needed and Josiah helped her carry them back to the weaving shed.

'I should thank you for your help with Effie's wages last Saturday. It took courage to stand up to Tate as you did. Effie's father is too fond of the bottle. She needed her wages to make sure her brother got some decent broth. He's better today, and she's back at her looms.'

'It's the least I could do for the daughter of Phillip Burrell.'

'How do you know I carry that title?'

'Don't worry, I may be a clerk but many more of us support your father's cause than people might think.'

'Don't bother flattering me,' she snapped.

'It's not flattery I assure you. I've often wanted to hear him speak.'

'Very well, I'll put your word to the test. My father will be speaking to the remaining turn-outs at Felsted's Hat Works on Sunday. Be near the gates at 3 o'clock sharp and you'll get your wish.'

*

There were 50 standing in a typical Manchester mizzle: that peculiar mixture of fine rain and mist which soaks everything. Those without hats or shawls stood very little chance of staying dry. There was, despite his stout coat and wide-brimmed hat, a trickle of cold water running down Josiah's back.

Burrell stood bare-headed, rain darkening his hair, his broad shoulders glistening from the water soaked into his jacket.

'Friends, thank you for coming. The reason we are here is that it has been nearly a year since you stopped work and turned-out, here at Felstead and Co. You did not do that lightly I know and the rest of us here and in the towns around have marvelled how solid you have been in your resolve. But there has not been the support of other hatters and I have come to tell you that I see very little use in you continuing this fight.'

There was a man's voice from near the front, 'What ye saying is we're beaten.'

'It's not been a complete loss Jeb, Felstead's have had to agree to better peace-work rates than you had at the start of the dispute, but they are rates that remain unjust.'

'Aye Mr Burrell,' said a woman near the back, 'that may be true and prudent, but we be hungry Phillip, well-nigh clemmed.'

'And I have brought you some help for that. I organised a collection from the other hatter works. There are ten sovereigns for you in my pocket to be dispersed for the relief of hardship.'

The crowd stirred, and Josiah heard mutterings of *well-done* and *fancy-that* going around. A cheer might well have broken out, but Burrell held up his hand to stop it. He looked at them as a father with bad news to tell his family.

'I would like to say that your suffering will be the last called for from workers seeking justice and proper returns for their labour, but the fact is everywhere I look I see storm clouds. There will be more, not fewer, disputes like yours in the future, and they will be across many industries, unless trade and attitudes buck up. The only comfort I can see is that, when that time comes, you will already have made your contribution and may avoid more hardship.'

After a collection had been taken from the crowd three cheers were given for Mr Burrell, and people started to disperse. Phillip came over to where Dianne and Josiah were standing. He was shivering.

'Father your chest, what were you thinking of, getting so wet?' scolded Dianne.

'Please don't fuss pet, I'll be warm enough when I get home.'

'Where there is no doubt a perfectly sound raincoat on the hook behind the door, and not on your back where it should have been.'

'The turn-outs had no coats, so why should one who has the honour of leading them, speak to them warm and dry, when they are wet?'

A tall man had come over; he had a craggy face and a substantial nose below kind blue eyes. 'Well, one good reason Phillip would be that they live in easy walking distance of here and can get dry quick after a wetting, while you have to go to the other side of Ashton to get home. But as it happens, my place is two streets away and my missus will have the fire stoked and something hot to drink, so you'll come and get dry there and I'll not take no for an answer!'

'You always were an interfering busybody Fred Sowerby,' said Burrell, 'but it would be bad manners of me to refuse hospitality so openly extended, and anyhow I'll not say that getting warm and dry isn't somewhat appealing.'

'What about you Dianne? Will you come as well? Bring your young man if you like.'

'I'll come to make sure Father does get dry and see him on his road home afterwards, but Mr Brakespeare here is not *my young man*, as you so delicately put it. He works at Leavington's and wanted to hear Father speak.'

'Well, in that case, I'll extend the same polite invitation to him as I extended to Phillip and make his attendance compulsory. A man in an all-women shop, and to add to that the only boy who's ever come with Dianne to a meeting, there's a puzzle-and-a-half for me to stick my long nose into. But we're getting wetter jawing here. Let's get going.'

Fred Sowerby was better than his word, his house was not even two streets away. The journey finished at a short tunnel between two houses. The courtyard beyond was mostly rutted mud, with two large puddles in one of which toddlers were fishing around with a stick, ignored by their mothers who were leaning against one of the sets of steps, sharing an earthenware bottle. One looked at Sowerby with bleary, bloodshot eyes.

Fred led them to the end of the courtyard and up some steps which allowed access to a sort of landing that stretched along the front of three houses built above a ground floor storeroom. He opened a door. In the room beyond a kettle sang on the range, in front of which washing was drying. Above the mantelpiece was a sampler edged with crowns, cups and pink roses which said *The crime of drunkenness dispels reason*. At a well-scrubbed wooden table, four children were being taught their letters.

'Hepzi, Hepzi. Where are you lass?' called Fred.

'Gone away with the gipsies Fred, where do you think I'd be?' The woman saw Burrell and immediately went over and embraced him. 'It's been too long a time since I set my eyes on you, Phillip.' She took his hands in hers, then she saw the condition of his jacket. 'And when I finally do, I find you're as wet as a fish. What were you thinking of, Fred!'

The washing was tidied away, and a chair was pulled up to the fire. Hepzibah Sowerby insisted Phillip's jacket was put to dry.

'His shirt's soaked as well,' observed Dianne.

'David is about your size,' Hepzibah said. She turned to the older girl who had been teaching reading. 'Martha nip upstairs and get one of your uncle David's old shirts for Phillip.' The girl did as she was bid and came back with a worn but service-able garment.

Hepzibah turned back to Phillip, got a towel and handed it to him. He managed to wipe his chest and arms but had trouble with getting to his back. Hepzi looked at him then took him by the shoulders and swivelled him round.

'You were always hopeless at drying yourself, Phillip.' She seized the towel and started to dry his back. Fred had been out in the back kitchen and came back into the room. The rest of the family were smiling, but for a tiny moment Fred scowled; he did not approve of something he saw in the scene, though the spasm passed.

'Now put this on,' she commanded.

'In front of everyone!' protested Burrell.

'Well, we've all seen your manly chest before Phillip, even me. Remember those evenings when we were young and used to go swimming,' She smiled at him and he smiled back at the shared memory. 'Come on Phillip, you need to get out of it now!'

'Oh, very well.' The shirt was changed Phillip started to warm himself.

Another of the children who had been at her letters stood in front of Josiah and bobbed him a curtsey, then held out her arm. 'Please, Sir, can I take your coat?'

'Thank you,' he took it off and also handed her his hat.

The girl looked him up and down. 'You Dianne's beau?'

As Josiah spluttered, Dianne rescued him. 'Caddy, really what a rude question to a guest. You take my coat as well in penance.'

'I'm only asking,' said Caddy. 'What's the harm in that? If I don't ask for myself, then I'll never get to know properly. Now that's what I reckon would be rude. Mum and Dad won't ask, though they'll be dying to know. I was just making use of the chance.' She turned to Josiah. 'Sorry if I was rude mister. No offence meant.'

'None took. But I hope we'll be friends, so you must call me Josiah.'

'Then you can call me Caddy,' she said and then she took the coats through to the back room.

Dianne sat on a bench at the table, Josiah next to her. Hepzibah began filling beakers with hot water from the kettle, offering them round. The steam that rose from Josiah's combined the smell of apples and an elderflower scent.

'Have you got any grog to go with this concoction of yours Hepzi?' said Burrell. 'It would warm me quicker than all these wholesome flowers and fruits.'

'And give you a headache later. You know full well this is a house committed to two things, the Charter and the Pledge.'

'One to slay the power of the rich,' said Fred.

'One to slay the power of the demon gin,' said Hepzibah.

Fred Sowerby raised his beaker, and they all followed, including Burrell, 'A toast brothers and sisters: The Charter and the Pledge.'

They all echoed his words.

'But Caddy was right,' said Fred. 'Just who is this mystery person, on the arm of our Dianne, is a question on all our minds.'

'Oh really,' said Dianne. 'I told you before Fred, this is Josiah Brakespeare. He works in the office at Leavington's and professes sympathy with our cause and has already been of such practical help to one of my fellow workers as his position allows. He just wanted to hear Father speak.'

'That's true Mr Sowerby. The reputation of Phillip Burrell has crossed the Pennines to Yorkshire where I was working, and so when I found I was a comrade of the no less famous Dianne Burrell I had the cheek to avail myself of the opportunity.'

'Talks posh, don't he?' said Hepzibah. 'Grammar boy I'd reckon, but no less welcome here for that.'

'Did I come up to expectation, Mr Brakespeare?' asked Phillip.

'Very much, Sir.' Josiah paused.

'There's a question in your noddle lad; I can see it from here,' said Burrell. 'Ask it.'

'I was taken by what you said about the storms to come. What gives you that impression?'

'An important question. Peterloo made me what I am, someone willing to fight for justice in parliament and mills.

'I see a pattern to disputes in all sorts of industries, from coal mines in Oldham and Stoke to the hatters you've just seen. Masters are trying to reduce wages, but it's not just a matter of making more profit. Owners have difficulties that are forcing more bankruptcies just as food costs rise for families. Both reduce the consumption of the goods factories produce. There's a cold wind blowing through commerce in general and I can't see it backing just yet. There'll be more and more disputes, and if enough occur together, then I don't know what will happen.'

CHAPTER 14

Practical arrangements

Josiah and Dianne were walking towards Stockport in what had turned into a fine evening. They had just seen a dry Phillip Burrell off in the direction of Ashton and were in no real hurry.

'They are a good family, or rather families,' commented Josiah.

'They are fortunate in many ways. The house is reasonably roomy as well as warm, and well maintained by the brewery store in the under-croft.'

'Now that has to be an amusing irony, a house of abstainers supported by the profits of the demon drink.'

Dianne chuckled. 'Supported in more ways than one.'

Josiah took a moment to see the pun.

Dianne laughed again, this time at his expense. 'Josiah your seriousness will be the death of you yet. I suppose they see it as one of those compromises people of principle have to make in these difficult times. But it's a good household. Hepzibah acts as the housekeeper and sees that the combined house runs well, which leaves David and his Jemmy to work as weavers. Even in hard times, it's rare that the hatters below and the weavers above are both out of work. Mutual support is the key to strong unions and well-founded families.'

'I agree, but I did wonder how they knew which children

were which.'

'I know what you mean, fourteen children in total, aged from two to fifteen. All of them who are old enough can read and write because of a combination of Sunday school and Hepzibah's determination. More than that, none of them, so far, have had to go to the mill or the hatters before they were twelve.' She broke off and stopped, looking at him in a solemn sort of way. 'There's something I want to make clear.'

Josiah returned her look.

'I hope you're not going to take the jokes about us walking out, or you being *my beaux*, as Caddy put it, seriously. If you are thinking in anything like that sort of way about me then forget it. I am dedicated to the cause of women's emancipation and justice for them as workers through strong unions.'

Having said her piece, she started to walk on past Josiah. He let her get a few more steps before speaking. 'Aren't you being rather presumptuous? Don't you think I might have an opinion of my own in the matter; one that you might not have anticipated?'

She stopped. 'And have you got such an opinion?'

'Yes, three opinions in fact.'

'So, let me hear them.'

'First, I know that you are the idol of every young, and some older, Chartists and I expect you have lots of them falling in love with you all the time, but that list does not include me.'

'Well, how rude.'

'Please hear my reasons before you decide to think less of me. My heart is not yet recovered from my last encounter with love. So, it's not about you nor what I think, it's about me. I'm not ready to love again. Next, you have your calling and I

83

respect that. Your dedication does you credit, and your cause is, in my opinion, just. To do that effectively you don't need followers to get in your way. You must plot your own course.'

She pursed her lips and frowned.

'Lastly, though I'm not in the market to be your *beaux*, I am in the market to be your friend, and I wouldn't care what people said about our relationship behind our backs or to our faces if we know when we are seen together in public, we are doing it as friends. If that is acceptable, I will look forward to more occasions like this afternoon and more chances for exchanging ideas and debating with you. Here, take my hand on it.'

She hesitated and looked at him quizzically. 'You are a very surprising young man,' she said. 'I watched how you talked to Caddy. A child that precocious is not easy to make friends with, but you did it with a few words in no more than a minute. Now you do the same with me. I don't know why I should take you up on this offer of friendship.'

'And you said I was rude.'

She paused again. Then she held out her hand to him. 'It's a bargain, but since I now have you as a friend I can walk out with and exclude romantic commitment, I think you and I might broaden out a little from turn-out meetings by having some entertainment as well.'

'Agreed,' said Josiah, and they shook on it.

CHAPTER 15

The Promenade of Wonders

Josiah was of no doubt that Dianne was a very determined self-educator. So, he was surprised when she produced a rather badly printed handbill that announced that the following week *The World-Renowned Promenade of Wonders is to be Available for the Visitation of the Discerning Citizens of Stockport and its Environs.*

'I'd like to go to see this.'

'Are you sure?' said Josiah.

'Quite sure. I've never been allowed to go to anything like this and so now, safely accompanied by you, is my opportunity.'

It took some time for Dianne and Josiah to locate the *Promenade of Wonders*; it had to be somewhere in the jumble of cheap houses and wharves near the canals in Droylsden.

'Could that mark the place?' said Dianne, pointing at what looked like the head of a giant, poking up over the buildings.

'I do believe it might be,' said Josiah. 'At least I've not heard of any giants on the loose in this area; especially ones which doff their hats.'

They found a piece of open ground where two lines of booths and tents were marked with burning torches. The giant, cut from wood and gaudily painted in someone's idea of eastern dress, had been fixed to the wall of a dilapidated factory. This figure had a beneficent expression on his face, which went along with the painted canvas next to him announcing *I am the Giant Pleasure. Welcome to my Promenade of Wonders.* Two boys tugged alternately on ropes which pulled the giant's arm so he repeatedly lifted his hat.

'At last,' said Dianne, excitement all over her face. 'So, let's make the most of the time we have. Both of us have to be up for work tomorrow.'

They passed through the entrance, where two men collected their penny entrance money, and a fat lady, who seemed to be twice as broad as she was tall, played a barrel-organ, accompanied by a tall emaciated man on panpipes.

The first tent they came to housed *The Ravishing Miss Rapunzel.* It contained a young lady with pink eyes. She had long fair tresses, but the join between natural hair and long coils of bleached horsehair was far too obvious. Even so, her vigorous efforts at brushing the horsehair seemed to please the onlookers.

'Do you think they dyed her eyes as well as her hair?' said Dianne.

Josiah cringed. The thought revolted him. 'It's quite possible.'

The next tent was far more macabre: wax models of terrible diseases, *rarely met with,* as it said on the sign outside. There were several bottled babies, one with two heads but only one torso. There was a small octopus, allegedly taken from the body of a fisherman, matched with the small skeleton of a sailor taken from the stomach of an octopus.

'Look at that, Martha,' said a noisy onlooker, pointing towards the babies.

'Pity they dain't live,' replied Martha. 'Would 'ave been a

boon to the parents. After all two 'eads are better than one.' They cackled in chorus.

One tent opened onto a crossbow shooting gallery where encouraged by Dianne, Josiah tried, unsuccessfully, to hit the bulls-eye.

Another tent had a particularly engaging sign, which said *Bear Lady*. Inside it was very gloomy and Josiah could just make out that facing a pair of curtains were some benches.

The tent was warm, and its air carried a musky animal scent. There were plenty of unpleasant smells around the place: the sulphurous torches, the sweat of other visitors, the rancid smells of cheap food, and of course the reek of gin on the breath or from the booth that was selling it at a farthing a snort.

Josiah and Dianne sat down, waiting to see what would happen. After a few more people came in, a small man came around soliciting halfpennies. Then without any explanation, he pulled back the curtains. Beyond sat a figure about five feet high. It seemed to have some sort of coiffure and wore a long dress. There was a shawl around its shoulders.

A first glance it looked like a stout woman, but her face was covered in coarse brown hair and had protruding teeth below an excessively long nose. Her hands, protruding from the sleeves of her dress, were also hairy and had very long nails.

The man returned and started to play on a penny whistle. The *Bear Lady* stood up and started to jig mechanically on the spot. There was a sound suspiciously like a jangling chain, and as she danced, she grunted. The man stopped, and as the music died the lady flung out her arms in rage at her torturer and roared. A woman in the audience screamed. Someone behind the scenes tightened the chains in restraint and the curtains were quickly drawn. The tent emptied, though the roars of the enraged bear, punctuated by the sounds of blows from a whip, followed the audience outside.

Appalled by the plight of the bear, Dianne's enthusiasm for the *Promenade of Wonders* was near to exhaustion. She looked at Josiah. 'How can human beings be so cruel,' she said.

'Have you seen enough?'

'Perhaps. I let my curiosity overcome my reserve. I see now why my father stopped me in the past. But I'll see all there is, so I never have to come to a place like this again.'

'There's only one thing left,' said Josiah. 'The penny-gaff.'

Josiah led the way to the door presided over by the giant.

'Penny for the benches, halfpenny for the pit,' demanded the man on the door.

'What's the difference?' asked Dianne.

'In the pit, you stand, on the benches, ye sit. Mek ye minds up, there's a queue.'

'Two for the benches,' said Josiah.

Beyond its outer walls, there was very little left of the factory. The roof was missing and most of what had been the ground floor had fallen through. The pit was the floor of the factory's cellars and was very much a male preserve with a lot of jostling and drinking.

The benches were perched on what was left of the ground floor. They were banked up on three sides, making a crude amphitheatre. There must have been about eighty people already seated. 'It looks like we're only just in time,' said Dianne as she and Josiah pushed their way to a bench and sat down.

A raised wooden stage had been built on the floor of the pit, level with the lowest benches. It had a raised section at the back of the stage next to the far wall and was illuminated by torches.

Josiah saw a midget with a painted red face, wearing a poorly made Punch's costume and a paper-mâché nose. He came in from the right of the pit carrying a ladder. He propped it up against the stage and climbed up. He made two low bows, right and left.

'Ladies and Gentlemen. Welcome to *Weston's Theatre of Delights*.' The crowd cheered. 'Now you may be astonished that these boards,' he stamped for emphasis, 'are uncarpeted and that there is no painted curtain on which to feast your eyes.'

'Up the spout, are they?' shouted someone in the pit.

'No such luck,' shouted a voice from the benches, 'Someone's ad 'em to make petticoats.'

The crowd laughed. The midget raised his hand to quiet them. 'Neither of your speculations are true. It is simply that we have nothing to hide at *Weston's Theatre of Delights*, as all is literally, above board.'

The audience groaned. 'Though here at Weston's, we do always keep one or two surprises up our sleeves.'

There was a flash and a bang of a small powder charge, which made Dianne jump. To Josiah's surprise, as the midget fell through a trap door, from two other trap doors to right and left, a male and female acrobat rose slowly into view.

They were extremely adept, starting with a display of weight-lifting by the man and tumbling by the woman, with repeated somersaults, cartwheels and handsprings. A trapeze was lowered over the stage for her. She hung from it by her knees, performing various perilous tricks to great appreciation.

For her finale, the trapeze was raised as high as it could go, and she swung it vigorously back and forward. On the final swing, at a fearful height, she somersaulted off the bar to be caught by her partner. As they took their bows the cheering and applause were deafening.

'Was that more to you taste?' asked Josiah.

'Definitely, I'm glad I didn't miss it,' exclaimed Dianne.

Unfortunately, the acrobats were followed by a rather incompetent troop of clowns, singing and playing the spoons and bones. These were a complete anticlimax to the acrobats. After a while, Dianne turned to Josiah. 'I think I've seen enough,' she said, do you think we could leave?'

Josiah glanced round but they were hemmed in and he did not see much chance to get out until the show finished. At least the clowns were leaving.

As they did so a gentleman emerged from the right-hand trap door. He was dressed to represent an Irishman, complete with a green coat and an oversized shamrock in his hat. As he wandered around the stage, he cried such things as, 'The Charter now' and, 'Home rule for Ireland'. Cries which some part of the audience took up and others jeered. There was a card across his back which said, *O'Connor*.

'Good heavens,' Josiah heard Dianne say under her breath. He felt her stiffen.

O'Connor was soon joined by another character from below the stage. He was portly, with a union flag on his waistcoat, but he was not John Bull, for the label on his back said *Cobden*, and his cries were, 'Down with the Corn Laws' and, 'Free trade'.

Dianne stirred again. 'Oh no,' but her worst fears, as well as Josiah's, were realised. After circling each other, the characters drew their swords and started to fight, this to the delight of the audience, who alternately chanted *Cobden* and *O'Connor*.

Dianne pulled at Josiah's arm. 'Can we leave,' she said, 'I'm feeling a little faint.' But they were so packed in there was no way for them to get out.

A door at the back of the stage opened and the female acrobat emerged. She was in an exaggerated cotton dress, with a crude black wig slapped crookedly on her head. She held in her arms a shawl wrapped round something that might have been anything from a bag of potatoes to a suckling pig. This new character stood high above Cobden and O'Connor, who continued to fight. The woman started to scream, 'My babies, my babies, save my bairns.'

Josiah was just beginning to be slightly amused at Dianne's embarrassment when from stage left rushed a figure in a black top hat and frock coat, to a tumultuous cheer from the audience. The newcomer's coat bore paper travesties of the badges of a police officer. He brandished a truncheon and shouted, 'I will save you miss, and your bairns.'

The policeman fought Cobden and O'Connor, finally, after some truncheon versus swordplay, smashing down their weapons. Having laid them low, to the biggest cheer of the night, he raced upstage, clasped the acrobat by the waist and kissed her on the cheek. Then he brandished his truncheon in victory. The fat lady and the emaciated man who had been at the gate appeared, and to finish the show the whole audience sang 'Rule Britannia' at the top of their lungs.

'Did you not like the play?' Josiah said to Dianne, as they started for home.

'I found the whole thing unrealistic,' was the only comment Josiah could encourage from her. At least in her personal embarrassment, she had not identified him as the Lone Policeman.

CHAPTER 16

A storm and its aftermath

After sunset, the night had gradually become humid and close and Josiah had slept badly. He had gone to bed at about eleven but tossed and turned until the market clock struck one when a breeze got up, and the temperature started to drop. But the breeze did not bring relief; as hard on its heels, one of the worst thunderstorms that he could remember descended on the town.

Lightning flashed overhead, and the thunder rolled simultaneously with every bolt. Rain was added to by hail, which rattled and bounced off every neighbourhood roof. At one point, when the noise from the hail was at its loudest, Josiah went down and opened the door onto the Hillgate to make sure the roof on his house was still in one piece. Water was streaming down the cobbles, mixed with melting hail and debris of all kinds. Not until three did the storm roll away north, leaving him to get some rest.

When he stepped out the following morning, it was sunny and bright, but as he made his way towards Leavington's, though the weather was now fair, there was plenty of evidence of the storm's destruction. The publican at the White Lion at the end of the street was bailing out his brewhouse and cellars and there was a bucket train of clerks emptying water from the ground floor of the Manchester and Liverpool Bank. Everywhere people were sweeping up water from kitchens, drying out mats, and in many other ways getting back to normal as best they could.

From the Lancashire Bridge, Josiah could see that the Mersey was swollen and running fast. In the middle of the river was a rowing boat containing two men who were battling with the current. The only thing that stopped the boat being swept away was a rope held by two policemen standing on a strip of gravel on the outside of the turn. Though their footholds were firm, they were still having a hard job keeping the boat steady in the stream.

As Josiah looked over the bridge, Constable Howcroft recognised him and shouted, 'Josiah, give us a hand or we'll lose the boat!'

Josiah took off his coat, giving it to a lady in the small crowd that was gathering, and ran down the steps to help.

'Why is there a boat out there at all Bob?'

'We're trying to retrieve a body. Charlie McGuinness, the knocker-up from Parks' Mill, spotted it at first light. It's snagged on one of the bridge supports.'

The men in the boat started waving furiously. 'That's the signal. They've got it. Come on lads, pull as hard as you can!'

Even after a couple of passing weavers came down and added their strength to the rope, it was still a struggle to get the boat ashore. The boatmen had not been able to get the body on board, so it hung macabrely with its arms over the gunnels, as if trying to clamber in.

As the boat neared the bank, Josiah and Constable Howcroft were able to catch a second rope thrown to them by the boatmen. The boat was beached, the body was lifted out and laid down. A man with broad shoulders, a working man. His hat and clogs were gone, but he still had his jacket, which was torn in several places from its battering from current and bridge.

On the back of his neck was a gash, which must have bled profusely, but which had been washed clean by the river. There was some bruising under this wound, as well as deep scratches on his knuckles and palms.

Howcroft pushed the hair back and Josiah felt sick. He knew the face, and the staring eyes still had the kindly shade of blue he had seen after the turn-out meeting at Felsted's. The last time Josiah had seen Fred Sowerby, he'd been the happy centre of his family, not a wet and battered corpse in a swollen river.

*

Ashton's Borough graveyard was not pretty: a parcel of land bequeathed to the town for the purpose of burying those who could not find rest in hallowed ground, due either to cost or, as in the case of Fred Sowerby, conviction. It was a patch of land hemmed in by the river and the mills.

It was a fine day for such a melancholy task, but even the colourful banners of the local Abolitionists and Chartists could not lift the mood of the mourners. Hepzibah, with a black shawl over her head, was supported by Caddy and her brother.

Phillip Burrell, who had agreed to give the eulogy, was so deeply moved by the death of his old friend that his gift of oratory escaped him. Finally, with one last effort, he rallied. 'Fred Sowerby was my friend, my oldest and dearest friend. The only thing that divided us was that he was a staunch total abstainer and I, well I like the occasional pint or a gin. But we were friends and fellow fighters in the cause of the improvement of the conditions working people endure in their employment. Aye, and we were united in supporting their right to a free vote.

'Fred Sowerby will not simply be badly missed; he will be irreplaceable.' Phillip took a deep breath and raised his voice as he looked at the crowd. 'To Fred, *The Charter and the Pledge.*' This valediction was echoed by all present.

Josiah was standing with Dianne. If Ned Ingliss, or indeed Inspector Fidel had seen him, they would have thought him very canny to have taken this opportunity to bond himself closer with Dianne. But the truth was that he had come to support a friend and to offer his prayers on this solemn occasion, whether Fred, the atheist, would have approved or not.

The chief mourners started to shovel soil into the grave. As banners were furled and people drifted away, Phillip came over to Dianne.

'We will have to get back to work Father,' said Dianne.

'Such is the slavery of toil that we cannot stop long even to mark the passing of a good man.' Phillip looked at Josiah, 'Thank you for making sure Dianne could come, you must have been most eloquent to persuade Tate.'

'I think I was pushing at an open door. Not to give Dianne time, as a known friend of the family, to attend the funeral, would not have been condoned by Mr Leavington.' Josiah did not mention that he had bought their presence by being engaged in a personal errand for His Nibs. 'Has the Felsted's turn-out finished?'

'Yes,' said Phillip, 'There was no more fight left in them after Fred died. But Felsted has not gloated; he's accepted people back on the new terms, and has had all of them back without any blacklisting.'

Hepzibah was coming towards Phillip. She touched him gently on his left shoulder and he turned. 'I don't expect you'll be able to come to the house?' she said.

Phillip took her hands in his, running his thumbs tenderly over the backs of her hands. 'I have to be off, lass. You know how it is.' She was crying and they embraced. Gently Phillip kissed her forehead as he withdrew.

Such tenderness, such fellow feeling, thought Josiah; they must have been close friends in the past when they were boy and girl.

After farewells, he parted from Dianne and set off walking alone to perform Tate's errand. There were still unanswered questions about how and why Fred Sowerby been swept downstream. He could have fallen in upstream and drowned before his body floated down to be caught on the bridge. But why had Fred been out in the middle of the storm in the first place? It seemed very unlikely that he had floated all the way to the Lancashire Bridge from the nearest place on the Mersey to where he lived. But if he had gone in the water closer to the bridge, what was he doing within Stockport much later that night? Josiah knew that he had to know the answer to that conundrum. It was bad enough to be concerned with how the Sneaker might threaten Dianne; his most important task was to protect her, preferably by catching the assassin himself. But now there was this puzzle about Fred, Josiah knew himself well enough to realize he would not be able to settle to the larger task of apprehending the Sneaker until he was sure how Fred Sowerby had died.

CHAPTER 17

Personal services

Josiah's errand was to Castle Mill, which dominated the lower end of the marketplace because it could be seen from practically every point across the town and because the builders had made the tops of the walls look like castle battlements.

The instructions from Tate had seemed clear enough: Josiah was to see a man by the name of Caine in the weaving shed. The way Tate had referred to Caine suggested he had done business with him for many years. But the way Tate continued his instructions, especially when he made it clear that Josiah was to see Caine alone, suggested to Josiah that there was more than met the eye. It seemed to him that Tate's interests always had priority in any transaction on behalf of Leavington's. In the event of a coincidence of Tate's and Leavington's interests, Tate would cooperate, but Josiah reckoned that such occasions were rare and Tate rarely, if ever, came off out of pocket.

In the weaving shed, a labourer was carrying three bolts of cloth that looked like he was taking them to be dyed. 'Excuse me,' Josiah, shouted above the noise of the shuttles, 'where will I find Mr Caine?'

The man nodded to the end of the shed, 'Beyond the green door,' then he leered. 'You'll find the "special services" you've come for on tuther side.'

Josiah walked down to the door, slid it back and stepped through. As the door closed, the noise from the weaving was absorbed by the stacks of cloth in the store. As his ears adjusted to the quiet, he became aware of a rhythmic creaking and soft human voices, one of which was female. As he listened, these sounds became more intense, rising in speed and volume. There was a small squeal before he heard a satisfied male sigh and the creaking stopped.

A tall man came around one of the larger stacks of cloth. He was tucking in his shirt and fastening his britches. He looked up and grinned at Josiah.

'Give her a few minutes and she'll be ready to go again. Insatiable she be.'

It was common for some working girls to sell their favours to the men or the overseers. Leavington's all women shop restricted that sort of practice, but in many other mills, and apparently that included Castle Mill, a bit of prostitution in return for better working conditions was common. Sometimes such services ran to having a few professional tails to offer *relief* to the men in general or married men in particular; special services indeed.

'Are you Caine?' Josiah asked, trying to stick to his errand for Tate, and hide his disgust.

'Yeah, what's that to you?'

'Mister Tate sent me to give you this.' Josiah took a small package from his pocket.

Caine snatched at it. He broke the seal and pulled out a bundle of banknotes. 'Tell Tate from me that the next time he sends one of his lackeys to deliver what he owes; the messenger will go back home with a few lost teeth.' He packed the notes back into the envelope, holding on to a few for himself.

'Princess, I've got your pay here.' A woman emerged from behind the stacks of cloth. Caine handed her a couple of the notes. 'One for this week's work and a bit more for a few considerations later.'

He looked at Josiah, 'Now get out, before I decide to batter you!'

Josiah thought about standing his ground and arresting Caine, but he could not break his disguise; the stakes were higher than an in-house brothel warranted. He turned and left the room and Castle Mill itself, as fast as he could.

The more Josiah thought about what Tate had sent him to do, the angrier he became. He was not surprised that Tate was involved in this sort of prostitution, but Tate had used him as something close to a pimp. Josiah felt degraded, soiled by the errand. His integrity had been insulted, in a way that offered him no means of redress.

He turned down a narrow alley that cut a corner off into Underbank. Only then did he hear the footsteps behind him. Looking back up the ginnel, he caught a glimpse of a man. He decided to run for it, but he had hardly moved, when someone threw a rough sack over his head and pulled him backwards. He tried to struggle, but whoever it was pinioned his arms to his sides. He heard a door slam.

He was spun around several times, as if playing a violent form of blindman's bluff. Dizzy, he was seized again and smacked face-first into a wall. Blood trickled down his nose. His head was ground into brickwork, making more of a mess of his face.

At last, the darkness was relieved by a vague light which permeated the sacking. Josiah panicked, 'They're going to set the sack on fire!' he thought, and he started to struggle again, but it was useless.

The light grew brighter. He could hear someone breathe, and he could smell the person's breath. It was tinged with the odour of cheap spirits, chewing tobacco and filthy teeth.

'Where is it?' The hand that was holding his face to the wall transferred to his throat. 'You're in hell and I'm the devil. Tell me what I want to know or…' the pressure around his throat increased until Josiah started to choke. 'Where is it?'

'What are you talking about?' Josiah rasped.

The hand tightened again, 'The silver watch. I know you have it. Give it me or your next breath will be your last.'

'I know nothing about any silver watch.' The fingers began to tighten again. 'Wait… What does it… look like? I might… be able to tell you if… I've seen it.'

There was a pause. 'Two fingers, letters round the edge. Where is it? Or I'll snap your neck.' The grip became implacable. Josiah's head swam, he was too confused to lie, all he could do was tell the truth.

'Never… seen… anything… like it.'

*

The darkness ebbed away, and Josiah found he could open one eye. The other was swollen and glued together with what felt like blood. He tried but failed to sit up. All he could see with his one good eye was a whitewashed ceiling with a few yellow stains. A face appeared.

'You know, I always thought you'd take that belligerent streak in your nature too far with someone!'

The voice had a familiar and friendly brogue. Josiah relaxed.

'Michael O'Carroll, you know I wouldn't hurt a fly, and as to *belligerent*, you're a fine one to talk!'

'Mary, he's awake and he's arguing, so he must be alright!'

The next person Josiah expected to see would be Mary O'Carroll, Michael's wife. He was surprised when it was Dr Kay, who carefully scrutinised him.

'Now Josiah, I'm going to push your face around a bit, which won't be pleasant but is necessary.'

Kay took hold of Josiah's head and twisted it to the left, which didn't hurt too much, and then to the right which was agony. Josiah was happy when his head was replaced gently on the pillow. 'Well first things first, you'll be glad to know your neck's not broken. But I'm afraid I'm going to have to inconvenience you further.'

Mary appeared and stroked Josiah's hand. 'Won't take long, Pet.' That was the first time Mary had ever called him Pet.

Dr Kay held up two fingers in front of the functioning eye. 'How many fingers?'

'Two.'

'And now?'

'Four. And before you ask, I can see clearly enough to know you bite your nails.'

'Yes, embarrassing but quite right, never seem to have managed to stop since I was a boy. Before I do the final part of this examination, how's your head?'

'Sore but not the worst headache I've ever had.'

'Good. Now the next bit will hurt. I'm worried about the condition of the other eye. I'm going to force the lid up, and to make sure your hands don't get in my way I'm going to ask Michael and Mary to hold them down.'

Josiah's arms were suddenly gripped, Kay put his thumbs on the top and bottom of Josiah's left eye and forced the lids apart. Josiah screamed but as the lids opened a smeared image of Michael appeared.

'Can you see Josiah?'

Josiah panted, but after a few gulps of air said, 'Yes.'

Mary and Michael sighed.

'That's good. You can clean him up Mary,' said Kay. 'The eye's intact, and while the bone may be cracked, it's not displaced. He'll need to rest for a couple of days to let the swelling go down and the eye open. I take it you know each other well?'

'Since Josiah was no more than a slip of a grammar boy and curious about the workings of the market,' said Michael.

'Well, he's lucky you found him when you did.'

Michael came over and looked carefully at Josiah's forehead. Now the pressure was off, there were two glasses of whisky in his hand. He gave one to Kay, took a sip from the one he kept for himself, and then turned to Josiah.

'Who did it, lad?'

'I got taken off guard and dragged into one of the Castle Mill lockups. Whoever it was didn't want to be seen; he put a sack over my head and pinioned me.'

'It'll need a couple of stitches,' said Kay, 'and before that, it will need a thorough cleaning.'

Michael's head appeared, took a good look, and then to Josiah's horror spat a mouthful of whisky onto the gash.

'Arrh!' shouted Josiah. 'Where did you get that horrible idea!'

'The Good Book lad, don't you remember that Our Lord did that when healing a deaf-blind man? The fact is the trouble with being teetotal is you can't take alcohol internally, so there's no choice but to have to take it externally. Do you think that the wound will pass muster now Mary?'

'Yes, get me that needle and thread I've had simmering in the kettle.'

In fact, the needle didn't hurt as much as Josiah had feared; the whisky had a numbing effect, but he didn't care to think about Michael's saliva.

After Dr Kay had gone, the O'Carrolls made Josiah up a bed in the kitchen. Josiah ached, but he was warm and safe, and he let his mind ramble a bit as he fell asleep. It was then, in the mysterious hinterland between sleep and waking, that the questions came to him. Had his attacker some reason to think he might have had what he had called a watch?

CHAPTER 18

Flotsam and jetsam

Three days later, face still sore but with only a very black eye to show for the attack at Castle Mill, Josiah watched Charlie McGuiness make his way down Tyesly Street on his four o'clock in the morning rounds.

Charlie carried a long cane in one hand and lantern in the other. He didn't so much walk as wander. He came on with a steady tread, but at times would cross the road for no apparent reason. Stopping at a house he would lift the lantern, reading something near the door. At others, he would bang on the main door, knock on the small window to the cellar rooms, or take his stick and tap on an upper window until someone acknowledged they had heard the call to arms of the mill.

Charlie came up to Josiah and stopped.

'Thought it was thee, Constable. I can recognise most people who are out at this hour from the shape of their shadow. Walk with me and I'll see if I can 'elp thee.'

They rounded the corner into the small cul-de-sac of Hollins Row. Charlie stopped at the next house. Using the lantern, he read the slate that hung on the wall. It had a printed heading, Park's Mill. Underneath, in a scrawl of different hands, was a list of what looked like times.

'They put the bog-trotters fresh off the boat in 'ere.' Charlie banged on the door. The hinges rattled, and the noise echoed around the street. But he kept knocking until a tousled young man opened up.

'What in the name of all our lady and the martyrs do you think you're fecking doing!' He pulled back his fist and made to swing at Charlie, who placidly pushed the lantern in the Irishman's face. The man's clenched fist opened into a flat palm to shade his dazzled eyes.

'Just doing me job. You and your mates don't want to get on the wrong side of the overseer in your first week, does thee?'

The Irishman stepped back. Charlie and Josiah moved on. 'They're no other houses to be visited until we get near the river. What's up?'

'I was told you were the one who spotted Fred Sowerby's body in the river after the storm.'

'Spotted a body. Like the rest of thee, didn't know it was Fred until we got 'im out.'

'Anything odd, out of place?'

'You mean apart from a drowned fellow human being?'

Josiah was frustrated by Charlie's glum, slow manner of talking. He was observant and reliable, but he could be annoying. 'Was the body stuck on the bridge pier when you saw it?'

'As it 'appens, no. First saw it as it came around the bend. That was peculiar. Flotsam like that usually comes around on the Lancashire side, but this didn't. It was on the Cheshire side and passed close to Park Mills. It was only when it tracked across the river that I realised it was a body and not a bundle of cloth.'

'Was there anyone about you didn't recognise?'

'Hard to say.' Charlie paused and sucked his teeth. 'The

storm had got people stirred up, so there were more about than normal, but none I recall as unfamiliar. It might be worth talking to Billy Scraff. He was about.'

'Surely too near dawn for Poor Billy?' said Josiah.

'Billy may be daft but he's no fool. He'd know a storm like that would wash things down as might be of some value to 'im. Fact is, he's been like a kid with a secret ever since, though what it is about he won't say. I'd 've a word with Poor Billy if I were thee.'

*

Josiah had spent three wasted nights looking for Billy.

Previously, when on night duty, he rather liked the shores of the River Mersey at three in the morning. But its charms were beginning to pall. The mill workers, the piecers and weavers, the carders and overseers, would not be stirred by Charlie McGuiness to get up to start their working days for another hour or so; those in the few mills which worked the clock round would have had no time to look out on the river as they served the tyrannical machines that fed King Cotton.

Tonight, as on the other three nights, he'd been raised from his bed by questions about Fred Sowerby's death that had been rolling around his mind since Fred's funeral. Indirectly Charlie had already answered one of his questions. The body had been on the Cheshire side before it snagged on the bridge, so it was very likely that Fred's body had gone into the water inside Stockport's borough boundaries.

Billy Scraff was the poorest of the poor nocturnal folk. A boy with no home and no permanent roof over his head. A scavenger on the banks of the Mersey.

Josiah saw the dim flash of a fire-fly lantern along the muddy shore; the faintest of lights which told him where Billy was. He walked down the steps on to the mud and quietly moved forward. The light went out, then on again. Josiah could see the young man's face. Billy was squatted down at the edge of the lapping water, engrossed in examining something he'd found.

'What is it, Billy?' said Josiah quietly. The boy shot up in surprise, seeming to leap into the air in a way half cat, half frog. 'Sorry, Billy. I didn't mean to startle you.'

'Yer very light on them pins of yourn, Constable.'

'Found much?' Josiah knew from experience that Billy needed coaxing. No one knew where the boy came from, not even Michael had worked it out. All that was certain was he never missed mass and always carried a crucifix. Some called him an imbecile, but Josiah preferred slow. Gaunt with cheeks marked by smallpox, the only teeth left in his head were blackened stumps, though he was no more than twelve.

People in the church had tried to take him in but it never worked; he ran away after a few days. It seemed he couldn't stand being indoors. The sky, the dark and the river were his home. Some said he should be in an asylum. Josiah thought that would be unimaginably cruel and was likely to kill him. Poor Billy Scraff, the saddest of the sad in this sad town.

'Looking for silver,' said Billy.

'Silver. That's good. Found any?'

'That 'ould be telling Constable. Billy 'as his secrets.'

'Who'd have thought it, silver in the Mersey. All of Stockport would be down here if they knew. You keep your secret safe Billy.'

The boy's temper flared, 'You don't believe Billy. Yen just

laughing like 'em all.'

'Sorry, Billy. Tell you what, how about some grub on me to make up? Ugly Tom's all right?'

Ugly Tom's was in a big house on the Lancashire side of the river. The property must have been a very fine one once, with a big garden, but now it was a ruin, only the cellars still intact. It was somewhere night workers congregated, where they could get a hot drink if it was cold and a bite to eat; a place to exchange news at the end of a hard shift. Josiah knew it well. It had been on his beat.

A few looked up as they ducked and came down the few steps from the outside. The foul miasma of excrement filled the air, only to be expected considering Ugly Tom's clientele was dominated by the night soil men who emptied privies during the night and disposed of the contents outside the town boundaries.

Except for a good fire, the only light was from a few candles on the makeshift tables, around which small groups of men sat. One or two nodded to Josiah and Billy.

They found a table in a corner. Josiah went to fetch a large bowl of Ugly Tom's speciality gruel for Billy and a large slab of bread. The boy tucked in. Josiah waited. He reckoned himself to have a strong stomach but eating or drinking at Ugly's was not something he could face.

With the last of his bread, Billy wiped every last drop of gruel from the bowl. Then, with evident satisfaction, he wiped his mouth on the filthy sleeve of his coat.

'When I find all the silver I'll eat 'ere every day,' he said.

'If there's enough silver you'll be able to eat at the King George everyday Billy. I'll be bound you'll have your own table.'

The boy grinned. 'True enough Constable, true enough.' Billy looked around, leant forward and whispered. 'I trust's ye Constable. I've found a big bit already. But I think there's more, 'ad a glimpse on it.'

'How do you mean Billy?'

'If ye promise you'll not welch on me, I'll show ye.' He stood up, rummaged in his britches and pulled out a bag. Again, the boy looked around. 'Keep all me precious things in 'ere.' He put his hand in the bag and pulled something out. Reverently, he placed it on the table under the light from the candle.

It was somewhat tarnished, but it was silver. It was a bit bigger than a large gentleman's watch, but there was no glass cover. There were two hands, one large like a minute hand on a clock, and the other a smaller, like an hour hand. The large hand pointed to the letters of the alphabet which ran clockwise around its edge. The smaller hand pointed to an inner set of letters that also ran clockwise. There was less than a full alphabet in this ring, and what letters that were there were placed in no intelligible order, running from W through to R.

'Bet you've not ever dreamt of somethin' like that, Mr Ainscough,' said Billy.

Josiah thought of his aches and pains of the past few days, as well as violence and terror of the original attack. 'Only in a nightmare, Billy, only in a nightmare.'

CHAPTER 19

A spark to powder

The latch on the outside office door rattled. 'Look out everyone, His Nibs is in,' warned Hugh. Immediately, Angel tidied up the battered mugs that had been used for early morning tea; hiding them away for washing at a more auspicious moment. Aristotle stood up from his stool and tidied his waistcoat and tie, paying particular attention to the cheap tie pin he was wearing. As a result, he knocked some papers to the floor which he had to scramble to pick up.

Josiah could hear Tate's slow step across the outer office flagstones, and then the inner door opened. Every time Tate made one of these dramatic entrances, Josiah tried very hard not to look at him, but it was not easy, the opening of the inner door was hard to resist. This time he couldn't and as if it had been planned, he looked towards the door, catching Tate's eye.

'You look a sight Breakspeare, and no mistake. You could do with something cold on that black eye of yours.' Then he started to laugh as he walked across to his office and shut the door behind him.

Josiah looked away. His bruised eye and cheek were much better, but Tate still found it very amusing. That was probably since Josiah had received the injury on Tate's errand. But at least he was back at work and able to resume his duties.

Work went on. Nothing happened out of the ordinary. Getting on towards midday, Tate came out of his lair. Hugh nodded at Josiah and mouthed, *Off for a pie and a pint.*

The only unusual event was a quarter-of-an-hour later, heralded with another sound from the outer door's latch. Angel went out to attend to whoever it was. No-one had been expected. Two quiet voices could be heard. Then the outer door closed, and Angel came back. He walked over to Josiah and gave him a small note.

'Said she wouldn't disturb your work, but the note would explain all.'

Josiah opened the slip of paper. It simply asked if he would mind walking her home that evening after work. It was signed Dianne.

The rest of the day took its toll, so by the time they were away from the mill and on their own, it was clear they were both rather reflective and taciturn.

'You seem quiet tonight,' Dianne said.

'I'm sorry. His Nibs has been particularly irksome this afternoon. I suppose he's got me down.'

'I know, it's like when the overseers get into their heads my work's not good enough, even though I know they say it just to needle me; it can still make me melancholy.' She wrapped her arm around his, and patted his hand, 'Let's walk on and talk of nothing but the weather and what we hope is to eat this evening.'

'Or in fact why you sent me the note.'

'Are yes, the note. That is rather embarrassing,' she looked a bit sheepish. 'You know that I lodge with two other politically like-minded sisters?'

'I have gathered that, but what has that to do with me?'

'Well they are high-minded and principled people, as we are Josiah, but…'

'But?'

'Well, I've never had the heart to tell them that you and I are not walking-out.'

Josiah laughed out loud. 'Let me guess. They want to meet me and have been on at you for some time, and now you can't get out of it anymore? Well let me see; playing your beau a little more actively than I have in the past seems within the terms of our agreement.'

'Thank you for saving this maiden's honour,' she said, and gave him a sisterly kiss on the cheek.

They walked on arm in arm. Chatting about the books they had read or were reading until they were in the street where Dianne lodged. By the front door of those lodgings was a familiar figure. 'Why there's father,' and Dianne waved.

Phillip came over to them, looked at the entwined arms and grinned, 'I see that you're getting closer by the day.' Josiah felt embarrassed and tried to disengage from Dianne, but Phillip patted him on the shoulder, 'No need lad, seeing you two arm-in-arm gives me more pleasure than you might believe.'

'Was the meeting a bad one, Father?'

'In short, yes, and since I think what I've found out affects you I came as soon as I could to pass on the news.'

'I'll make myself scarce,' said Josiah.

'No need. It's news that might affect you as well, indirectly.'

They went inside the house and sat down at the kitchen table. 'What has happened?'

'There were some representatives from the south present. A

few weeks ago, the mine masters in the Staffordshire coalfield proposed to reduce the wages of the colliers by seven pence a day. That much is common knowledge and has been in the newspapers. At first, it looked like a bargaining ploy, but it seems the masters were serious.

'The miners called a mass meeting at Hanley where they passed resolutions: a nine-hour working day with a break for food, four shillings a day wages, the abolition of the truck system, and they resolved to strike until these conditions were met.'

'Did they go on strike?' asked Josiah.

'They did lad, and two days after the original resolutions they added an incentive to the masters that they could draw coal to keep their mine pumping engines going and further demanded that the practice of paying six days wages for five nights work continue without interruption. But there was no sign of any movement in the masters' position.'

'That's fairly typical,' growled Dianne.

'There's more lass. A few days ago, there was a mass meeting at Burslem of the Society of Mining Paupers, reckoned at 10,000, following a procession of 2,000. They committed themselves to back the strike and linked their call for a fair day's wage for a fair day's pay to the People's Charter, believing that only the passing of the Charter can solve their problems. That means that the strikes are now backed by the Society of Mining Paupers.'

'Which means what?' asked Josiah.

'The paupers are not workers in the mines in dispute, they are miners who have become ill by working in the mines or who have been laid off,' said Dianne.

'But if they are not in dispute, by linking the strike to a call to the terms of the Charter haven't they committed sedition?'

'I think that would be arguable. The only saving grace is that the Chartists themselves have never said anything like that, so it's hard to see how a given Chartist or even the national leadership altogether could be charged successfully with sedition, but that might not stop the government trying.

'In any case, the miners are now committed to a strike across the whole of the Staffordshire coalfield and will probably try to extend the strike to the Shropshire coal mines where the same coal seams are mined. A delegation from today's meeting was to be sent to Shropshire tomorrow.'

Josiah remembered what Phillip had said about the possibility of dire consequences after the meeting at Felsted's hat works. Then Phillip had indicated that he feared that there were so many potential disputes in different industries that they might all link up, given the right conditions. It would probably only take one confrontation between the turnouts from the mines and civic authorities where the Riot Act might be read to provoke an armed response from local dragoons.

Dianne voiced what Josiah was thinking, 'Father do you think that there's going to be a general strike?'

'I think it very likely, and if other organised workers follow what the miners have done and aligned individual disputes together under the banner of the Charter, then we can expect difficult if not dangerous times ahead. But I must go, others need this news. Take care of yourselves and each other as you can. God bless both of you.'

After Phillip had gone, Dianne and Josiah sat still. Then they realised that they were still dressed in their outdoor coats.

'We can't sit here like this,' said Dianne. 'Let's at least take off our coats and have a drink.'

Josiah was not so much thinking of the effect in general on the body politic but his relationship with Dianne. Perhaps she might be thinking similar thoughts?

'Things are not looking good.'

He thought, was she speaking for herself or to him?

'After all, it doesn't come as any real surprise. But I could not have expected us to be parted so soon. Though I know we thought it would be a convenient relationship, now breaking it in a few days or a few weeks, that seems very sad to me, very sad.' She rallied, 'I'll put the kettle on.'

As she took off her coat one of its sleeves got caught on the cuff of her dress.

'Oh drat. Can you help me, Josiah? Its caught, and I can't get it free.'

He went over and managed to unhook the button on the cuff of the dress sleeve from the coat. As he released it, the coat fell to the floor and two arms gently pulled him towards her and she kissed him softly but fully. He drew her to him and responded in kind.

They must have kissed for several minutes before the front door opened, and Dianne's fellow lodgers found them in a charming, if embarrassing, embrace.

CHAPTER 20

Rain in the wind

Josiah extricated himself from the smiles and winks of Dianne's fellow tenants and got away as quickly as he could. Two things stood out as clearly as if they had been written in pure sunlight across the evening clouds.

The first was the personal mess of his relationship with Dianne. While she would only think of him as being sad because she would soon be called to high trade union matters, she did not know who he really was, or why he had been sent to stand guard on her. When that became apparent Josiah reckoned that she would be enraged, partly on the basis that she didn't need a man to look after her, but even more so that she was being spied upon. Josiah hoped that when that moment arrived, he was not in the vicinity. He might be a protection to her, but he knew that she would never see things that way.

The second thing was of much more of immediate concern. Phillip's information was very likely to be much more detailed and up-to-date than anything known by Inspector Fidel. Josiah needed to update the good Inspector as quickly as he could. A smart walk to Deansgate was required and he set off in that direction.

The sun was down before he arrived. He walked in through the door of the station. Sergeant Sandiway was minding the desk, his whiskers as luxuriant as ever.

'Well, you were the last person I'd expected to see this evening. What can I do for you?'

'I've got some news the Inspector may find useful.'

'Sounds important and you're in luck. He's in the back with Ned. Go right through. I'm sure he'll be glad to see you, even if he's heard your news already.'

He knocked and went into the Inspector's office.

'To what do we owe this honour?' said Fidel as soon as he saw it was Josiah. 'Have you come to your senses and decided to join us at last?'

'It might come to that yet, but not at this point. In this case, I have news you might not have heard yet.'

'Reputable source?'

'Does Phillip Burrell count as reputable?'

'You've got our interest, so speak.'

'There's been a development in the miners in the Staffordshire coalfields. The strike is now official and an all-out dispute. What's more, they're sending a group of their own to try to raise support in Shropshire.'

'So much for that not coming to a head,' said Ned.

'Well, Mr Burrell thinks that the dispute will widen from there and then take in other industries. He thinks we are headed towards a general strike.'

'How do you know?'

'I was there when he warned his daughter.'

'I told you he was psychic,' said the Inspector. 'If Phillip Burrell's only half right we can expect the same happening here very shortly.'

*

The following day Josiah was back at work as if nothing was disturbing him. The reality was that as he had always been, from an early age, nervous about future events with unknown outcomes. Objectively, there was no reason to think things were any different from the day before or would be different the day after. Tate was as spiteful as ever, Hugh tolerant, Angel amusingly eccentric, Aristotle vain and tedious. Nothing new, nothing out of the ordinary, except Josiah's tension concerning things he could not control or affect, and which were about to change; whether for the worse or the better was an open question. He did not see Dianne at all during working hours, but if he knew anything, it was that she would feel the same as him.

The day ground on until the bell on the mill tower began to ring, another of Mr Leavington's principles, interpreted by Tate as an excuse to get a bit of free overtime from the hands if he could.

To Josiah's relief, Hugh offered to tidy up the office, so Josiah was free to walk Dianne home. She was waiting, a discrete distance from the mill gate. Silently they linked arms and walked on, the occasional entwining of fingers the only visible sign of how they felt.

Inside Dianne's lodgings coats were taken off and hung up, then still in silence they kissed several times before sitting down, on opposite sides of the kitchen table. They both knew they needed to talk, and this was the moment.

'Have you heard anything from your father.' As a paltry opening gambit.

'No, not even a note. Though I'm not surprised. Whatever is happening, it doesn't seem that close to being critical.' She sipped her drink, 'At least not yet.'

'Same with me. Not that I'd expect to hear much before you heard it.' There was the first lie, or could he call it an untruth, even a fib, to diminish the impact it had on his conscience. In fact, he had seen Ned Ingliss shadowing him in plain clothes on his walk to work that morning. Inspector Fidel thought his position at Leavington's at least that important. He also expected that Ned had been in the shadows watching Dianne and his walk to this house. It looked as though the Chosen Men were watching out for his wellbeing and would inform the good Inspector if he needed to send a message to the Manchester's.

Dianne sipped again. 'I find myself divided in a way I never felt possible.' She put her hands in his. 'You know I am committed to my cause, but it would not take much for me to follow my heart with you, rather than stick to my principles.'

'Dianne, that would be a very foolish thing to do. Your principles are so much a part of the person you are. We may have been naïve to think we could share as much about ourselves as we have and not run the risk of developing an attachment, but there is no chance that we could be happy unless we act according to what we think is right. At this point, that choice falls on your shoulders. Don't give up what you have so often defended.'

'Didn't someone say that conscience makes cowards of us all? Well, it seems that I am sorely tempted to prove whoever said that correct.'

Josiah lent forward and kissed her hands.

She smiled at him, 'Thank you,' she said. 'I wish I was not so alone. Father will not be tracing the same path that I have. There will be other sisters with me, but they idolize me, and I find that in the position I am at present, more of a burden than a help.'

Josiah swallowed hard; another lie was required. 'You will not be alone; you will be able to draw strength from other people. You will not find yourself alone.' He might have added, not as alone as I am at this moment. He was a lover and deceiver in the same instant. 'If I could do anything to help relieve your feelings and uncertainty at this moment I would do it.'

She looked at him. It was the look of a child, trusting, sad but impossibly hopeful. Then he understood. He let go of her hands and stood up. Going over to the empty fireplace he looked into the dead ashes. 'I can't do that.'

'Can you not?'

'In many ways, I am not as free as you. There is my mother to consider. He didn't know what sort of morality invoked one lie to defend another.

'I thought she was much better?'

'That is true. And before you ask, it is not her health that keeps me here.' He looked at her, 'that has much to do with my affection for you.'

'So, you might come with me?'

'I cannot at this moment say yes. Give me a night to decide. I will give you my answer tomorrow.'

There was a knock on the door. Dianne got up and opened it. On the step was Caddy. Dianne frowned, 'What are you doing here?' she said.

'I have a message from Mum.' She saw Josiah and it seemed to him that she took on a more cautious expression. 'Sorry, mister didn't expect to see you here.'

'Well, you better come in.'

Once Caddy was inside, she sat at the table. It was Dianne she had come to find, and all her attention focused on her.

'It's a personal matter,' she said. She glanced at Josiah before she looked again at Dianne. 'You know how she's been. She's been so sad since Dad died. She'll not rest till she's spoken to you face to face.'

'Very well Caddy, I'll come with you.'

Coats were replaced, and they left, Caddy and Dianne in one direction, Josiah in the other; it was clear that Josiah was not needed or wanted on whatever errand Caddy was engaged on.

As he walked towards home, he considered his position carefully. To leave his post would not be a proper repayment of Inspector Fidel's generous personal support. But he would be being true to the primary objective of guarding Dianne. That was a point he could argue with Fidel. He might even get the Inspector's blessing. But Josiah would know it was not out of a sense of duty that he would go with Dianne, but for the sake of love.

Affection was one thing, but to take to the high road as her guard and personal assistant, that would be a very different matter and would step over the line that converted affection to a declaration, and a public one too, of active love. The sort of love that led, in his moral world, to marriage, children and respectability. But once asked, even after being her brother-in-arms, would she see the inevitability of their relationship?

If he went with Dianne, then that would be a risk he would have to take, which would be added to the complications of knowing what he had been doing up to now. Also, he would have to embrace the fact that his loyalties had been changed by these new circumstances. No longer would he be the unbiased upholder of law and justice for all and every person in the community, someone who held the ring in the boxing match between masters and workers, the law-abiding and the criminal.

He would be counted as an activist in the grievances of the working people, as Dianne was herself. He had, as many Methodists had, stood aside from such a role. Was he ready now for such a commitment? That was more of a vocation than even marriage might be considered. He did not know where he would stand when he had to make that choice, though he was aware that it might be a choice that he had to make in no more than a few seconds and not in the cold meditation of wise consideration.

CHAPTER 21

In play

The following morning, Angel was the only one in when Josiah arrived at Leavington's.

'God lad,' *whistle, croak, hand-gestures for pains in the belly and head*, 'you look as if you'd lost a sovereign and found a farthing.'

Josiah couldn't agree more.

'Anyway, this should get your day off to a good swing. There's an urgent note left last night by His Nibs. The weaving shed needs to prepare for an urgent order. I was going to take it, but if you go then a view of Dianne Burrell's dark eyes may cheer you up.'

There was no Dianne about, but he did have long discussions with the overseer and several senior weavers as to how to manage the transition to the new order to keep everyone, even Tate, happy.

It was a good hour before Josiah got back to the office, and there had been a change in mood. Tate came out of his office. 'A very good morning to you Mr Breakspeare.' The way Tate emphasised Breakespeare was odd. Josiah thought, for a second, the old martinet was going to wink at him.

The other change was that Angel and Aristotle seemed more formal. Even Hugh was rather aloof. A little while later Hugh went out on an errand of his own and Josiah made an excuse and followed. When he cornered him, Hugh was awkward. 'What happened while I was out this morning?'

Hugh looked at his shoes before he met Josiah's eyes.

'Are you telling me that you did not anticipate what happened? His Nibs had a visit from a court official this morning. He was asking for you.'

'Why would someone from a court be looking for me?'

'Well, he actually came for someone called Ainscough. Know anyone by that name? Because Tate said as much when the visitor had gone. We've all got the impression that you're a spy of the government and not our colleague and friend. Tate hinted that Breakspeare is not your real name.'

There was no point in yet more subterfuge. 'My real name is Josiah Ainscough and I'm a Constable of the Stockport Police.'

Hugh looked incredulous.

'Hugh, I am not a spy for the government. I was placed here at the request of the Manchester force to ensure the safety of Dianne Burrell.'

'So, you're trying to tell me that you're a spy, but not for the government?'

'I know it sounds strange, but that's about the size of it.'

'It does not sound strange – it sounds ridiculous! I know I'm not very bright, but I will say this to your face: I do not believe you.' Hugh made to push past Josiah.

Josiah felt utterly frustrated. He had lied to Dianne, her family and friends, all of who he liked and respected. Now the secret of why he had allowed himself to be trapped in this invidious situation had come out and he was to be branded as a traitor, a deceiver for doing what he thought had been for the best.

'You do not understand.'

'I think I understand all too well.' Hugh's temper was rising.

'No, you do not! I was at the Hall of Science to hear Feargus O'Connor and foiled an attempt on his life.'

'What sort of lie is that?'

'It's no lie, it's the truth! I am the man who has been called the Lone Policeman. It transpired that it might have been one of the Burrell family who was the real target.' He paused, wondering if to say more.

'In that case, you're now in the wrong place. Dianne Burrell has disappeared.'

'What?'

'Maybe disappeared is a bit dramatic, but she no longer works at Leavington's. She has left, done a flit. You're guarding not one-person Constable Ainscough if that really is your name! You don't need to be here anymore, and no one wants you.'

Hugh finally pushed Josiah out of his way and headed in the direction of the works' office. Josiah watched him go, realising that whatever use he could be, he could not be it as Josiah Breakspeare. He knew he must try to find Dianne, as well as tell whatever he found to Inspector Fidel.

As Matthew's Gospel had it, he was about to shake off the dust of Leavington's from his feet, when he saw Effie Wheeldon come out of the weaving shed. He called and she came over.

'Have you seen Dianne this morning?'

'No, Mr Breakspeare, but then no-one has.'

'That's what I've heard too.'

'You don't sound surprised? But then you're not what you seem yourself are you, Mr Ainscough?'

'How do you know my real name?'

'Well I don't come from these parts, and I used to live in Stockport on the north bank of the Mersey. I used to see our local policeman from time to time, and when you appeared here, I couldn't get it out of my head that you were the officer who used to walk the beat around us. I asked my dad. He may be useless for most purposes, but he still has a good memory. He happened to meet me one evening from here, saw you and confirmed what I suspected, that you are Constable Ainscough.'

'Why didn't you tell Dianne?'

'I considered it, but I thought it wasn't my place, especially when it became clear to most of us how smitten she was with you. Anyway, I owed you for the deal you did to get the money Tate tried to stop from my wages. It would have been wrong to return a bad turn for a good one. I didn't think that would be fair.'

'Thank you. Any idea where she would have gone?'

'Outside it being about Union work, no. But if you're looking and she's done a flit then I think I'll try to find her. I owe her a lot of things. Now might be a good time to join her side of the cause. What about you?'

'Much the same. I think she might be in danger and I need to make sure she realises – whatever she thinks of me as a result.'

*

There were not many leads to pick up about Dianne's whereabouts. Her father had certainly gone as well, he'd said as much; that he would go if a general dispute developed.

Josiah went over to Dianne's lodgings. She was not there, but her two friends were packing up their things, ready to move out to play their part in what was coming. They said they did not know where she was, and he could not get further information. He gave up and went his way.

Now he was standing outside one door of the long front of the three houses above the brewery store in Ashton. The door opened and there stood Caddy. She looked amazed and pleased that it was him. He heard a voice from inside, it was Hepzibah, but the voice was not as strong or as commanding as it had been when Josiah had last visited.

'Who is it pet?'

Caddy turned her head so Hepzibah would hear clearly. 'It's Dianne's beau, Ma.'

'Mr Brakespeare? Well, let him in lass, let him in.'

Hepzibah was sitting in a simple rocking chair near the fire. One shawl covered her shoulders, another her lap. She looked pale and hunched. It was as if she had aged more than ten years since Josiah had last seen her at Fred's funeral. He was shocked and saddened.

'How long has she been like this Caddy?'

'It came on slowly after Father's funeral.' The way the young girl spoke showed that it was not only Hepzibah who had aged. Caddy had been forced to become more responsible. 'She got through all that well enough, but then we started to find her sitting down and just looking at the fire or out the window, where normally she'd have been up and doing. Then one day she drew up the chair and that's where she spends most of her days now. Come and talk to her, she'll like that. I'll make you a drink of cordial.'

Josiah pulled up a stool and sat next to Hepzi. She looked up at him and gave him a big smile; somewhere inside lived the fire of the Hepzibah he had first met, but it was damped down and barely warmed the centre of her house. Gently he hugged her and patted her hand, leaving it resting on hers on the arm of the chair until Caddy came back with his drink.

'What brings you to my door, Josiah Breakspeare?'

'I wondered if you knew where Dianne or Phillip are?'

'That you asking', or the government, young man?' There was no rancour in her voice if anything merely a world-weary tone of regret.

'It's for me. I'm worried she might be in danger.'

'I wish I could help you, but I can't. The battle Phillip feared would happen has started. They wouldn't tell me where they were going, and I wouldn't ask even if I'd had the opportunity. Look for them in the hottest places.'

Caddy took Josiah's empty beaker and put a small book in his hands with a place marked with a scrap of cotton cloth.

'Why don't you pull up a chair and abide with me for a while. I'll tell you stories of the past when there was hope. And you'll stay out of trouble.' She put her head back on the chair and closed her eyes.

Josiah looked towards Caddy. She signed he should read from the book. He turned to the marked place and started to read. The poem was one of Byron's: *For we'll go no more a-roving, so deep into the night...* Hepzi settled more deeply into her chair.

An odd poem for such a full-square woman, whose principles included the Pledge and the cause of Chartism. Even outside that, she was staunch in the defence of her wider family, their education and their well-being, though open to seeing the good in people, himself at this moment, who she would have been excused from thinking unkindly of.

Hepzi's head had settled on her chest and her breathing had become more rhythmic. She was asleep. She slept the sleep of the just. If she had been a Methodist she would have been as staunch as his mother. But atheist that she was, she was no less a person of substance in pursuit of justice and service of her neighbours. As Mr Cooksley had remarked about Robert Owen before they entered the Hall of Science to hear Feargus O'Connor months earlier, she was like Owen in that she would do good, when or if Christian people failed. Her righteousness would serve as a reprimand to the believers if they failed the Kingdom of God.

Hepzi had a tough, dedicated life. Perhaps her fondness for this most passionate of Byron's poems gave pleasure because it reminded her of her love and solidarity in marriage with Fred. It was not surprising then that she had so easily collapsed in sadness now her strong right arm was gone.

Caddy came over and made sure Hepzi's head was comfortable. She took Josiah on one side and spoke softly. 'I heard what she said. I've heard they may have gone in the direction of Macclesfield but after they meet with the leaders of the turn-outs down there, they'll go where they're needed.' She paused.

'Something is troubling you,' said Josiah.

She nodded. 'Ma collapsed so quickly. If anyone caused that, did her harm, as you might say, then I will want to know how and why.'

'You've got a wise head on young shoulders Caddy. To think that grief from a death could do such terrible things to someone so indomitable.'

'Father's death hit her hard, that's true, but there's something more. She sometimes talks in her sleep, and then it seems to be about way back when she was a young woman. You're a churchman Josiah, pray for her, where I cannot.'

He nodded, embraced her and left; his thoughts full of all those caught up in whatever trouble had arrived on their doorsteps. The day was ending, and he was exhausted in spirit as well as physically. He made his way back to his home in Hillgate and closed the door on the confusion of the world for at least one night.

CHAPTER 22

By the Queen's Warrant

There was a knock at Josiah's door. He opened it, to find a young man in black with a top hat. His tunic was tight, short at the waist and trimmed in generous layers of silver braid. He carried a short ebony staff with a silver pommel and collar.

'Good morning Sir. Do I have the pleasure of addressing Constable Josiah Ainscough of the Stockport Police Force?'

'Yes... Yes, you do.'

'Good, I am tipstaff to Sir Grancester Smythe Bart. He asks you to attend him this morning at the local magistrate's court at nine o'clock sharp.' The man handed Josiah a note. It was impressed with the motif of a lion seizing a deer by the neck.

'This summons is issued under the authority of a Queen's Warrant. Good day, Constable.' The officer touched his hat with his staff and was gone.

The message inside the note confirmed that indeed Josiah had been summoned. He had no idea who Sir Grancester Smythe was, but a Queen's Warrant could not, under any circumstances, be ignored. As a result, he presented himself just before nine at the court's main door. When he knocked it was opened by Constable Giles.

'Come in Constable Ainscough. You are expected. Please

131

go up to the room at the top of the stairs and wait there until you are called.'

'Very formal aren't you, Tom?' said Josiah. 'Can't you tell me anything about why I'm here?'

Constable Giles closed the door and, rather furtively, looked up the stairs. He put his finger to his lips. 'You'll find you're not alone.'

He was right, there were three other people in the waiting room. The tipstaff, who had summoned him, was playing sentry on a second door which led through to the courtroom. The other two were Inspector Fidel and Mr Prestbury. Both were deep in their thoughts. Josiah nodded respectfully to both and sat down on one of the benches usually reserved for witnesses.

The courtroom door opened, and a small, grey man looked out. 'Good you are all here. Please come in.'

Sitting at the clerk's table was a smartly dressed man. 'Gentlemen, may I introduce to you the Right Honourable Sir Grancester Smythe.'

Sir Grancester was expensively dressed: a dark blue velvet frock coat set off by a damask silk waistcoat and full lace cravat. Lace could be glimpsed at his wrists. The clothes exuded quality but were also slightly foppish, certainly far more extravagant than the austere tastes of local manufacturers or merchants.

Sir Grancester rose to greet them. 'Thank you for attending gentlemen. I hope I have not inconvenienced you.'

Josiah thought Mr Prestbury must be extremely put out, having been summoned in the same way as a Manchester police inspector, let alone a humble constable from his own force.

'Sir Grancester,' he spluttered, 'I feel I really must protest...'

Sir Grancester held up his hand. 'Of course, Mr Prestbury, I perfectly understand how very vexating this morning's arrangements must be to you.' Prestbury tried to interrupt, but he was powerless in the face of that hand. 'You must understand that I invited you to attend as a matter of courtesy.' He nodded to his secretary, who handed Prestbury a letter.

'Please read. You will see it is clear that I am to oversee the investigations into the matter of the attempt on Mister O'Connor's life at the Hall of Science, and other connected matters, including the death of Frederick Sowerby. Since the last matter is the most pressing, I felt it best to come to Stockport first. I thank you, Mr Prestbury, for your forbearance in this matter, but I would not wish to detain you now you have ascertained that I am here on the very highest authority.'

Sir Grancester turned to Josiah and Fidel. 'Please, sit gentlemen.'

Prestbury read the letter and handed it back to the secretary. For the first time, Josiah saw Prestbury at a complete loss for words, but he pulled himself together, looked Sir Grancester in the eye, and accepted the inevitable. 'That seems quite clear your grace.'

'I am much obliged to you Mr Prestbury, much obliged.'

Prestbury bowed, turned and departed, closing the door behind him. The secretary gave the warrant to Fidel, who read it quickly and then passed it to Josiah. Not only did the document carry the royal seal and the signature of the Queen herself, but also the signature of Prime Minister Peel—on the highest authority had been no understatement.

'Now gentlemen, having got over the formalities, shall we have some tea?' The tipstaff immediately brought in refreshments, serving everyone from an exquisite porcelain tea service.

Sir Grancester began in earnest. 'First, let me make it clear to you that the government in London has been watching with concern the situation in the north for some time. We have been concerned about tensions between supporters of the Anti-Corn Law League, I believe you call them Leaguers up here, and the Chartists. We are also concerned about the growing amount of industrial disruption.

'In London, we have wondered whether there was an element of external agitation in the industrial unrest. To put none too fine a point on it, whether there is any sign of a guiding or shaping hand in these matters.' Sir Grancester looked steadily at the Inspector, indicating that he expected a reply.

'In terms of industrial unrest, the Manchester force has not encountered any patterns of that type. There have been outrages inspired by specific disputes and cases of harassment of people who have not turned out in some strikes, but these sorts of incidents have been common over many years. Nothing has changed recently to suggest a new element is in play.'

'Mr Ainscough, is that the view of Phillip Burrell?'

Josiah realised belatedly that he must have looked surprised.

'Come now Mr Ainscough, we are aware that the Inspector has placed you in the office at Leavington's to keep an eye on the safety of Miss Dianne Burrell. Because of that assignment, you have been drawn into her father's circle and have attended a turn-out meeting at which he spoke.'

It was Josiah's turn to pull himself together. 'In my hearing, Phillip Burrell has stated that relations between masters and workers are, in a wide range of industries, worse than for many years.'

'What is his explanation, if that is the case?'

'The general economic state of the country.'

'Could that be a fiction intended to hide his own and the Chartists' involvement in fermenting unrest? Is it not unwise, or at least naïve, to take at face value the word of such a well-known radical agitator as Burrell?'

Josiah swallowed hard; time to tell the truth and shame the devil. 'I realise why that might be an attractive hypothesis, Your Grace, but he impresses me as honest.'

Sir Grancester smiled. 'Even Phillip Burrell's enemies vouch for his personal integrity. As a result, I am inclined to agree with you Constable. Of course, Burrell may not be involved in any conspiracy that might exist, and thus would not be in a position to know.'

Sir Grancester turned his attention back to the Inspector. 'Mr Fidel, you have been acting on another assumption; that there is a conspiracy to ferment general disorder using murder and other acts of violence against important members of different radical organisations. Is that the case?'

'Yes, your grace. The attack on Feargus O'Connor was the first direct suggestion that it might be so. There is circumstantial evidence of other instances of harm to possible targets which may have occurred.'

'The unfortunate Mr Sowerby was a potential target in that category, was he not Inspector?' Grancester turned to Josiah, 'I am informed you helped pull him out of the river. Was Sowerby murdered?'

The more garrulous might have thought this was a very good opportunity to make known his private opinion on how Fred had died, but this was not such an occasion, thought Josiah.

'Impossible to say, Your Grace. His injuries were consistent with a fall, as far as I saw. He was not the first person to drown in the Mersey near where he died. The river was very high that night, but there was no way to tell if he fell or was pushed.'

Sir Grancester steepled his fingers and frowned. 'Thank you, Gentlemen. It seems to me, Inspector, that you have acted commendably in this matter and done more than expected under the heading of general duty. I will ensure that your superintendent is appraised of my opinion. I would be obliged if you could appoint an officer to liaise with me and Constable Ainscough as he continues his activities at Leavington's.

'In the meantime, can I have from you a list of cases of violence that you feel might be part of any second conspiracy. I will consider them in more detail.'

Sir Grancester looked down; the meeting was at an end as far as he was concerned, but Josiah could not leave until both Inspector Fidel and Sir Grancester knew that Dianne had disappeared from Leavington's. He coughed and Sir Grancester looked up.

'Constable, have you more to add?' His manner oozed a variety of polite anger. Josiah knew that he was thinking, how dare such a minion raise more business?

'I would have had to meet Inspector Fidel this morning in any case. Dianne Burrell has gone from Leavington's. It seems she has joined her father.'

'Are you sure?' asked Fidel.

'I spent most of yesterday trying to find her, but it seems she has left.'

Sir Grancester sighed. 'Now it is my turn to be vexed, but it cannot be helped. Please go with the Inspector and he will get you sworn in so you can become a part of his Chosen Men.

I'll see you in Manchester this evening. I think this meeting is now closed.' This time the meeting was over.

They were outside and well away from the court before the Inspector spoke. 'If the Burrells are gone then that's the best indication possible that the disputes are growing and headed in our direction.'

'I'm sorry I could not forewarn you about Dianne and Phillip Burrell. You would have been my first port of call this morning.'

'You did your best and it isn't as if we didn't know it was a possibility. Get your travelling clothes together and come to the city as quickly as you can. I'll arrange to have you sworn in as a special constable, which should cover the legalities. Don't be surprised if you don't see your own bed for a few days at least. I'd bet my pay that watching the turnouts as they come up from the south is one of the extraordinary services Sir Grancester will have in mind for my lads, and that will now include you. This evening's meeting is going to be very interesting.'

CHAPTER 23

Call to arms

Josiah followed Inspector Fidel to Manchester as soon as he could, but there were things he had to do, most particularly making sure his Mother and Father knew what he was about and that they shouldn't worry if they didn't see or hear from him for a while.

There was also the problem of Billy's silver watch. Josiah had persuaded Billy to part with it, having sworn to the boy that personally he would make sure any reward for its return would be Billy's. But there was no time now for Josiah to investigate what its purpose might be, and his intuition was that he should not part with it until he had examined it in detail. It needed to be safe, but where could he put it? After a moment it came to him — how about the chimney?

A bit of scrabbling discovered a loose brick in the flue. He wrapped the watch in a cloth and put in the crevice created by removing the brick, then resealed the whole with the half a brick he normally used to prop open the back door when needed.

It was early evening before he got to the Manchester station house, where he received a friendly welcome from Ned.

'The Inspector is in a meeting.'

'Let me guess — it's with one Sir Grancester Smythe, whose secretary is with them?'

'There's a military gentleman as well, a Colonel Wymes. Arrogant cove to my way of thinking from the way he parades himself in his uniform, complete down to his spurs. Typical regular cavalry.'

'Definitely regulars? There'll be a meeting of all available officers at the change of duties in a while, then it's the turn of us Chosen Men, which you are to formally join.'

It took a bit of time for the magistrate who was swearing in special constables to be free to deal with Josiah. There had been a change of plan since the meeting at Stockport; Sir Grancester had asked for Josiah to be made a Manchester officer. As a result, Josiah's swearing-in was more complicated, and he had to be issued with a Manchester uniform. By the time he'd obtained it from the store, which was a couple of streets away, the station house was full of officers.

Sandiway got everyone into squad order in the yard at the back of the station house.

'Watch him, Sergeant,' Ned said as he walked past Sandiway, but near enough for Josiah to hear what he said. 'He has a reputation for being a drill sergeant's nightmare in the Stockport force.' Ned must have thought the Sergeant would see this as a joke, but as soon as he could Sandiway came over. Josiah came to attention and tried to salute but made his usual mess of the whole matter.

The Sergeant chuckled. 'I think I'll hide you at the back, if I may. After all, you're here for your brains and detective skills, more than marching. Just don't try any stamping or we'll both be embarrassed. The Inspector may not worry if we don't cut a dash as a body of men with this lordling, but it's my professional duty. I like my lads to shine.'

'Of course, Sergeant.'

The door at the back of the station house opened and Sir Grancester appeared. Sandiway immediately brought the men to attention. Josiah did not stamp. He wondered why it had never occurred to him to go softly like this in the past. It protected the reputation of the squad as well as relieving his sense of uselessness.

Together with the Inspector, there was the officer Ned had mentioned, dressed in full scarlet uniform. His spurs jangled as he walked. He even had at his belt a well-polished but rather incongruous sabre. Did he expect to be attacked here? The whole effect was a combination of impressive military swagger and an air of threat, somewhat undermined by vanity.

Sir Grancester surveyed the men, holding them at attention sufficiently long to impose on them his general authority. The man with the uniform might be flashier but Sir Grancester was the real commander here, and everyone at the muster knew that without anyone saying it explicitly.

'Thank you, men, please be at ease.' A subtle difference but significant; not a case of stand easy, but at ease; meaning they were still under the control of his authority.

'I do not intend to delay you in your duties, but I thought I should introduce myself, and make it clear why I am here.

'As your Inspector will confirm, I have the authority of a Queen's Warrant to guide and assist the local forces of civil governance in the emergency that is growing south of us. Many of you will be aware that there has been unrest in the Staffordshire area. I can confirm to you that all the mines in the Staffordshire coalfields are now turned out. Other industries are being drawn into this action, and Colonel Wymes and I anticipate that there will be groups of strikers moving north who will attempt to disrupt legitimate enterprise in and around Manchester. You will be at the centre of assisting the military and other civil authorities. Thank you.'

Inspector Fidel stepped forward. 'Thank you, men. Those of you who are coming on duty please proceed. Will my Chosen Men stay behind.'

Once only the Chosen Men remained in the yard, they filed into the main meeting room. At the head of a large table, on which was a selection of papers, sat Sir Grancester, Wymes and Sir Grancester's secretary. There were three others Josiah did not recognise. There were enough chairs for the rest of the men to sit.

'Good,' said Sir Grancester after everyone had settled. 'Colonel Wymes has already been introduced to you, but no doubt you will be wondering who these other gentlemen are. They represent the towns to the south of Stockport: Alderman Cooper from Wilmslow, Alderman Hardcastle from Poynton and Alderman Dee from Macclesfield. It is these three towns which we believe to be under most immediate threat. Wilmslow and Macclesfield are on main routes to the south-east. It is thought that Poynton will be a major target because of the importance of coal to the success or failure of the strikes.

'Perhaps we should start with questions from these gentlemen?'

Alderman Cooper held up his hand. 'Gentlemen, we are already aware of at least one column of strikers moving towards us. We are as prepared for their arrival as well as we can be, but it is clear that we do not have sufficient police or local dragoons to deter even a medium body of turnouts coming into Macclesfield, let alone Cheshire in general. Will the army be able to help us?'

'I think that is a question for Colonel Wymes,' said Sir Grancester.

The cavalry officer got to his feet. 'There have been several encounters between militia and turn-outs, but those engagements have not deterred the strikers.'

The Alderman was not satisfied. 'Sir, can you give us an assurance that regular army units will help us if need be?'

'Sir I wish I could tell you otherwise, but I cannot promise you any help of that nature.'

'So that's a no then,' whispered Ned, who was sitting next to Josiah.

'Gentlemen, the best way for you all to be safe is if you each can protect your areas and communities separately. Supplement your forces with as many special constables as you can swear in and wherever possible coordinate your activities with local detachments of dragoons and militia. We will attempt to raise forces to strengthen areas where pressure from turn-outs becomes violent.'

Sir Grancester intervened, 'This might be an appropriate moment to inform you that the Colonel and I have been asked by the Prime Minister to help coordinate your efforts with each other and with those of the army. We will also be liaising with the local authorities.

'The officers of the Manchester police force you see with us here provide another source of support. They are an elite group of officers who will be able to gather information about how the strike is progressing. They will make available that information to you where appropriate, either directly or through myself or Colonel Wymes.'

Alderman Cooper spoke, 'That is good to know Sir Grancester, but in any event, we will not be able to withstand on our resources for very long. It is inevitable that once north of Poynton, Stockport will be the next target, followed by Ashton and Bury, then Rochdale. Then the turnouts will march on Manchester.' The other aldermen murmured their agreement.

Sir Grancester raised his hand, 'Gentlemen, I am sure you will do your best. I do not think I need to remind you that you can read the Riot Act to make your legal rights clear to the mob, that you have the legal power to arrest and detain whoever threatens the Queen's Peace. Rest assured Her Majesty's Government believes the stability of the manufactories in the north-west of England, especially around this great city of Manchester, are vital to the well-being of the nation's economy.'

*

Despite it being relatively early Josiah was stuck in Manchester; not even Ned could find him any sort of train back to Stockport. The only way he would be able to get back to Leavington's in time for work was to get off on foot early in the morning.

As the evening wore on the comings and goings in the station house subsided. Sergeant Sandiway arranged for Josiah to use an empty cell, made a bit more comfortable with spare blankets and a couple of extra mattresses. A sandwich and a mug of cocoa were provided.

Finding an old copy of a local newspaper, Josiah settled down to read until his mind became calm enough for sleep. The warmth of the cocoa in his stomach was comforting, and he was quickly at rest for the first time that day.

The newspaper was a copy of the *Manchester Trumpeter*. It

fell open at the pages that carried the personal advertisements. Josiah scanned them. *Upright man in his sprightly years seeks the company of a young woman for social intercourse.* It was the sort of personal message that was common in popular papers like the *Trumpeter.*

Many such personal messages were probably genuine attempts to find company in the lonely city, but most, Josiah had always assumed, were really about obtaining sexual gratification, with or without payment.

This one was definitely in that category, as the use of the word *intercourse* made very explicit. The signature was just a made-up name — Jolly Peter. He finished his drink.

Sandiway stuck his head around the door. 'You comfortable enough Constable? I could always arrange a nightcap from the local tavern if it would help.'

'Very generous Sergeant, but I don't drink, except cocoa of course, if you've got another.'

'Coming up,' said Sandiway.

Josiah settled down. Thoughts about the silver watch swirled in his tired mind along with a half-formed idea about the advertisements in the newspaper. He remembered that there had been a year in grammar school when secret codes had been a popular pastime for the boys. He recalled that he had been very good at devising them, especially where the codes were of that class known as cyphers.

In a cypher, the letters of a message were shuffled in such an away that they made no linguistic sense. How the encoded letters came out was determined by a keyword or phrase. *Jolly Peter* was a phrase which was just short of being a potential keyword. In a cypher, the letters of *Jolly Peter* could be at the start of a line of letters. Then they would be followed by all the other letters of the alphabet not included in the keyword. To code a message you would write the alphabet over the top and rewrote the message using the letters shifted by the keyword.

It was Sandiway again. 'There's your cocoa. I'll say goodnight and let you get some rest.'

'Thank you, Sergeant. Goodnight.'

Josiah yawned and then nearly fell from his makeshift bed. *What if Jolly Peter was a keyword?* If that was the case, he knew where the keywords were to be found. But where might the encoded message itself be?

He flicked through the paper. Several pages on he found what he was looking for — a short list of letters that appeared to be in random order. He carefully folded the newspaper and put it in the waterproof pocket inside his new uniform. Now he would have to wait to see if the silver watch might be a way of making encoding or decoding easier.

CHAPTER 24

3,317,702

J osiah looked out from beneath his tarpaulin and was hit
in the eye by a large drop of rain from the tree above him.
Though he had enjoyed his two nights in the open, most people
would not have agreed with him, but life in the fields was far
less complicated than in the town, especially when dealing with
Sir Grancester Smythe.

A pair of mud-encased boots appeared in his line of sight.
Ned was wet through, but he had got a loaf of bread in his
hand. 'Budge up and I'll share what I've scavenged.' Ned pulled
off two lumps from the loaf.

Josiah fished in his pack and brought out some cheese.
'Thanks, brother, I wonder what else is in that cornucopia
of yours?'

'Has Maggie said anything useful?'

'Who? Maggie? No, moved on from her, she has a friend
who seems to know one of the union men from Stoke. I've
been talking to her. I've convinced her I'm from Ashton, here
to support the cause any way I can. You?'

'Talked to a fair number last night. All manner of trades and
motives. Only a small group of miners left. The main group
split off towards Poynton before we tagged along.'

'Ned, these people aren't unreliable types. There are a few

146

hotheads. They're polite, though underneath they're very angry.'

'What sort of cause have they to be angry?'

At first, Josiah thought that Ned was just kidding, but the inflexion in his voice had been harsh. He caught a glimpse of Ned's expression. He'd meant the way he'd said it, with all the bitterness of a bad memory.

A grey-haired man walking with a stick and shoulders sagging came up. The man might have looked hale and hearty but for his demeanour: the depth of the creases in his face, the air of sadness that surrounded him. He stopped in front of them.

'What can we do for you?' said Josiah.

'Listen to my tale, that's all I ask.'

Ned finished his bread and got back on his feet. 'Can't hang about here – girls can't have too much attention.' And was gone.

'Tell me your tale, Sir, if it helps you.'

Shot through with pain, the old man lowered himself and sat next to Josiah.

'Like you, I was young once. I had a sweetheart. We married and three sons and one daughter came along. My sons deserted me, but my daughter was true. She married and had a daughter herself. When she and her husband died my granddaughter survived, but she was murdered by a thief. She was innocent sir. Tell me what was the good in all of this?'

Josiah was shocked. 'How did this terrible thing happen?' To lose a daughter was bad enough, but a granddaughter murdered. Whatever the details of the story, it would explain the old man's demeanour.

'Thank you, Sir.' He offered his hand to Josiah. 'I am called George, George Blandford.'

'Josiah,' He offered George his hand, and then some of the

bread and cheese.

'It's a long story, sure you've got the time lad?'

Josiah nodded.

'I was on the procession that delivered the National Petition to Parliament. Now… where to begin?' The old man thought for a moment, the resumed more confidently. 'Someone was shaking me, "Wake up Grandad!" I tried to wake up but after a few seconds, I was back in the arms of Morpheus. The shaking started again.

'"Wake up Grandad!"

'"Let me be Pet."

'"Come on Grandad, it must be soon!" Another shake.

'"It's not time yet."

'"How will we know?"

'"Someone will wake us up for breakfast," I said, turned over and hoped that sleep would return, but I was wide awake.

'I'd never been anywhere a servant would come and call me, and as soon as I thought it there was a soft knock on the door. "Morning Mr Blandford. Master hopes you slept well. I've some hot water for a shave, and I've strict instructions to help Millie get a good wash in the kitchen for the big day, while you get time to collect your thoughts. I'll leave the water by the door."

'Millie was already up and at it. "Don't forget to get up for breakfast Grandad," she said as she closed the door behind her. I pulled on my trousers; in case anyone saw me, as I collected the hot water. Then I washed, shaved and finished dressing.

'Next problem was breakfast. Supper the night before had been more like a banquet, but then this was a well-to-do house. It belonged to Mr Cain, a high up clerk in a big bank. I never knew folk like him were on our side. When we got there, everyone, all the guests, family and servants were on the doorstep to welcome us. Almost the first thing that they had asked was where *it* was.

'At first, I couldn't think what they meant. But Millie tugged at my pack until I got the gist. Then I unpacked it. It was still as battered as it had been the day that I yanked it from the hands of that bastard hussar in St Peter's Fields. The bell was all skew-whiff and the tassels faded from the bright blue and gold they had sported on that day. I was ashamed of it in the company.

'But the maid put out her hand and delicately touched the tarnished brass. "Does it still sound sir?" I must have smiled, then I blew it. Clear and commanding, as it had been every time I'd sounded it over the years, as it had been only a few months before at the Hall of Science, calling people to rally to the defence of Mr O'Connor.

'I got down to breakfast with the help of another guest, a Mr Bax, a smart posh man, who turned out to be one of the Birmingham representatives.

'Millie was afore me and already eating, sitting next to an earnest young man who seemed to be explaining what the things on her plate were. Millie got up as soon as she saw me, ran over and hugged me. Then she twirled around showing me a dress I'd not seen before with a beautifully embroidered bodice. "What do you think Grandad?"

'The young man who had been talking to Millie came forward. "I'm Jonathan Bryant. Mr Cain realised that you would not want anything for yourself to remember this day by, but he thought a few things for your granddaughter might be acceptable. This dress is for today and there are two more for every-day and a full range of underclothes that should last as she grows. I might add all the women in the house have had great fun making all the things. They are all on tenterhooks and hope you will like this gift." The kindness brought tears to my eyes.

'We walked to where the procession was assembling in Lincoln Inn Fields. There were thousands of Chartists there. I was amazed; you know they were still adding in signatures from petition forms that had only just arrived. The final total was 3,317,702. When they had done, they reeled it all up into a huge roll of paper and mounted it in a frame, with long wooden handles, so that teams of men could carry it all the way to the Houses of Parliament.

'Jonathan came up. "I've found where our cart is. When the procession starts, we can join it."

'The Petition was complete and the first group of men who would pull it towards the Houses of Parliament were moving it along using ropes. It began to circle the whole of Lincoln Inn Fields, being shown to all there. As it passed, a great cheer went up from every quarter as the many people who had worked to create it saw the final form of all their efforts. Two horsemen appeared to act as marshals to the procession. Behind them was a brass band. This was followed by a phalanx of flags and banners. From our wagon, I could see a green, red and white tricolour which seemed to be the flag of the Welsh delegates. On another were a cap and a bundle of liberty rods bound with a ribbon which said, *Justice*.

'But my favourite banner was the one on our cart, the cart of the Peterloo Association. On its front were scenes from that fateful day. There was even a decent likeness of "Orator" Hunt, who was the main speaker, but the most dramatic was the scene of the hussars charging the crowd. Over this picture, it said *Peterloo Massacre, Manchester, August 16th, 1819*. On the rear of the banner was the message *Murder Demands Justice*.

'The wagon was soon in line and the bannermen had taken up their burden. Then came our chance to parade around the field on our way out. Wherever we went there was a great cheer and I tried to respond as well as I could on the bugle.

'So many people, so many sights, so much noise. Wherever the road was wide enough there were omnibuses and cabs sporting colours, as well as crowds of supporters.

'Only on Pall Mall was it different, where the windows and balconies of the expensive gentlemen's clubs were full of silent members of Parliament and others high up in government circles; there it was the marchers who took up the cheering and waved their banners in the faces of their opposition.

'I blew the bugle for all I was worth. I was catching my breath when I looked up at one of the balconies. Standing at the rail was a tall, well-dressed man. He was leaning forward on the rails. He looked relaxed but his hands were clenched so tight his knuckles were white.

'As we came into Whitehall we saw the Houses of Parliament for the first time, but only the Petition stopped at the parliament building. I could see a whole crowd of men struggling to get it through the door.

'We crossed the Thames by another bridge and the carts were gathered in a park near a big church, which Jonathan said was Southwark Cathedral.

'We ate what we had brought with us, then and there were some wine and good water provided for those who needed it.

Millie had started to show signs of feeling tired, and I found her a place to have a nap, while I and Jonathan listened to some speakers who were addressing the crowd.

'When she woke, we started towards Mr Cain's house, using another bridge which Jonathan thought would be less crowded. Millie now had enough energy to carry my pack. We were in no hurry, strolling as Millie skipped and danced.

'I asked Jonathan how a well-educated lad like him got involved with the Chartists.

'He said, "Well I have the time to get involved with the movement as much as I do because I work for Mr Cain, so I could just be going along with the flow. But the truth is I became interested in the cause in '39."

'You must have been just a whelp then?' said I.

'Jonathan laughed, "I've not been called a whelp for many a year."

'I must have looked embarrassed because Jonathan laughed again.

'"Don't worry I'm not offended; whelp I was and whelp I still am and proud of it. My father ran a butcher's shop. I ran errands from the moment I was big enough. Father served the well off and the poor. So, I was admitted to the kitchens of the wealthy to be petted by the cooks, and into the kitchens of the poorest where I was invited by their children to a bit of skipping or fisticuffs. I grew up knowing as my parents did that the poor needed help. A place at a grammar school gave me the education, a head for figures gave me my profession, Mr Cain gives me the time and opportunity."

'I imagined the young man stepping into the light of politics. "Will you stand for a seat in parliament?" I asked.

'Jonathan stopped and looked hard at me. "I've never confessed it, not even to myself. But yes, I would, no better than that, yes I will if the chance comes my way."

'I stepped forward and gave him a big hug. I said something like, "God strengthen your arm lad, and may you sit in a Chartist government one day."

'Then a tall man came out of the shadows. He punched Jonathan, knocking him down, then made to hit me with a cudgel. I threw myself at him to try to protect Millie, but I was too slow. The blow that was meant for me hit her and she crumpled, blood pouring down her face onto the beautifully embroidered bodice of her new dress.

'The last thing I remembered was seeing the man kick Millie's body aside and carry off the pack and the Peterloo Bugle.'

CHAPTER 25

Quarry Bank Mill

George Blandford shook Josiah's hand and moved away. Josiah felt that he should be doing something to bring justice for the old man but there was nothing he could do, only remember and pray.

He put his things together in his pack and waited for Ned to return. His partner arrived just as the column of turn-outs was starting to move again. Soon they came to the bank of the River Bollin and the path to their target, Quarry Bank Mill owned by the Greg family, leading members of the Anti-Cornlaw League.

Though the Bollin was not very deep, it was deceptively swift, causing at least one drowning a year. But a swift-flowing river was an obvious attraction on a site for a cotton mill, as was placing a mill in a farming area. With the ups and downs of the cotton industry, being able to move workers to the land in times of low demand in the cotton cloth production, would make any mill easier to manage.

Something was depressing about the valley. The trees were dark, and the clouds, full of rain, gathered above their heads. The marchers became quiet. Josiah kept his eyes sharp. Before long he noticed a gamekeeper on the opposite bank with a shotgun. He was accompanied by another man, who could well be a special constable. Josiah pointed them out to Ned.

'That looks like our sort of company,' came the whispered reply.

Sightings increased; single heads glanced down on them; faces in the undergrowth were visible for short periods. Then the marchers started to come to the part of the river that provided the main source of water for Quarry Bank's great wheel. The river deepened and broadened here. The marchers had to walk on a path between the river and a series of large ponds. Finally, the river roared over a thirty-foot weir.

As they got close to the mill, Josiah heard a groan from the marchers behind him. He could guess what that meant, the path the turn-outs had just come along had been sealed with more 'specials' and lads from the workforce. They had no choice but to go forward into the narrow mill yard.

There was a small barricade to their left and another further up the slope that led to the road towards the village of Styal. The marchers did not have much time to assess their situation; once they were through the gate in front of them, they were trapped in the mill yard.

A walkway ran across the top of the office from the warehouse on the right and across the space between the buildings behind the smaller barricade. On to it stepped a smartly dressed man, who walked to the middle and looked down on the turnouts.

'Friends, for so you are to me, and I hope you always will be. I know that times are hard and what effects that is having. I defend the right of people to strike in good faith. I was approached this week by five of my own men asking permission to have leave to join you. I gave them my leave and told them clearly that they would have their jobs back, no questions asked, when this civil war is over; and we can be friends and fellow workers together again.'

There was a half-hearted cheer for this, half the turn-outs thinking they agreed with the sentiment, the rest wondering which way Mr Greg's mind was working.

'But friends, we know that these actions are utter folly. Would you draw the plugs from the boiler of our steam engine here, only to insist that the mill pay for the repair of the boilers? What a jolly idea such a plot, a plug plot, would be, provided there is still money in the factory to put things back when the turn-out is over. Many of you will be union men. You will be fighting for your family and its future as I do.'

That produced jeers. 'You ain't clemmed,' shouted a voice from the back.

'We're getting better victuals on this march than we get at home,' shouted another. Arms were raised, fists shook. They may have been trapped but they were not cowed.

Mr Greg raised his hand in apology. 'You are quite right to chide me, my friends. I do not starve, nor do my family. Many of you do and I regret it. But look at it from my point of view. When trade is slow there are no profits to make unless my costs diminish.'

'Yen could cut profits!' jeered several voices.

'You know friends that I choose to improve the conditions of my workers when I have a superfluity: housing in the village, gardens for growing extra food, schooling for children, privies on every floor of the mill.'

'So, you can make sure there's no time lost when nature calls.' The heckle raised a laugh.

Mentioning the privies had been a slip, it sounded trivial. The emotion of the crowd started to change. Mr Greg realised what had happened and tried to recapture the moment, but he knew he was now up against it.

'Friends, I support charity in hard times and charity may do much.' A slow handclap started.

'Friends, the hunger you feel is nothing to the prospect of the thousands of hungry people who will be on our streets if the Corn Laws are not repealed! That is the way to get better conditions; not this reckless turnout.'

Now Greg had lost momentum. All the people in the march who Josiah had talked to were of a single mind that this strike, in whatever industry, was caused by the reduction of pay to protect owners' profits. To them the Corn Laws, though they might be important, were secondary to the problem of wages in hand and bread on tables.

More people began to clap. The sound got louder and Mr Greg tried to speak again, but the clapping grew in pace and finally, he could not be heard above it and he stood mute, downcast, both hands on the rail of the bridge.

Over the heads of the men and specials at the main barricade, Josiah could see up the track that went towards the Styal Road. It levelled out at the top so he could not see beyond. Over this rise came a small group of young people who Josiah recognized as having been part of the turn-out column. They were cheering and waving something in the air: loaves of bread.

'What's up towards the Styal Road?' Josiah whispered to Ned.

'Nothing much, except the Apprentice House.'

'It seems to me they have out-flanked the main barricade.'

The youngsters started running down the slope. Though they were shouting and cheering, the attention of the men and specials was focused on the main group of turn-outs, but there was something else they all missed. There was a figure with them who had not followed, a person who was now watching what was happening. Only when the youngsters were in earshot of the barricade, did this figure turn and saunter away. The way that figure walked was engraved on Josiah's memory: it was the Sneaker.

Chapter 26

A plug plot

One of the men on the barricade finally heard the halloos. He turned and immediately grabbed at the shoulder of his neighbour. They stepped forward; staves raised. These solidly built workers were in no danger from a small group of youngsters, but in the atmosphere of heightened tension, Josiah knew they would not see that. They would hit out and the youngsters would fall.

A few other heads in the crowd that had seen this distraction as an opportunity. They charged, not at the main barricade, but at the one that protected the space on the left between the two buildings. The rest of the crowd followed. The men and the constables were overwhelmed. Bits of wood and furniture flew every way. Many turned, now armed to defend themselves, but one group charged on as soon as it had got through. They could go to the left into the weaving sheds or to the right and invade the carding and spinning sheds.

'That lot are up to no good,' said Ned and started after them. Josiah could do nothing but follow.

The cobbled surface between the buildings sloped steeply. The six marchers who had got through could not be seen, but no doors had been damaged, so wherever they had gone it must have been further into the mill buildings.

The yard doglegged and around the corner was a door which was hanging off its hinges. Locked and bolted it might have been, but it had not resisted the concerted effort of six men.

'They know where they're going,' said Ned.

'It looks like they're after doing damage to the great wheel or the steam engine.'

In the basement the great wheel, even at idle, sounded remote and wet. The dribble of water from the pen-trough seemed very small but the impression it made, in the echo of the wheel chamber, was as if the sea was lapping on the shore. When something knocked against the wheel it made a noise like a heavy cracked bell. The chamber smelled of the river beyond the wheel, where Josiah could see a couple of ducks.

It was clear that the turn-outs had broken into two groups of three. Three were attacking the wheel gearing with crowbars and an axe. Ned ran down three flights of slippery steps and started to lay into them. He seemed to be enjoying himself and he pushed one into the centre of the wheel which rattled him over and over like a bag of stones. Josiah left him to it.

The other three must have gone further into the basement. Once away from the wheel, Josiah could hear a steam engine gently turning over. The power room was full of transmission shafts. These came and went by a jumble of routes. Bevelled gears took power through the ceiling on shafts leading to upper rooms. Away from the great wheel, it was virtually dark. If you knew your way through this maze of machinery you could probably traverse it without injury, but Josiah cracked his head several times before he made it to the end brick wall, behind which must be the steam engine.

There was a door, which showed a glimmer of red light.

Josiah pushed his head around it to see what was beyond. The steam engine made its own orchestra of sounds. As the steam from the second half of its stroke was exhaled it caused a gurgling sound in the small dish that collected condensed water over the exhaust valve. The room was hot and foggy with dust, smoke and steam.

Like the water wheel, the engine was idling. The turn-outs had surprised the engineer who had been minding it; he was lying unconscious next to a wall, blood running down his cheek from his head. Josiah crept past the engine and mounted the walkway to the left of the top of the boiler. It was hotter here and sweat ran down his spine. He could still not see the men, but he could hear they were arguing. The attackers were trying to work out how to draw the plugs from the engine's boiler.

'This is a bleedin' waste of time,' said one. 'Why don't we just smash the plugs out with a hammer?'

'If you do that without venting the steam pressure, yen bloody fool, then you'll be scalded to death or worse. The fire out first and steam released before we get to grips with plugs.'

Josiah came to a stairway which led down into a pit. In front of him was a pile of coal which had been poured in from the outer world. Beams of light which caught the dust and smoke illuminated the stokehole of the boiler. One man was busy with a hoe, raking the coal from the boiler's hearth. The two who were arguing were just standing there. One practical person out of three thought Josiah. It was fortunate for Mr Greg that the two arguing had not taken their lead from the third, who looked as though he might have some practical experience of steam engines.

'It's not all the plugs that need to be removed, just the fusible ones on the crown sheet,' Josiah said in a casual voice. The men looked up. Josiah continued as if he were an expert. 'There's probably only one on this boiler, but since Bolton's specified it, there might be two or even three.'

The man who had been raking the coals out stood up. 'Bugger, I'd forgotten that. Thank you, young man, for your advice.'

Josiah moved gently down a few steps of the stairs. 'Of course, if you really wanted to do some serious damage to inconvenience Mr Greg, you'd stoke up the boiler and let out some water and wait until it blew up. Too bad you've lost your opportunity.'

All three of them looked more sharply now. 'But you're a turn-out like us, I've seen you as we've gone along.'

'Yes, I have been with you, but I'm not a turn-out and I think it's my duty to stop you, three gentlemen, trying to harm Quarry Bank Mill or that boiler. Will you come quietly?'

One man picked up a cudgel that he'd left near the coal pile. He charged up the lower steps, but Josiah was ready. He sidestepped and hit the man in the side of the head. The second man followed his mate. Josiah was now off balance and had to retreat backwards up the steps before he felt steady again.

The second man threw himself at Josiah, who dropped onto one knee. The man went headlong over, and as he did so Josiah stood up sharply. The man somersaulted, missed the walkway, landing with his hands and buttocks on the hot surface of the boiler. His britches saved his body but not his hands from contact with the hot metal; he screamed with pain; both his palms burned.

The man who had been raking the hearth put down his hoe,

making sure that Josiah could see he was not going to use it as a weapon. Then he walked up the steps. 'I'm not taking ye on, you've won. Nice footwork youngster, if I was your age, I'd have relished a few turns in the ring with ye.' Ned came in and led them off to join their comrades.

Robert Hyde Greg came through the door from the power room. 'I won't embarrass you with exactly why you and your colleague are here Sir, I'm content to be happy you are.'

A couple of workers who had followed Mr Greg went to help the engineer, who was showing signs of coming around.

'Thank you, but these turn-outs are not the most belligerent who could have arrived at your door.'

Mr Greg turned to a figure who only then who had come into the room, Sir Grancester. 'I take it that you think there might be worse to come, Sir?' said Greg.

'I think the young man is essentially correct. The troops dispersed the strikers yesterday in Bollington. They were greater in number and much more vexatious. But I doubt they will be gone for long.'

'In which case, I will cut my losses. I will pay off this group and then I will stop the mill until the present situation resolves itself. Thank you, Gentlemen,' said the owner of Quarry Bank Mill, who then withdrew.

CHAPTER 27

Precepts of revolution

*If you have been instructed to make us leave this place,
you should seek permission to use force, for only the power
of bayonets will dislodge us.*

Honore Mirabeau

Well, it seems it was a draw between us at Quarry Bank. I tracked you easily as you came up with the turn-outs to the mill along the river valley. I reconnoitred how Greg would lay out his troops and barricades, all very predictable. My strategy to get a few hot-headed youngsters to provide a distraction so the hard-core turn-outs among the crowd could get through to the wheel worked well, but again you managed to thwart me.

I have to admit you were most adept and quick to respond to your opportunity, though I would have succeeded if you had not been so aware of what was going on. I had outwitted you, but you turned the tables and had the last laugh on me. But do not be too sure of your success, do not preen your feathers just yet. There will be other occasions that will provide me with my opportunity.

If you did not see me then you are not forearmed. If you saw me then you should be afeared. I have my rifle and you are mortal.

CHAPTER 28

Encoded

It was about mid-afternoon when Ned and Josiah managed to get themselves back to Manchester. Inspector Fidel eyed them up. 'The pair of you have looked better, but Sir Grancester thinks you did a good job, so let's see if I agree.'

The Inspector said next to nothing while they reported both about what they had seen and heard before they got to Quarry Bank and what had happened there. It was clear that the Inspector was pleased, but he was very concerned about how the turn-outs had been able to pick and choose the targets.

'Going to Quarry Bank was a good idea. If they had managed to stop the mill that would have been in every newspaper in the country over the next week.'

'There was indeed very little damage done, but the mill is stopped and has to be guarded,' said Josiah.

'What are you saying?'

'That while they didn't win an outright victory, they have achieved their main aim. As time goes on, every time there's a threat from the strikers; the owners of any and every factory will remember that Robert Hyde Greg could not stand against the workers, and that will make them more likely to cut their losses.'

'I hear they got a bloody nose in Bollington,' said Ned. 'That will give them pause for thought.'

'That may be, but troops were involved, and they are a scarce commodity. At present the route into Manchester is open. We have to hope they don't realise it until the city is better organised. Tidy up a bit and get some rest. Be back here midday tomorrow. There's bound to be more to be done by then.'

Ned went off quickly hoping for some food, but Josiah delayed leaving.

'Something more on your mind, Constable?'

'The Sneaker was there.'

'Are you sure?'

'Positive, the way he moves is engrained on my memory. He put the youngsters up to ransacking the Apprentice House. That distraction nearly got a big group of turn-outs into the mill.'

'That's a really serious development. But how would anyone manage it?'

'You said yourself they had been canny when the columns divided. Someone wanted them to succeed and whoever that was, sent the Sneaker to help.'

'I hope you're wrong about that,' said Fidel.

*

Once Josiah was back in Hillgate he cleaned up and changed his clothes. He'd be welcome for dinner at Tiviot Dale Manse, so he would have time to do what he had been itching to do for several days.

Before lighting the fire, he retrieved the silver watch from its hiding place in the chimney. Then he put the kettle on to boil and got the newspaper that had been in the pocket of his uniform since the night he'd spent in a cell at the Manchesters' station house. He sat down in a chair next to the table, placing on it the newspaper turned to the personal advertisements on one side, another copy of the *Trumpeter*, and finally the silver watch.

He had already tried to see if *Jolly Peter* would decode the possible message in the paper from Manchester, but it didn't. But there was a possibility that *Jolly Peter* was the keyword for the next week's paper, a copy of which he had obtained from Manchester.

The kettle whistled, and he made the tea. As he left it to draw, he took down a jar from a shelf and helped himself to one of his mother's shortbreads she'd given him the last time he'd managed to get to church. He put it on a small plate, poured the tea from the pot and sat down again. He took a bite of the biscuit.

There were letters inscribed directly into the metal of the outer track of the silver watch, all in alphabetical order with a space between the letter A at the start of the track and the letter Z at the end of the track. Thus there were twenty-six spaces all in alphabetical order, with one extra space.

The inner track had the same arrangement but there were only twenty-six spaces and no permanent letters inscribed on the track. Indeed, the track had small holes in the centre of each space where a letter might have been inscribed. Then Josiah remembered that there had been a few separate letters which had been mounted on pegs in the material Billy had given him. He found the letters, slipped the letter J into the first space of the inner track. He filled in the spaces with the letters he had and then cut pieces of paper to fill in the rest.

He had managed to clean the mechanism before having to hide it and remembered being surprised that the two hands were not mounted on a simple spindle but joined by a small gear train, very similar to the one that would be found in a real watch or clock. That arrangement allowed the hour hand of a clock to go around at a different rate to the minute hand. Did a small gear train do the same for this silver watch?

He moved the mechanism so that the hand that swept the outer track was pointed to the letter A. Then he disengaged the short-hand and reengaged it so it pointed at the letter J on the inner track. Then he pushed the larger hand round and back to A. After one complete revolution of the large hand the shorter hand now pointed to the O in Jolly Peter.

He looked at the silver watch for some time. What had happened was exactly what an encryption machine used to encrypt any of the letters in the outer ring, should have done. What was more, provided you did not encode more than twenty-six letters into the encoded message no letter in that message would be doubled, even if they were doubled in the message to be encoded.

Then Josiah realized that the silver watch was not just an encoding machine. If an encoded message was spelt out letter by letter on the inner ring then the original uncoded letters would be spelt out on the outer ring. He had in his hands a way of reading encoded messages. There was at that moment no way to prove that because it was most likely that the keywords Jolly Peter would not allow him to decode any encoded messages in the first copy of the *Trumpeter* but what if there was an encoded message in the second paper?

He searched through the paper. There was only one candidate for an encoded message: a sequence of twenty-three random letters at the foot of a single page about halfway into the paper.

He carefully reset the silver watch so that both hands pointed to A and J respectively. Then he moved the inner hand round so that it pointed to the first letter in the sequence. The large hand pointed at A, the second letter he selected was decoded as L, the third also L though the encoded letter was not a repeat of the previous one. As he went on the message developed. In the end when he had separated the words by adding sensible choices of spaces it read '*All force P or D Burrell at HS.*

So Dianne had been the target the Sneaker should have gone after when it was clear that her father was not at the meeting. She had avoided being attacked because of her devotion to getting the children to safety. The Sneaker had decided to play a lone hand by going after the most important alternative target at the meeting, Feargus O'Connor. Josiah himself had thwarted that attempt.

Josiah sat back in his chair. The most shocking thing about the discovery of the purpose of the silver watch was that, though he had no idea who had sent the message or anything about the details of the conspiracy they were engaged in, he could read any messages they sent, provided he could find the appropriate key phrase and the coded message.

The use of a mechanical cryptograph constituted an incalculable advantage for the conspirators for it meant that messages could be seen in plain sight but if one fell into the hands of an opponent, such as himself, the conspirators were running a corresponding risk. They would not know Josiah could read their messages unless he revealed it to them.

There was also something else. This single message was highly suggestive that the messages were sent for the benefit of the Sneaker.

He poured a second cup of tea and took another piece of shortbread. He would not have the time to work on finding the other messages and keywords that had appeared. But those messages needed to be found and decoded. He carefully packed up the silver watch, along with the issue of the *Trumpeter* he had been using, and a detailed set of notes. The cryptograph would be much safer in Michael Carroll's possession than being left in Josiah's lodging. Josiah was also virtually certain that Michael's imagination would not allow him to rest until he had confirmed Josiah's deductions by using the silver watch to find and read more secret messages

CHAPTER 29

Preparations

The following morning Josiah left the silver watch and his notes at Michael's house. Then he walked across Lancashire Bridge. He was still feeling sorry for himself and that, combined with the knowledge Dianne might remain in danger, meant he didn't look properly where he was going. As a result, when he turned the corner into Underbank, he walked straight into an ample figure, emerging from the Manchester and Liverpool District Bank.

'Watch where you're going lad!' said the man.

'I'm dreadfully sorry,' said Josiah.

'Hang on son I know you, don't I?' It was Porthos, one of the 'Three Musketeers' and Josiah's companion in arms at The Hall of Science.

'It's the Lone Policeman, as I live and breathe.'

Josiah found himself embraced in the butcher's copious arms. 'I'm surprised you'd want to own me.'

'Nonsense lad. These are troubled times and some days we may be opponents and some days friends. Best to remember the good times. It will make healing the division easier when all this is over. In any case, it would be difficult for any Chartist to ignore the service you did for our cause by saving Mr O'Connor's life.'

'I wish I felt as sure as you seem to be of my virtue.'

'Why?'

'I'm worried about Dianne.'

'So are several of us.'

'I was given the responsibility to keep her safe from the man who tried to kill Mr O'Connor.'

'Let me guess,' said Porthos. 'You don't know where she is so you can't satisfy yourself your duty's done?'

'That's about the size of it.'

'In which case, I'll give you a hand. Miss Dianne is on her way, along with twenty of her sisters, to settle a score with Leavington's, especially that bastard Tate. If you leg it over there quick you should be in time to see the show.'

*

Everything was calm at Leavington's gates when Josiah arrived, but it was not going to remain that way. Josiah could not see Dianne and her regiment of women, but he could hear them approaching. He found himself a discrete position, where he wouldn't be seen, and waited.

They came down the road in a column, three abreast. They even had a banner carried on two poles at their head: a petticoat, flying proudly in the wind. There were about fifty women, arm-in-arm. In front of the banner, Dianne looked as beautiful as ever, her determination all over her face. The column turned through the gates and stopped opposite the office doors. On every floor, Josiah could see the faces of the women inside the mill pressed against windows.

'Tate, Tate, show yourself, you arrant coward!' Dianne was in no mood for compromise. She had come to turnout

Leavington's and turn it out she would. Josiah desired to run over to her and kiss her; she was noble, brave and his heart went out to her.

The door to the office opened and Tate strolled out. 'Well Miss Burrell, it's not Saturday, so if you're hoping to collect the pay you think we might owe you, you'll be disappointed. When you left, since you didn't complete the week, I'm afraid you are not entitled to a farthing! You've been sacked! We laid you off. I don't think even the clever Mr Brakespeare, or should I say Constable Ainscough, could argue your case in this matter.'

At the mention of his name, Josiah looked for any reaction from Dianne, but there was none.

'You know damn well what I'm here to do.'

'Tut tut, Miss Burrell, no swearing please, we are polite folk here. Please be clear Miss Burrell, what do you propose to do?'

'To turn your workers out!' At this, the girls Dianne had brought with her began to chant: 'A fair day's pay for a fair day's work, a fair day's pay for a fair day's work....'

'They're women, not men; they don't do a fair day's work, not now, not ever!'

Tate's loss of temper did him no good.

The chant changed, 'Equal pay for equal work, equal pay for equal work....'

Tate's reaction was to call towards the open office door. From the darkness within, Angel, Hugh, Archibald and several of the male overseers emerged. Each had a pickaxe handle in his hand. Tate had thought they would intimidate the women. He was wrong. Except for Archibald, they didn't go to stand behind Tate, but passed him by and went to join the women. This brought a great cheer. Several of the flightier girls gave each of them good kisses in return for their support. Josiah noticed that Angel blushed to the roots of his hair when two girls kissed him simultaneously, one on each cheek.

Tate retreated smartly behind the office door. The women rushed forward, but Tate was prepared. The door would not give way, no matter how hard they pushed and cursed. They went to all the doors that led into the mill; none of them yielded.

Thwarted, Dianne's amazons became enraged. They started loosening stones from the yard and throwing them at the mill's windows. There were screams from within as glass shattered. Then a group of men led by Tate appeared on the roof. They had a supply of stones of their own laid aside and started throwing them down at the girls.

The amazons shouted and shook their fists, and though some scattered, Dianne remained in command. With a few stalwarts, she attacked one of the doors which was hard for Tate and his forces to bombard. The tactic seemed effective, though some stones got through. Tate had to move position, and that meant men skittering across the slate roof, always in danger of a fatal slip over the edge. One man got above the door and dropped a large brick, which caught Effie Wheeldon square on the nose. She screamed and went down like a ninepin. Josiah winced; Effie's nose was sure to be broken. Dianne ran over to her. When she stood up there was blood on her hands. All this must stop before someone was more badly injured or worse.

Josiah stood up and yelled at the top of his voice. 'To me, to me!' The men, who had stood by, not really sure of what to do, rallied and joined Josiah in a charge to support the women's attempt to get through the door. A combination of staves, fists and the extra weight of the men did the trick. Three united heaves and the door first creaked and then gave way.

Tate played his last card. His small troop came running at the girls from the main stairway which linked with the store that the women had broken into. But Tate's men were outnumbered and very quickly had their arms pinned.

Dianne looked at Tate and his men. She was wild with anger. She turned to her amazons. 'Bring them all and follow me.' She led them round to the back of the mill where the filthy river flowed that had once driven Leavington's wheel.

'Throw them in,' she commanded, and in they went; the river might have been hopelessly polluted, as bad as the worst midden anywhere, but it was not deep enough to pose a risk of drowning, but ample to cause disgrace.

Having seen Dianne's revenge on Tate, Josiah went back to the yard to find Effie Wheeldon in a bad way. The brick had cut the skin on her nose and cheek, and plenty of blood had flowed down over her lips and out of her damaged nose. It had been staunched, which made it clear that the worst injury she had received had been to the bridge of her nose. Where it had been straight and one of her prettiest features, it now had a small kink in it, one that Effie was doomed to carry for the rest of her life, but Josiah suspected she would consider that a proud token of battle.

Dianne came over to him. 'So, Mr Ainscough, have you now decided which side you are on?'

'I remain divided, but I know I am definitely on yours.'

'Well, I suppose that is a blessing. But you admit you were spying on us all the time?'

'No. I have been forced into spying on the movements of turn-outs over the last few days, but I was never spying on you.

I was sent to protect you and you are still in danger.'

'What have I to fear? Surrounded by my sisters we can accomplish anything.'

'You may be named after the huntress and surrounded by your amazons you may fancy yourself Hippolyta, but you are not indestructible. Believe me Dianne, the night I saved Feargus O'Connor from a bullet in the back...'

'...You were the Lone Policeman?' she said astonished.

'Yes, and you were the real target of that assassin.'

'Ridiculous, how can you be sure of that?'

'I have read the original message that sent the assassin to the Hall of Science that night. It says clearly that you or your father were both possible targets, and since he was not there, it was you.'

One of Dianne's lieutenants came up to them. 'We're ready to go sister. The plugs have been drawn on the boilers. Mr Angel says that he will secure the mill and make sure the girls who don't want to join us are safe and sound.'

'Thank Mr Angel for me.' She turned back to Josiah. 'We will be moving on towards the centre of Stockport to join up with those coming from other places. Josiah, if you walk with me, we can talk of this more.'

CHAPTER 30

The workhouse

They formed up again, their numbers swelled by women from Leavington's. They crossed the border into Heaton Moor and could easily have turned out other mills and works, but they pressed on towards the centre of the town. By the time they crossed the Mersey at the Brinksway Bridge they were over a hundred marching behind Dianne's petticoat banner.

'Josiah you said you had seen a message?'

'Yes, a coded message placed in a newspaper. Mr O'Carroll and I have found a means to decode them.'

'Them? You mean there has been more than one?'

'Yes, someone is trying to ferment violence.'

'But you said there was a message about the Hall of Science meeting.'

'Yes. This conspiracy goes back some time. How long we don't yet know. It has been well prepared, and the development of the trade disputes has provided its opportunity.'

'I suppose that since you know, the authorities know?'

'You would be wrong. Dianne, I do not know who to trust. Someone attacked me believing I had the key to this matter, but I didn't until I connected it with the accident which befell Fred Sowerby.'

Dianne was horrified. She went pale and held out her arm

so that Josiah had to steady her. 'Connected to Fred's death! Fred was murdered?' But they were close to the Workhouse at Shaw Heath and discussion would have to wait.

The Union Workhouse was a depressing building at the best of times. There was a small gatehouse with a lancet arch opening, on which was carved the words Stockport Union Workhouse. Beyond that was a single gravel path that allowed a small coach access to the main entrance with its impressive-looking door. But as Josiah knew well, once beyond that door there was a cold, bare waiting room.

Josiah had been hardened to many things by being a policeman but delivering people to the workhouse was something he had never reconciled himself to. It was an inhumane place set up to label its inmates as the *undeserving poor*. You might survive better in the workhouse than outside its walls. You might be fed better, but your dignity and self-respect rarely, if ever, returned after the separation of your family and enduring the stigma of once having been an inmate.

Outside the gatehouse were some starving people: more than braced, truly clemmed. They had come to this of all doors because the workhouse was thought to have a store of bread.

There was a low moan from the amazons leading the march. The column faltered and stopped. A woman was pleading with the gatekeeper. 'Please mister, just some bread for my daughter. You can see how hungry she is.'

The gatekeeper seemed moved but there was nothing he could do. To comply was to lose his job. Josiah wondered how far the man might be away from the workhouse himself if that happened. 'I can't pet,' he heard the man say. 'It's more than my job's worth.'

There was another low moan from the amazons. The gate-keeper looked up and the woman turned. The amazons at the front of the column moved a few steps forward. Then a few went a little further. The hand of the gatekeeper began pulling on a rope. It was no more than the warning bell he would have rung if he'd let a coach through; it rang in the waiting room. But the amazons interpreted the action as being some sort of appeal for reinforcements and rushed forward.

The gatehouse was overwhelmed, and the gatekeeper relieved of his keys. The turn-outs swept up the path and banged on the front door. There was no reply. None was needed since the waiting room was not locked. Through they went.

Dianne and Josiah looked on in awe. There was a pause, then they began to hear screaming and people started to emerge. A human chain formed, and hand to hand, loaves of bread and other victuals came out. The woman and her children were the first to receive this largess. The word quickly spread and the poor of all the local rookeries came running. Josiah felt he was standing on the hill of the Sermon of the Mount, watching the miracle of the Feeding of the Five Thousand.

Dianne was dancing in joy, 'You see Josiah it can change, it can all change.'

*

Everyone worked hard to empty the workhouse's bread store. Eventually, the column reformed and on they went towards Wellington Road, coming out opposite a scrubby piece of open land that had been designated as an extension to the town's cemetery. It was full of strikers. A cart had been dragged to the centre of the land. Then Josiah saw Phillip Burrell being urged forwards; he was going to speak to the crowd. Dianne saw him, 'There's Father,' and lost in her excitement she waved, completely forgetting Josiah. Then with all her amazons, she ran forward to join him.

Suddenly, Josiah realized he was at a loose end. He could follow, which would have the advantage that he could hear Phillip's view of the current situation, instead of Sir Grancester's, but there was a nagging doubt at the back of his mind. This might be a very good hunting ground for the Sneaker. Here there was an opportunity to use *all force*, to disrupt the Stockport turn-outs; killing one or both of the Burrells might be very effective, but how might the Sneaker attempt it?

A close-quarters attack on either Phillip or Dianne would be difficult, but if the Sneaker was proficient with musketry? Josiah looked round. There wasn't much in the way of vantage points. The nearest was the roof of Fellows Hatting Company's building. Fellows was not a big firm, but its building was notable in that it stood on a small triangular plot and because it had a restricted footprint, was five storeys high. It was known locally as the Smoothing Iron, because of its shape. The roof of Fellows and Co. was the best vantage point overlooking the field, but to threaten anyone in the crowd would require a very good shot. As he considered the Fellows building, Josiah saw a head appear above the parapet of the roof. The head disappeared then reappeared. Something with a slight metallic glint was pushed over the parapet.

Josiah moved away from where he was standing, suddenly conscious that he could be a target as much as the Burrells. He headed off, but not in the direction of the Fellows building. Once he was sure he was out of sight, he doubled back towards the company's gate. He sauntered into the yard and looked for a way to the upper storeys. The main door to the stairs was open and he followed the invitation they offered. Everyone seemed engaged in their tasks and preoccupations, and no one took any notice of him. When he reached the top of the stairs there was a solid door that opened out onto the roof.

He had seen the head near to the sharp end of the smoothing iron. Where Josiah had emerged was nearer to the back and he was well obscured by the paraphernalia of pipes and chimneys that emerged from the roof. He dropped down to the parapet and doubled up to creep along. When he caught a glimpse of the figure he'd seen, Josiah hid behind a chimney. The figure was not looking his way but was concentrated on the view across to the crowd. He was using a telescope, but beside him, leaning against the parapet, was a short-barreled musket, and next to it what looked like powder charges and ammunition.

Josiah was temptingly close, but not certain he could rush the man. If this was the Sneaker, then he already knew how agile he was, and that knowledge made him cautious. The man stood up and any doubt Josiah had was dismissed. This was the Sneaker; he bent down and picked up a bag, in which he packed the telescope. He stooped again collecting the ammunition from the roof. The range of any target in the crowd was probably too long even for him, Josiah thought. But he was engrossed with packing and this gave Josiah his chance.

He was only three strides from the Sneaker, but that was one stride too many. The musket was pulled over the shoulder along with the bag. Then he was gone. He had been no more than a few feet from another door that Josiah had not seen from behind the chimney and it was barred from inside; Josiah would have to go back to the stairs he had come up by.

He went back to where the Sneaker had been preparing. There he found a couple of cartridges that had been missed: normal cartridges carried by any soldier, containing powder and round shot. But as well as normal round shot there were five conically-shaped objects.

Made of lead, they had pointed ends and three rings around their diameters on the main body. At the bottom of these devices, there was cut a cone that pierced the body of what Josiah began to think was a projectile. He measured the diameters of the body of the conical devices against the standard balls. At their broadest point, the cones were all smaller than the balls. If these were projectiles, they would be easier to load using a normal ramrod, but they would not fit very tightly. He could not guess what advantage they might have. He pocketed the cartridges and the projectiles, and then returned the way he had come up from below.

CHAPTER 31

The precepts of revolution

When Henry IV came to Paris he came as a king who had conquered the people.
Now we are a people who have conquered the king.
Parisian Newspaper

When I watched you lead the turn-outs from Leavington's under their petticoat banner, I could have killed you easily. It might have been amusing to see your brains splash over the hair of your doxy. To hear her scream and see her fear. But I thought it might be much more fun to reverse the sacrifice: to kill her slowly before your eyes. So, I foreswore the shot and let you live. I pray to the cruel god I serve that I might get that chance in the future.

At the workhouse, I had another opportunity but since you were feeding the poor, I let that chance pass. That was a mistake for which you nearly made me pay.

I could see you well enough from the end of Fellows Mill. But I was there to see if I could disrupt the meeting that Phillip Burrell was conducting. I had no time for you, and in any case, I was concentrating; weighing up the prospects.

I had prepared an escape route; if I had not you would have caught me, though it's likely I would have done for you this time. But you stalked me well and without my exit route, I would not have escaped. I would have stood my ground if I had not already prepared to leave, the shot being far too far. Did you find the cartridges I left? Even if you did, it was unlikely you made anything of them. Nothing at that moment, but a chance for a demonstration was fast arriving.

CHAPTER 32

The Riot Act

Back on Wellington Road the turn-outs were excited and renewed in their zeal by what Phillip had said. Josiah fell in with Dianne.

'That was a great speech, don't you agree Josiah?'

'Certainly, as good as any I've heard,' he replied. 'Where are we going?' No point in alarming her by telling her what he'd just discovered, he thought.

'You don't pay as much attention as people give you credit for,' she replied. 'Didn't you hear?'

He shook his head, trying to look as much like an errant schoolboy as he could.

'The market square, silly. The news came that they're going to read the Riot Act, and so we're going to see if they dare to do it in the face of our crowd.'

Josiah's heart sunk. 'What will you do after the Act is read?' He had a horrible feeling he knew.

'Why we'll turn-out Castle Mill and be done with it.'

The second message had been *All force* to keep Castle Mill open.

The march swung off Wellington Road and went up Churchgate, from where there was a straight path down into the market square.

Josiah struggled to keep his eye on the rooves of the buildings. The Sneaker would need a vantage point to threaten the marchers, but where? They turned into the market square. There were barricades around the Castle Mill manned by lines of soldiers in tight formation, muskets at the ready. The turnouts went as far as they could, then stopped. A tense silence fell.

Phillip Burrell stepped forward. He stood tall and strode with determination towards the town hall. As he approached the line of soldiers in front of the town hall steps, two infantrymen barred his way by crossing their muskets in front of him.

Sir Grancester's tipstaff stepped forward. 'State the nature of your business here,' he declaimed. Everyone in the square could hear him.

'I wish to speak with the mayor. A confrontation where firearms are involved is in nobody's interest. I hope he will agree to speak with me.'

If Phillip was shaken by the force being displayed against him and his people, Josiah did not hear it in his voice.

A small group stepped onto a first-floor balcony: The mayor, Mr Prestbury, the town clerk and of course, Sir Grancester.

The mayor leant over the rail of the town hall. 'I have nothing to say to you Mr Burrell or the rabble at your back.' The mayor looked fleetingly towards Sir Grancester. The holder of the Queen's Warrant nodded. The mayor was not confident he was saying the right thing, but he continued nonetheless. 'We know of your seditious schemes and conspiracies, but we will not tolerate them here. These are the only words you will hear from us.'

Mr Prestbury, Chair of the Police Watch Committee stepped forward, his *pince-nez* in place. He held up a piece of paper and began to read. '*Our sovereign lady the Queen Victoria chargeth and commandeth all persons, being assembled, immediately to disperse themselves, and peaceably to depart to their habitations, or to their lawful business, upon the pains contained in the acts for preventing tumults and riotous assemblies.*' He folded the paper and put it in his pocket, 'The Riot Act has been read. God save the Queen.'

A quiet gripped everyone, what would now happen? There was a single shot and Mr Prestbury's head jerked back: a splash of blood spattered the mayor and Sir Grancester. The sound of the shot had come from behind Josiah, from St Mary's Parish Church.

Several things happened at once. The soldiers immediately fell back to the town hall steps and others emerged from behind barricades and from the gates of Castle Mill. This left Phillip on his own in the open, which Josiah remedied by racing over to him, barging him and half dragging him to cover.

'What the hell just happened?'

'Someone has shot Mr Prestbury.'

'For the love of God why?'

'They may have been trying to kill you.'

'What!'

'Just keep low and out the way. Keep a wall or something solid between you and the tower of St Mary's.'

For the first time, Josiah realised that Phillip Burrell was confused. He explained, 'I think that's where the rifleman fired from. Trust me, Phillip, I had good reason to fear this sort of outrage before I found Dianne.'

When Josiah reached Dianne, she was already doing her best to protect herself and others around her.

'Get as many as you can to cover,' he said. 'If the marksman starts picking off people at random, nowhere in this square will be safe.'

But even as Josiah attempted to keep the turn-outs safe from the Sneaker, he saw that Sir Grancester had come down onto the town hall steps to talk to the lieutenant who was in command of the soldiers. After listening to Sir Grancester, the officer gave a series of orders. The soldiers in front of the town hall formed a double line, with the front-line kneeling on one leg. Then they fixed their bayonets. The same message got out to the other barricades where soldiers formed single or double lines as they could. They were wary of the crowd, but they were prepared for the worst.

CHAPTER 33

The Stockport Riot

Anyone who knew nothing of the Sneaker might easily think that the shot had come from the crowd: a piece of defiance aimed at the man who had just read the Riot Act. Josiah looked at Sir Grancester. The bearer of the Queen's Warrant was impassive; there was no sign of shock at the death of a man who he knew, even if Mr Prestbury had not been one of Sir Grancester's more popular of collaborators.

Josiah was also becoming suspicious of the absence of any regular police. No doubt Castle Mill would have many special constables in reserve for any attack, but there were no regulars who might calm the situation more effectively than either specials or infantry. There were no calm heads like Sergeant Smith, able to use his experience of battle to see through the confusion of events. Even so, the rearrangement of the soldiers had not gone unnoticed by men in the crowd who had military experience. Voices were raised.

'You lot thinking that was us?'

'You're here to protect us, not shoot us.'

Fists were shaken at the young and intimidated troops. They didn't look like they had much experience of action to fall back on.

'You going to sort us out as you did them at Bollington?'

'Think of your mothers and families,' one woman shouted.

People were starting to gather stones and other objects which were to hand to throw at the troops. Then there was a second shot and one of the soldiers in the front line near the town hall slumped down, blood on his tunic.

This time Josiah was quick enough to see the rifle smoke as it drifted away from the tower of St. Mary's. He must stop the Sneaker before anything else happened. He started to run towards the church. This was a tinder box. One more shot and the crowd's anger and the infantry's panic would boil over and a battle would start.

Josiah was getting near the wall of the church grounds when he heard hooves and the jangle of harnesses. The rhythm of the hooves increased, and the sound of harnesses intensified. Josiah looked up Churchgate. There was a small detachment of horsemen, led by Col. Wymes. The horses quickened from the trot to the gallop and at their head, Wymes drew his sabre. Helped by the downward slope into the market square, they charged into the rear of the crowd as the Sneaker shot a third soldier at a barricade.

Josiah scrambled over the church wall as the cavalry passed. A great roar went up from the turn-outs and they ran at the troops in front of them, matched by a similar roar from the horsemen. The cavalry spread into the crowd like sea flowing around rocks as the tide comes in. Groups of turn-outs were trying to surround individual horses and pull their riders down. In some places Josiah could see dragoons lashing out with sharpened steel; sometimes someone would fall when hit by a blow, to be dragged out of the way of the horses' hooves by his or her comrades.

Some of the soldiers were trying to hit people with the flat part of their blades, using them as battens, but some had lost all discipline, and as at Peterloo were slashing out with the cutting edges, intending to maim.

In the centre of the mêlée, he could see Wymes. The colonel was slashing away with the best of them. He had lost all self-control, and Josiah could see his arm rise and fall repeatedly as he wheeled his horse and looked down for his next target. Eventually, the crowd pulled back and a space cleared around him. No one would approach him and when he spurred his horse towards them, they fell back. But a figure appeared from this ring: George Blandford. The old man had asked Josiah what the point of Millie's death was, and Josiah had promised to give him an answer, though he had never managed to formulate or deliver one.

The old man sprang at Wymes. The rider was surprised by the strength of the man's onslaught, as was his horse, which shied. Wymes tried to get into a position to bring his sabre down on Blandford's head, but when Wymes managed to strike, the old man avoided the blow and grabbed the Colonel's arm, holding on to it by the wrist and elbow. Try as he might, Wymes could not get free and pinned in this way the horse pirouetted, lifting the old man off his feet at each turn. They quickly became a spinning top, moving towards Josiah.

'Let go you old fool, let go!' Wymes was desperate. Though they were getting towards the back of the crowd their contest was attracting a lot of attention. If Wymes fell, he ran a certain risk of being killed by the enraged crowd.

'You will not pass. I will have it, Sir, I will take it as a trophy!'

The horse bucked, and the combined effect of the horse's

strength and the old man's weight ripped the sabre from Wymes' grasp.

'See you, bloody-handed tyrant, I have it now!' shouted the old man brandishing the sabre above his head.

Seeing Wymes disarmed, the crowd advanced on him, but the colonel was not done yet. He took out a pistol from a holster buckled around his waist. He cocked it and fired at the crowd. Then he turned his horse away from the market square and galloped away up Churchgate.

Josiah's attention turned back to the Sneaker. He ran to the church porch at the base of the tower, but a shout from near the town hall steps made him turn. The shout was from one of the officers. He could not hear what the order was, but he was high enough to see over the heads of the crowd. There was a rippling sound of musket fire and a cloud of white smoke from the infantry near the town hall. The soldiers had fired a volley into the crowd which was matched by the screams from the turn-outs.

*

The crypt of St Mary's looked like a battlefield dressing station; Ladies with nursing experience and strong stomachs were assisting Dr Kay in tending the wounded. Mary O'Carroll and a group of her Catholic Sisters were there as well as Mrs Cooksley and some others from Tiviot Dale, along with members from St Mary's. A Catholic priest was offering comfort and prayer, as was Mr Cooksley.

At the far end of the crypt, a row of bodies lay covered in white sheets. There were seven at the current count, but Kay expected more to expire before the evening was out.

Mrs Prestbury and her son had come to collect Mr Prestbury's body. They stood around and looked on as an undertaker's man, assisted by Sergeant Smith, transferred the body to a temporary coffin and placed it on a handcart to wheel it out of the church.

Josiah was comforting George Blandford. The old man still held Colonel Wymes' sabre. Though he had received only superficial cuts and bruises, the effort of his attack had been too much for his heart. Josiah's objective was comfort, but he also wanted to know why the man had attacked Wymes in such a recklessly heroic manner.

'Sir, can you hear me,' said Josiah softly.

The old man looked at Josiah. 'Yes son, I can hear you. What are ye doing here, I met ye near Wilmslow?'

'Do you remember attacking the man on horseback.'

The old man nodded. 'He'd charged into the crowd, blowing that bugle of his. I took it off him lad, me on my own.'

Josiah found tears welling up in his eyes. He remembered part of Shelley's poem The Masque of Anarchy, written about Peterloo:

Rise, like lions after slumber
In unvanquishable number!
Shake your chains to earth like dew
Which in sleep had fallen on you:
Ye are many—they are few!

'I saw you do it. You were like a lion. You took his sabre.'

'I got the bugle,' came the reply. 'Orator Hunt was speaking when those bloody bastards came, hallooing and yelling, waving cold steel at honest English men and women. They thought to cut us down as if we were no more than corn before the scythe.'

Josiah saw his memories of past and present were merging.

'We stood firm we did. As that bloody bastard passed me I grabbed at his wrist and hung on. I pulled it from his grasp and held it high. I have it still. Give me a tune on it before I go, Jonathan.'

Josiah held his hand; George Blanford was slipping away, leaving this life.

'Millie is that you? Bless me child, where you been? I've been looking for ye everywhere. Don't fret now Grandad's here. Take my hand and we'll walk together.'

George's hand squeezed Josiah's and then relaxed. Josiah bowed his head and started to say the Lord's Prayer.

Michael O'Carroll and Mary came over. As Josiah fell silent, they started to recite:

> *May light eternal shine upon him, O Lord,*
> *with Thy saints forever, for Thou art kind.*
> *Eternal rest give to him, O Lord,*
> *and let perpetual light shine upon him.*

Dr Kay came and closed the old man's eyes. 'So the grand old man has gone. One more eyewitness of Peterloo will be laid to rest. A pity that we will not be able to place the Peterloo Bugle that he wrested from a dragoon that day on his coffin so that people can remember him as they should. That would have been fitting.'

CHAPTER 34

The principles of a revolutionary

A true revolutionary should be ready to perish in the process.
Maximilien Robespierre

The tower was ideal. A clear view of the market square. No one saw me come in nor did they see me climb the inner stairs. The trap door at the top opened easily and everything was quiet. I jammed the door on its top side. If things went wrong, then I would need time to fight my way down those stairs. I arranged my cartridges and checked the sights on my rifle.

There was a spotter who raced back to the town hall steps and warned the troops that the turn-outs were coming down into the square. By the time they started to arrive everything was quiet except for the barricades. The people looked surprised and uncertain. They paused and went quiet with fear. Then the group of officials emerged from the town hall. The crowd faced them. I could not hear anything, but Phillip Burrell stepped forward; probably reasoning with the officials.

Then I saw a man in black. He put on a pair of glasses and held in his hand a piece of paper from which he began to read, what had to be the Riot Act. When he was finished, he put the paper in his pocket, and I shot him through the forehead.

The echo of the shot came back to me, reflected by the mill and the other buildings.

Backwards and forwards, backwards and forwards. I shot soldiers on the lines behind the barricades and I shot turn-outs to make it appear that both sides were firing. It was a joy, a thing of beauty and symmetry. I was beyond joy, all my skill, all their ignorance; I do not know how many I shot but I had to stop after the horsemen charged into the square.

My soul sang, and my heart lifted. Ignorance defeated, stupidity massacred, terror sown on the wings of destruction. Nothing of all that I know is better than this, to kill without responsibility.

Chapter 35

Unexpected messages

Sir Grancester Smythe swirled the brandy in his glass. He held it up so that the light from the candles illuminated the patterns that the spirit made as it wept down the insides. This fascinating effect of light and translucence was merely a matter of refraction and reflection within the thin layer of liquid that clung to the glass, but it pleased him. No matter how much desperation the liquid showed as it tried to resist gravity, it could not prevent itself from gathering in the bottom of the brandy balloon for him to consume. What was true of the brandy was true of the turn-outs: they were trapped. The strikes were far from over, but with the Stockport riot and the successful way he had discredited the mob and foiled their intentions he thought matters were going well. It was very early days, but the events in Stockport might prove to be the beginning of the end of the General Strike, as it was now being termed.

His secretary entered with a tray of coffee, which he placed before him. 'Will you be needing me any longer this evening?'

'I was just considering that matter. I think we should not let things lie. We have the advantage in north Cheshire for the time being. Have you ever seen a prize fight, Madden?'

'No your grace, I can't say that I have.'

'Pugilism is both savage and uplifting. You should go to see a bout or two to improve your education.'

'When we get back to London I shall make it my business to take your advice, My Lord.'

'I have found the very best prize-fighters to be rather gentlemanly when not in the ring, but when fighting, with their opponent at bay, they are ruthless. They go after their man as soon as they know they have the upper hand and they are not satisfied until they have knocked their opponent senseless or so badly mauled them that they cannot come up to scratch. This is what we must do with these seditious turn-outs.'

Sir Grancester set down his glass and picked up one of two pieces of paper on his left. He passed it to Madden.

'Encode this message and place it in the earliest newspapers in the usual manner. The Burrells have gone to ground, licking their wounds no doubt, but I want them flushed out. I want them harried and given no time to regroup.'

'Yes, My Lord.'

'That will be all Madden, you may go.'

'Thank you, My Lord, but Colonel Wymes is here asking to see you.'

Sir Grancester sighed. 'Send a maid with another cup for coffee and a second glass.'

'I have them ready outside in anticipation My Lord. If I may, I will bring them in before I summon the Colonel.'

Madden left the room and returned with the extra cup and glass. He bowed before leaving. Sir Grancester finished his first brandy and poured himself a second. A talk with Wymes was not what he had looked forward to when planning this relaxing evening, but it could not be helped. There was a knock at the door and Wymes entered before Sir Grancester had time to permit him.

'Sit down Richard,' he indicated a seat opposite. 'Pray help yourself to coffee or brandy or both.'

Wymes pulled the tray over and poured a measure of brandy twice if not three times the one Sir Grancester normally drank. Wymes held his glass, 'Too long life and victory,' Sir Grancester nodded in response.

'It was a great victory today,' carried on Wymes. 'Did you see the charge we made; did you see how those ruffians cowered before my sabre!'

'Yes, most gratifying, but somewhat undercut by you being frightened from the field by one weak old man.' Wymes' cheeks coloured. 'You can be as angry as you like Colonel, but you cannot deny that you are no longer in possession of the sabre you so proudly brandished as you rode into the crowd this afternoon. No doubt it now sits on the table of some gin-shop as the man who took it from you tells the tale, with advantages, to any deplorable who will listen.'

Wymes half rose in his chair but thought better of confronting Sir Grancester.

'As it was, it was our anonymous friend who won us the victory, combined with the resolution of that young infantry officer. The turn-outs will not forget the volley of shot into their ranks, and perhaps even more important, the flash of the sun off those fixed bayonets. They will remember next time they dare to defy the Riot Act that it may be enforced with lethality.

'And while you have been celebrating your great display of valour, I have already sent Madden off with this message to our friend.' He passed the second piece of paper to Wymes.

'As you will see, I have instructed him to offer money on the head of the female Burrell to persuade someone to betray her. A price on her head places pressure on her father and should make them move from place to place more quickly than they will like.'

*

'How many?' said an incredulous Josiah.

'Thirty in all.'

'Thirty, that's astonishing!'

'That's a minimum. There must be others I haven't found. These are all the ones decodable using the key phrases in *The Manchester Trumpeter*. From the first message about the Burrells and the Hall of Science, from the key phrase *Jolly Peter* I could follow the thread forward and back each week. Each week, the key phrase is given only in the *Trumpeter*.

'It was harder to spot the messages. For the most part, they are in local papers such as *The Stockport Advertiser* or *The Ashton Courier*. Sometimes the message is repeated in several papers as if whoever is sending them doesn't know the general where-abouts of the Sneaker.'

Michael took out his pipe from his waistcoat, scraped at the bowl with his small penknife, then packed and lit it. There was a huge grin of pride and success on his face. Josiah was in awe of the Irishman's energy.

'Thank you, my friend, for all this,' Josiah waved his hand at the documents on the table.

'Think nothing of it, lad. I enjoyed doing it.'

'Have you found any messages from before events moved to the North West?'

'I did find messages that seem to cover other parts of the country. One concerned what looks like a murder in Birmingham.'

'How many messages are like that?'

'Only two or three, but none later than a few weeks ago, about the time Sir Grancester and his staff arrived.'

'Are you saying this has something to do with Sir Grancester?'

'It may be only a coincidence, but there are no orders to the Sneaker since then, as well as there being no questions about information issues.'

'That proves nothing, Michael.'

'Agreed, it's not proof, but it's an interesting double coincidence.'

'Past messages might help us understand what is going on, but what about orders that were placed while I was away?'

'How about, *Disrupt turnout at QB* or last week, there were two messages *All force disrupt Stockport turnout,* followed by *All force preserve Castle Mill.*'

Josiah laughed. 'It would certainly fit if Sir Grancester was the head of the conspiracy. That would make the use of the silver watch as much a matter of disguising who was the puppet master, as making the messages unreadable.'

Michael chuckled. 'In which case, perhaps it was Sir Grancester who ringed the *Jolly Peter* advertisement at the meeting at the Manchesters' station house.'

Josiah paused. What they had just been saying was no more than a joke among friends but what if the fighting in front of Castle Mill was orchestrated by Sir Grancester? To keep control of its progress he would have had to have had the Sneaker there. The Sneaker was the only one who could have shot individuals on both sides from range. 'Any predictions for the coming week?'

Michael passed Josiah a message. 'As far as I can tell only one, but it's of a different kind.'

Josiah read what was on the paper; *Place price on head of DB.*

CHAPTER 36

Counter moves

From Sir Grancester's point of view, the next few days were busy with matters which fell into the ambit of his official work. The Stockport riot might, in the short term, have stabilised the south-eastern segment of the insurrection, but there were continuing disturbances elsewhere. In Preston there was a similar situation to Stockport, where the Riot Act having been read, the crowd reacted badly and a group of troops fired, killing four people. Preston's police force was also involved, laying about the marchers with truncheons.

Manchester was soon under threat from groups of turn-outs from Rochdale, Oldham and Bury. But a new pattern for the strikes emerged, spontaneous disturbances breaking out in Manchester but not coalescing into a unified disturbance all over the city. All these disturbances eventually required visits to calm things or assess local resolve. However, when his coach drew up in the courtyard of Wythenshawe Hall Sir Grancester was not thinking about anything other than a good bath, a decent meal and a good night's sleep. These were not to be.

The footman hardly had time to accept Sir Grancester's hat and help him with his coat when Madden came walking briskly down the hall, in his hand a newspaper.

'Sorry to be rushed My Lord, but this was in today's

Manchester Trumpeter. On the right-hand side of the paper in the column of small advertisements, there is a small piece of code.'

'Madden please get a grip on your feelings, it must be one of the messages I sent before I left.' Then he thought more carefully. 'But it would have to have been put into the *Trumpeter* rather late.'

'We did not put it in My Lord.'

'Are you sure?'

'Positive My Lord.'

'What does it say?'

'*Cancel interest DB. New targets follow.* Whoever placed it in the paper was directly countering your instructions, My Lord.'

'Whoever put that in the paper has the cryptograph that the Sneaker lost and has therefore been in a position to decode all our messages over several months!'

'Provided they knew appropriate key phrases, My Lord.'

'They knew the one we had just used to send the last messages. Find one key phrase and it's like following links in a chain. Ask Cook to rustle up some food for me. I'll take it in my study.'

*

Sir Grancester puzzled over the problem all night. All the first light of the early dawn showed for his efforts was a study strewn with an array of that week's newspapers. He had examined all of them for other messages but there were only the ones he had placed, and the single mysterious one, which was in a couple more papers than just the *Trumpeter*.

At about six o'clock a maid delivered some hot water so he

could wash and shave. Soon after that Madden appeared.

'I was wondering if you would like some breakfast, My Lord?'

'Yes, but I will not admit defeat. All I've found out so far is that single message, and whoever sent it seems to have a special interest in Dianne Burrell.'

'Why Miss Burrell?' asked Madden. 'After all, she is not as important as her father in terms of the overall effect on the strikes.'

'I take your point. If this was done by a member of the Burrell family surely, they would have used the message to protect Phillip as well as Dianne. If it was placed in the wider interests of the strikes then it might well be Phillip alone, but more likely it would not have been placed at all so that the insurrectionists could use the information gleaned to be more effective in their turn-outs.'

'Are you suggesting that the sender has a personal interest in Miss Burrell?'

'Given her ability to infatuate a wide range of men that would not be a shortlist, but the perplexing question is how did this person get hold of a cryptograph?'

'Could it have been stolen?'

'I doubt if anyone would get close enough to steal from such an effective and murderous agent as our friend.'

'But our friend did lose it, we know that because we had to replace it. Certainly, if I'd been him, I would have hunted high and low before admitting it to you My Lord.'

The Sneaker's whereabouts were deliberately obscured from Sir Grancester, as he intended. But Madden had a point. When the Sneaker lost the cryptograph, he would have looked for it before he used the emergency code that had warned Sir

Grancester of the situation.

Who might know about that search? If anyone, then it was most likely that it would be one of Inspector Fidel's Chosen Men.

'Madden, get a bath put up for me, followed by a hearty breakfast.' An hour later, looking and feeling much more himself, Sir Grantchester ordered his carriage.

'Where to My Lord,' asked the coachman as he opened the door for his employer.

'Central Manchester police station.'

*

Sir Grancester was sitting in Inspector Fidel's office while Sergeant Sandiway went to find the Inspector. He turned over what tactics would best be employed. It was very unlikely that even if the Chosen Men had heard anything concerning the lost cryptograph that they would have realised its significance. He could be more direct in the matter of Ainscough's intimacy with Dianne Burrell.

The Inspector came in. 'A pleasure to see you Sir Grancester. I thought you would be engaged for a few days more in seeing what was going on in Lancashire.'

'I managed to deal with that expediently; it was as we thought. Manchester has a little more time to collect itself, though not as much as many will assume.'

'What was the situation in Preston like after the shootings?'

'Not as quiet as Stockport and its area. I am beginning to think that killing a few rioters does not have as much effect in reducing their insurrectionist tendencies as I had hoped. Maybe the people further north are hardier than those from the softer plains of Cheshire.'

'You might well be correct on that account.'

'What is the current position here in Manchester?'

'Hard to say. There has not yet been a big press of turn-outs coming to the centre of the city, but there have been some serious incidents. Political activism has increased with the approach of the Delegate Conference of Trades of Manchester. They will convene for a day or two in the Hall of Science, but I estimate that the meeting will produce a battle of words rather than one of fists and staves.

'The incidents that have occurred have been attached to local disputes, long-standing things about pay and sackings, though they have attracted more people and more stones have been thrown. That sort of thing is very difficult for us to contain. By the time we get to such disturbances the whole thing is usually over.

'So, nothing of too much import. My impression is that it's a bit like a pan on a stove just before it comes to the boil. Manchester's a big place and even with an army of specials sworn in we can't cover everything.'

'You'll be asking me about troops next,' said Sir Grancester with a smile.

'Well I think quite often about them, I must admit.'

'All I can say is that there are plans afoot, and you'll be among the first to know when they are on their way. You'll just have to be patient.'

There was a pause then the Inspector went on. 'You'll pardon me Sir Grancester for asking, but usually, you have something specific on your mind when you turn up at my door.'

Sir Grancester looked at Fidel, 'How perceptive of you

Inspector, but in this case, I don't know how to approach it.'

'Well tell me as it comes, and I'll try my best.'

'The accepted account of the Stockport riot says that an unknown assailant from within the ranks of the turn-outs started the killings by shooting Mr Prestbury.'

'That would be my view Sir Grancester. I would go further and say the same assailant shot the individual infantrymen as well.'

'Indeed, but there is a persistent rumour that those original shots were fired by an expert marksman'

Fidel whistled, 'I have not heard that rumour, Sir, but there are often wild stories after such events.'

'This rumour has a second part, that Constable Josiah Ainscough was there in the company of Dianne Burrell, saw where that marksman was and tried to catch him.'

'If Ainscough was there then that would not have been an explicit part of his orders.'

'Can I say that I am not looking to blame Constable Ainscough for his concern for Dianne Burrell. In many ways, the Constable might legitimately think of that care as part of an uncompleted duty. However, it would useful to me to know whether the rumour is true or false. Given the sensitivity of this matter is there anyone who could confirm or deny that Ainscough did pursue the alleged marksman?'

'Not that I know, but Ned Ingliss would be the best person to ask. They were operating as a pair in Cheshire, up to Quarry Bank.'

'Is Constable Ingliss about?'

'I think so.' Fidel went to the door and shouted for Sandiway, 'Is Ingliss in?'

'Depends what you mean by in?' called back the sergeant.

'Don't be coy Sandiway. Where is he?'

'He's in the McInly's gin shop sweet-talking the barmaid.'

'Well tell him to get his arse round here; Sir Grancester wants a word with him.'

It didn't take long for a rather flustered Ned to appear. Sir Grancester had already made it clear he wanted to talk to Ingliss alone, so Fidel left them in private.

'Sit down Constable. I have a couple of questions for you concerning your colleague Constable Ainscough. I want frank replies and only the truth. Do I make myself clear?'

'Yes, Sir Grancester.'

'Have you ever had cause to think that Constable Ainscough's relationship with Dianne Burrell was, how can I put it, closer than duty required?'

'No, Sir Grancester, Josiah has never in my experience done or said anything that was not in line with his duty. Duty is very important to him.'

Sir Grancester frowned, 'Are you, sure Constable?'

Ingliss paused, 'I think it's very likely he's more attached to her than he thinks he is. They have been spoken of as walking out together, which given the original duty of protection of her, was probably very useful. That sort of social contact with a woman as attractive as her can promote passions even the most moral of us would not admit to ourselves.'

'Thank you for your frankness. May I ask you one more thing. Have you ever heard of anyone looking for an unusual watch or similar?'

Ingliss' expression became slightly more attentive. 'I may have Sir Grancester,' he said. 'For instance, I know that on

Stockport market they talk of someone asking around for such an item as well as telling story that Constable Ainscough was hurt quite badly in an attack by a masked man who was looking for something very similar.'

CHAPTER 37

Hobson's choice

The coach left Sir Grancester on the Lancashire side of the bridge across the Mersey. 'I won't be long,' he said to his coachman, 'Take the coach up to the market square and wait near the town hall. I will meet you there when I am done.'

Sir Grancester walked across the plain bridge of this mean mill town. He glanced down into the silted bed of the Mersey. This was a great river for the people in this God-forsaken place. It would be humorous if it was not so full of pathos. At Liverpool the wide expanse of this river was of some note, harbouring the great array of trading ships on the Liverpool side of the water, but here it was hardly a stream.

He still deplored the end of the slave trade. It had devalued his family holdings in the West Indies. Like many of the merchants and factory owners, he was waiting to cash them in when the government granted a sufficient bounty to produce an end to slave ownership. Likewise, he did not cry crocodile tears for Irish workers or any campaign for the repeal of the corn laws. It was all a matter of money not of morality.

He passed Tiviot Dale Methodist Church, with its portico which aped one of the better London Anglican churches. He was not a believer in any sense. He went to church as little as possible. When he went it was for the purposes of political or social advancement. But Sir Grancester deplored the way Methodists like Ainscough set themselves up in mock superiority to the members of the Church of England.

There was a lavender seller at the corner of Hillgate. It was a tight corner and she leaned towards him offering him a bunch of the flowers, 'Lavender Sir? Lavender for Sir's Lady?' He barged past her.

He hated these narrow northern towns, their smoke, their squalor, their narrowness of mind. Every part of his being longed to be back in London where he had all the pleasure and vices his heart desired. But soon he would be home with the plaudits of Queen and government ringing in his ears. A few yards up the hill and he came to Ainscough's door and knocked.

The Constable's face was a picture of astonishment when he opened the door. Wearing a simple shirt and wiping wet hands with a cloth, Josiah made a homely tableau.

'Sir Grancester... I,' He pulled himself up to attention and bowed slightly. 'An honour Sir.'

'I was passing, and I thought rather than summon you to Manchester I would simply call. May I come in; I don't think we should be discussing the matters I must raise with you in the street.'

The house was narrow: a simple kitchen-come-sitting-room downstairs and upstairs a bedroom. What was at the rear probably included some privy and other such inhospitalities that did not bear thinking about. Sir Grancester sat in the chair next to the fire.

'Constable, I need to have a private word with Phillip and Dianne Burrell, and when I say private, I mean unnoticed. I believe we have an opportunity to bring the disturbances in

Manchester and Lancashire in general to a close. Further, I believe you may be able to arrange such a meeting since the Burrells have some confidence in you.'

'That may be, Sir Grancester, but after the shootings in Stockport they will be very sceptical of you.'

Sir Grancester glanced at Josiah. The young man was looking steadily at him and did not drop his eyes. There was a flicker of something like uncertainty and it evoked a brief memory of a master at school appraising, with disfavour, his declension of a Latin verb.

'I know this is irregular Josiah, but I do not relish violence to our fellow citizens.'

'You assume I know where the Burrells can be contacted.'

'If you do not, then I am sure you can find them and get a message to them. You know the daughter better than anyone else I have access to; you were guarding her for some time.'

'When would you like to meet?'

'The day after tomorrow.'

'Where?'

'How about the magistrate's court in Stockport? That would be an unexpected place in present circumstances.'

'I will see what can be done. I will leave a message for you with Inspector Fidel if I am successful.'

*

The magistrates' court was empty. Perhaps it pined for the presence of Mr Prestbury if buildings could pine. Grancester Smythe sat where he knew Prestbury used to like to sit, hoping that this hiatus would not be long. There was the creak of the door from the street opening. Followed by footsteps on the stairs.

Into the court came Phillip and Dianne Burrell accompanied by Constable Ainscough.

Sir Grancester beckoned to Josiah. ' Well done, you have done exactly what I wanted, though I suppose you would see it as no more than your duty.' Sir Grancester waved a languid hand at three objects in front of him on the desk. 'Before we move to business, I am curious to know what you make of these objects. Regard them carefully, for they symbolise your future.'

Josiah was impassive, but Sir Grancester could sense the weariness in the way he was standing. The first object was Sir Grancester's cryptograph. Josiah shifted slightly as he looked at it.

'I see you recognise my little toy, which simply confirms to me what I already knew, which was that you had the one that is missing and have been using it to frustrate me. But what of these other objects?'

There was a pair of familiar handcuffs and a silver tube with a wooden handle. It looked like a truncheon, except that it was a mere six inches long. At the top of the silver tube, there was a carved silver crown. Josiah pointed to the object, 'That is a tipstaff.'

'Correct,' said Sir Grancester. 'Humour me for a moment, for you know its purpose.' Josiah nodded. 'It is carried by my clerk as a symbol of his authority, but in fact, the crown unscrews and there is space inside for a small warrant, no more than a note really; there isn't even room in the tube for a seal. But that small warrant carries enough authority to arrest a man or woman and consign them to jail awaiting trial. Can you guess what I am offering you?'

Josiah did not move a muscle.

'I will tell you. I am offering you the job of a tipstaff to a new court that is being formed. It is a *nisi prius* court especially called for its purpose, which is to try and convict all the chief conspirators of the current insurrection. It will sit at Lancaster.'

Josiah tried to look impassively at Sir Grancester, but sir Grancester smiled. 'Your gaze is steadfast Constable, but your cheeks are white with what I suspect is rage. Yes, Mr Ainscough, I have trapped you.'

'What would this job of tipstaff entail?' said Josiah.

'You would be given the responsibility of finding and arresting those who will be arraigned in front of the new court. The first person to suffer that fate is here.' He looked past Josiah and over to Phillip.

'Do I take it that Mr Burrell is on your list?'

'Yes, Phillip Burrell will be taken into custody today and held. I was rather hoping you would oblige me on that front.'

'And if I refuse?'

'Then your name will be added to the list and you too will be arrested to await trial. What is no doubt worse from your point of view is that I will also use my cryptograph to call your amour, Dianne Burrell, back to my assassin's attention. He will kill her, how of course is up to him, but she is a fine woman and he might well indulge himself a little before the *coup de grass*. Checkmate my young friend?'

Methods of terminating this interview flashed through Josiah's thoughts. Could he seize this foppish excuse for a human being and throttle him before he was killed or constrained himself? But the commandments said you should not kill. He wondered if he could get Phillip and Dianne away to freedom in the streets of his familiar hometown. With Michael's help, they might all get to Ireland. But that would leave his family here in disgrace. There was only one way out at this moment and that was to acquiesce, to play the coward's part, to suffer Dianne's wrath and Phillip's regret.

'You will give me your word you will not have Dianne harmed?'

'I give you my word she will not be harmed by my order until after the *nisi prius* court has deliberated.'

Josiah picked up the tipstaff and walked over to Phillip where he stood with Dianne.

'What does he want to say to us?' asked Phillip.

Josiah raised the staff and tapped Phillip on the shoulder. 'Phillip Burrell on the authority of the Queen I arrest you to be arraigned before a court at Lancaster on charges of sedition.'

There was a rustle of a skirt next to him and the aroma of violets. He looked into Dianne's eyes before her hand lashed him across his left cheek.

CHAPTER 38

Dying and bleaching

Ned Ingliss' situation had taken a turn for the better after Josiah had been transmuted to tipstaff. After a few days, he had been summoned by Sir Grancester and instructed to go to Stockport.

'They are expecting you at the town hall there. I want you to watch what is happening in the town and report back to me anything that you think may be of interest,' was what Sir Grancester had said. Dutifully Ned had done what he was told and now had a place to hang his hat overlooking the market square.

The fact was that there was not much going on in Stockport. The wave of action that had brought the turnouts to the town and caused the riot had dwindled away. Sergeant Smith had taken charge of the local police force and was running it well enough. Most of the mills had, with discretion, closed their doors, and were either locked-out or turned-out, depending on who you asked. Stockport was closed for business.

Ned was crossing the market square when he saw her with her mother. In truth he'd forgotten her, his fancy and favour having been distracted by several other ladies since seeing her at the Hall of Science. But coming across her suddenly, he was conscious how pretty she was, as well as how innocent. He went over and paid his respects. Rosemary brightened when she placed him, but her mother looked more than sceptical.

As chance happened, a few days after, another opportunity arose to get closer to the Hopgood family. He was in the town hall when he was called to assist in a meeting between a local manufacturer and the mayor. They were in the mayor's parlour when he arrived.

'Ah, here he is now,' said the mayor as he entered. 'Ned, this is Mr Hopgood.'

They shook hands and Ned drew up a seat. So, this was Rosemary's father.

'He needs your special talents. Explain the situation to him, Richard.'

'I run a dye-works down on the Portwood. A few days ago, three men turned up, pushed their way into my study and told me to my face to close the works. They made it clear to me that if I did not comply, they would be back with their compatriots to make it forcibly clear to my workers where their best interests lay.'

'Did they come back?' asked Ned.

'They didn't have to; I had no choice but to close. It's a choice many have made in the town since the riot.'

'So, you are now sitting out the strike?'

'Yes, I am quite prepared to close, but I have a seri-ous problem.'

'It's a dye works, Ned,' interjected the mayor, as if Ned was sure to know what significant difference that made.

'I see you don't know much about dying,' said Mr Hopgood. 'We specialise in cotton cloth in bulk, mostly calico or similar. That means we dye very large bolts of cloth in a single process which takes days. Cloth from the bolts is fed into a series of tanks where they are exposed to various chemicals, some of which are corrosive. They are dyed or bleached as required. They don't stay long in any tank; we keep them moving from tank to tank until they come out the far end as coloured cloth, which is washed and dried before it goes off to the customer. But if the cloth is not kept moving some of the chemicals can destroy it.'

'Mr Hopgood has a complete order halfway through his dying tanks,' added the mayor.

'If I can't restart the process then the cloth will spoil, and I will lose the order. It's worth about £500. A loss that large would bankrupt the firm.'

'Can't you get your men back and reopen?'

'They will not take the risk and I can't say I blame them. I've tried to negotiate with the men who came and closed the works in the first place, but I couldn't find them. Then a neighbour pointed out this article in the local paper.'

Ned read the headline, *French Revolutionaries in Marple Bridge*. It seemed that there was a local organisation calling itself a Committee of Public Safety.

'Do I take it that this Committee is something the French radicals used in the Revolution?'

'Quite so, at the height of the Terror in fact. Mr Ingliss, they are my last hope. Could you find these people and negotiate so that my men come back and save this order?'

Ned considered the matter. It seemed unlikely that such an outlandishly named organisation existed at all. But if it did then Sir Grancester would certainly be interested in it, and if he succeeded Mr Hopgood would be in his debt and that would get him closer to Rosemary.

'I'll do my best Mr Hopgood. I'll certainly do my best.'

Having left the mayor and Mr Hopgood, Ned considered the matter of the Committee of Public Safety, wondering where to start. What he needed was a manager of a largish mill who might have reason to deal with such people on his account. His Nibs, lately of Leavington's, was likely to keep an eye on such matters, just in case he might profit from the information. It would be worth squeezing Tate.

Ned knew where Tate lived, so he sauntered over. The house was in a reasonable area; it even had a token small patch of earth behind the iron railings and a short path to the front door. The curtains were still closed, and it took two or three goes of determined banging on the knocker until there were signs from inside.

'Bugger off. I'm not in.' Tate was very much worse for wear.

'Constable Ingliss, Manchesters. Open up or your well-off neighbours will think you're letting the area down.'

There was a rattling of keys and locks until at last Tate opened the door. He was a mess. Unshaven, dressed in a shirt that had not been washed for several days. Ned thought it looked as though he'd been sleeping in it. He pushed past the wreckage and closed the door behind him.

The house smelled of stale smoke, bad food and boiled cabbage; the last from the drains. Ned headed down the hall corridor and opened a door into what turned out to be the kitchen. Sunlight streamed in and Tate groaned while trying to shade his eyes. Tate followed Ned into the kitchen. Ned sat in the only comfortable seat near an empty grate, forcing Tate to sit stiff-backed on a stool.

'I've come to ask you one simple question; answer it correctly and I'll leave you to wallow in your sty. Make up a lie to see the back of me and I'll be back to make you pay. Understand?'

Tate nodded, 'Ask.'

'Where will I find the Committee of Public Safety.'

Tate laughed, 'What a bloody stupid name.'

'It's from the French Revolution.'

'It should have stayed there. But if it's from the Revolution then chances are it will be something to do with Monsieur Smith, that's what he calls himself. He's got an obsession with France; says he's a Chartist Jacobin.'

'Reckon he would have set up such a committee?'

'Drunk with him a few times until I decided it was too dicey to continue. He used to say that the French had the right idea; how they'd controlled the mob with terror. If he ever had the chance that's what he'd do. If you're going to see him take my advice and go armed.

'It may all sound very childish Ingliss, but he's a dangerous man. You'll find him and his mates in one of the dives near the river. If he's not there, then try Ugly Tom's. If he's got a committee, he'll need a place to hold court, and Ugly Tom's is perfect.'

CHAPTER 39

Committee of public safety

It had taken Ned a couple of blind alleys and empty gin shops, where Monsieur Smith had been seen in the past but not recently before he'd done what he should have first and gone to Ugly Tom's. So, it was a rather bad-tempered Ned who stooped under the low door at about half-past-six one morning. He went over to where what passed for food and drink appeared from a hidden kitchen, God knew where. There was an old hag serving.

'What yer want, love?'

'Looking for Monsieur Smith,' he said. 'Seen him lately?'

'Seen 'im, can't get rid of 'im and 'is crew; like bleeding cockroaches.'

She had no teeth that Ned could see, and her lips, or was it her gums, slapped together. They weren't very good at containing her spittle and so as she spoke white flecks of saliva formed at the corners of her mouth, some of which were projected forward.

'He's here all the time now. He's dozing in the back.'

'I'll go and disturb his sleep. Want a word with him.'

'If you're looking for a word then I'd be polite and wait 'til 'e wakes. The last person who disturbed his beauty sleep was found downstream in the Mersey with a smashed face; 'ave some gruel while 'yen wait.'

Ned took the noxious brew that was Ugly Tom's speciality over to a back table. There seemed to be some sort of scum on its surface, though the chunk of bread looked palatable. When he gave it an exploratory nibble he found it was gritty. Still, better the bread than the gruel.

Ned had taken Tate's advice and had a brace of pistols in his pocket. He finished his bread and waited. Before too long a man with grubby vest and britches came out from the back. His main distinguishing garment was on his head, a soft conical cap that curled over at its top. It had been dyed red and was adorned by a tricolour cockade on its band.

'Breakfast Mags.' Plain statement, no please nor thank you.

Ned itched to clout the man, but he was here on official business, as well as his extracurricular, personal interest. The man waited, then after a few minutes took the plate of what smelled like bacon and eggs and sat on a table near to Ned. The hag looked over and nodded. Ned waited until Smith was tucking in before he went over.

'May I disturb your breakfast, Monsieur?'

'Do I know you, citizen?' Smith did not look at Ned.

'I believe you run the Committee of Public Safety in these parts?'

'What if I do?'

'I have a friend who wishes to make an application to you.'

At last, Smith looked up. There was a scar down his right cheek, acquired from being slashed with a knife by the look of it.

'What sort of friend?'

'A dyer who wants your committee to permit his turn-outs

to do some work.'

'Why would I be interested in that?'

'General wellbeing of your fellow man?'

'The Revolution requires that there be no quarter given, even if asked. Citizen, this is the beginning of the end of the ruling classes here, just as the Terror was the end of the ruling classes in *la belle Français*. Remember you met me when you see me pass in glory in my later days. All that matters citizen, is whether you love freedom even to the point of death: *Vivre libre ou mourir* citizen, *vivre libre ou mourir*.

It crossed Ned's mind that this fool might find death a bit closer to him than he would like if one of the pistols in his pocket was pressed firmly to his temple. But natural inclination was no substitute for patience and cunning when poaching a young pheasant, at least that was what he had once heard a countryman say.

Smith finished his breakfast. He called over his shoulder, not acknowledging the presence of Mags in any way. 'Beer over here. Have your *bourgeois* friend present his case tomorrow to myself and my brothers and we will decide in the interests of the citizens of this,' he fought for the word but all he could come up with was, 'parish.'

'Where and what time?' asked Ned.

'Here, nine tomorrow evening, sharp. Mags where's my sodding beer?'

*

Ned met Richard Hopgood at the Lancashire Bridge the following evening. A simple note had explained the situation and asked the dyer to bring some coin with him, at least twenty

224

pounds in the form of gold half-sovereigns.

'Evening Mr Ingliss,' said Hopgood.

'Evening Sir. We should walk on. I'll explain as we go along.' They started to walk towards Ugly Tom's. 'First thing is, have you ever been in Ugly Tom's before?'

'No, not as far as I recollect.'

'In that case, try not to be too shocked, and try even harder not to vomit at the stench. You get used to it after the first five minutes. The person who runs this Committee of Public Safety looks like one of the biggest fools you'll ever meet, but he is very dangerous. He's been involved in several murders, though never caught.'

'Is he trustworthy?'

'I doubt it. I doubt it so much I'm carrying two pistols. If it comes to shooting, get in front of me and run for it. I'll be right behind you. Have you got the cash?'

'As instructed.'

'I have a feeling that while Monsieur Smith puts on political airs and graces, in the end, he will be bribable as any other vagabond.' When they arrived at the path to Ugly Tom's, Ingliss said, 'Follow me, speak only when you're spoken to.'

Inside Monsieur Smith was waiting for them. He had a coat of blue with a tricolour sash, as well as his cockaded cap of liberty. There were about ten other men more or less poorly dressed, all with their versions of the cap.

Smith stood as he saw Hopgood, took off his cap and bowed low to the floor in what he must have thought was a very proper bow indeed. His supporters laughed and jeered at this mockery.

'Mr Hopgood, I am gratified to see you are willing to attend our Revolutionary Tribunal. Pray accompany us to the back room, where we will hear your case.' He led the way. Hopgood followed Ned at his back. The rest of the rabble followed close behind. Ned took several sharp jabs in the back. At one point the tip of a knife was pressed firmly against his spine so that he could be in no doubt that the threat of violence was real.

The room was larger than Ned had expected, perhaps the largest cellar in the old house. It was lit by four blazing torches, the heat from which made it feel reasonably warm, or at least less damp. There was a table opposite the door with three chairs set behind it. Smith took the middle one and two of his friends, the only other two with revolutionary sashes, sat either side of him. Smith waved Ned and Hopgood to stand before them. The door was shut. The rest of the group were between Ned and the only way out.

Smith took out a brace of pistols and laid them on the table. One of his compatriots placed a sword in front of them. They were going through the rituals of a real tribunal. Though the rituals of the French Jacobins had very likely been rather abstemious, this was a British tribunal, and yet no one had a drink.

Ned whispered to Hopgood, 'Put two half-sovereigns on the table.'

Ned expected Hopgood to be all fingers and thumbs, but the dyer was not as overawed as Ned had expected. Richard produced his heavy purse.

'Monsieur Smith, thank you for seeing me. I notice that your comrades have not had time to acquire any beverages.' He placed two gold coins on the table. They glowed in the flickering torchlight. Ned saw Smith lick his lips. He couldn't take his eyes off the gold and Smith knew there was much more where those two small tokens had come from. 'In business, I have often found that a drink aids judgment.'

'I agree,' replied Smith. He nodded to someone behind Ned, who pushed between him and Hopgood before picking up the coins. The door shut behind him as he went to get the drink.

'Now Citizen Hopgood, the way we run this committee is simple. You put your case, we ask a few questions, then we vote and you accept the result.'

The drinks came in were put on the table from where they were distributed.

'Just one formality before we start.' Everyone stood and started to sing the Marseilles in French.

To Ned's surprise, Richard Hopgood was singing along with the best of them, in what seemed like reasonable French. The chorus ended with great cheer and a toast of *Vive la Revolution*.

'Now Mr Hopgood, what is your case?'

'Monsieur le President.' There was a chorus of *ooh* at this form of address. 'My case is simply this. There is a £500 order for dying calico in the dying tanks at my works. If it is not processed, then the cloth will rot in those tanks and when this is all over my men will have no jobs to return to. They will not come back to work and process it, though willing, and then go back on strike because they are frightened of reprisals. If your committee were to permit them then I think they will come back and we can complete the order, Monsieur le President.'

One of the judges sat forward in his seat. 'Why should we worry about the plight of the poor? The more miserable the labourers now, the riper for the revolution they will be. I say let your cloth rot and you with it.'

The speaker might have expected good support for such a statement, but Ned thought the response from the meeting was rather restrained. He hoped the drink was working.

'As much as I might respect your revolutionary zeal, Citizen, I ask you what will happen if the revolution does not take hold as you hope. The workers will be worse off having lost their places.'

'This seems just a way of breaking the strike,' said a man from the side-lines.

Smith took up his point. 'Why will you not just stay open permanently?'

'You have the force with which to stop me.' Hopgood nodded towards the pistols on the table, 'In any case you have my word I will not. Once the order is completed the works will again close. I will keep the bargain that Mr Hyde Greg keeps at Quarry Bank.'

'Citizens you have heard this *bourgeois'* case. I say permit him. How say you, my fellow judges?'

'Deny,' said the judge who had spoken against.

'Permit,' said the other.

Smith stood. 'Let the message go out that this Committee of Public Safety approves and will protect the workers of Hopgood's in completing this order but nothing else, come the Revolution.' There was a great cheer and singing broke out again. Ned and Hopgood turned to leave. Before he went Richard piled half-sovereigns on the table.

'For the good of your cause Monsieur. *Vive la Revolution.*'

Once away from Ugly Tom's a thankful Ned turned to Hopgood. 'That gesture with the cash was generous.'

'Not as generous as it might seem, it was less than half that was in my purse.'

CHAPTER 40

The letters of Rosemary Hopgood

Wednesday 7ᵗʰ September 1842

Dear Cynthia,

How quickly things can change. I told you about the cloth in my last letter. Well, things did not get any better and Pappa decided he would ask the help of the Mayor. I don't know all the ins and outs but apparently, this gambit worked, and to put it bluntly a couple of days ago a gang of men from the factory turned up and they saved the cloth and with it the finances of the business.

Overseeing the men on the first morning was a very smart and attractive young man. I recognised him immediately. He had been at the Hall of Science when we went in, but then he was dressed like a common workman.

I badgered Pappa, and he told me he was called Mr Ned Ingliss, that he was not a workman but a member of the Manchester Police Force, stationed for the time being in Stockport. Pappa warned me that we all owed this Mr Ingliss a great debt of gratitude. I believe he also said honour, but I didn't follow that.

The upshot is we will be entertaining Mr Ingliss next

Sunday and I must be sure to be friendly to him. He also said I should try to be a bit more sensible than normal. But I think that's just Pappa's sense of humour.

Rest assured I shall be on my best behaviour and will not repeat the mistake of being head-over-heels as I was with that milksop Josiah. But it is very nice to have a new and eligible man back in one's circle.

Your perpetual friend and cousin,
  Rosemary

CHAPTER 41

The Hopgoods' at home

'Martha my dear are you ready to go?'

'Just coming Thomas, I'm sure Elizabeth and Richard will not be worried about us being a few minutes late.'

'No, but I gather that part of this luncheon is for us, or perhaps especially for you; to see the quality of their new live-in cook. If I were her, I would be nervous and so I would prefer to reduce the period of her suspense to a minimum.'

Martha came into the hall where her husband was waiting. She was pulling on her gloves, 'Well I'm ready now.' She straightened her bonnet in the hall mirror and they started on their way.

'Do you think the young man I've seen the last few Sundays will be present?' asked Thomas.

'I would expect so. After the success he had in saving the calico contract from destruction in the dying vats he seems to have become a firm favourite of Rosemary, as well as of Elizabeth and Richard.'

'Rosemary has certainly become his constant companion at chapel. He is a very affable young man, though I haven't talked to him much.'

'I haven't talked to him at all. Though there is one thing that puzzles me.'

'What is that my dear?'

'I cannot rid myself of the thought that I have seen him before, not in chapel, but somewhere else, somewhere very different.'

They had reached the gates of Hopgood's dye-works and turned into the yard. At the top of the steps up to the front door of the manager's house, which the Hopgoods occupied, was a middle-aged woman in a smart white pinafore.

'Oh, mercy me,' said Martha as they started up, 'What ridiculous measure of vainglory!'

*

Hopgood's cook had produced a good meal. The meat was deftly roasted, the vegetables crisp and the apple crumble simple but well spiced.

'Well that was a fine meal, I think we can all agree on that,' said Richard Hopgood. Martha caught Elizabeth's eye, Elizabeth agreed on the meal's competence, but there was a certain resolution in her face that suggested she was not prepared to give the idea of a live-in cook unquestioning support.

As Martha had surmised, Mr Ingliss was present and seated next to Rosemary, who spent far too much time looking adoringly up into his eyes or hanging on to his every *bon mot*. Martha had to admit his charm, but after a little while, still trying to place where she had seen him, she decided to ask the young man some direct if not frank questions.

'Mr Ingliss,' said Martha. She was going to continue but he interrupted her.

'Please call me Ned, Mrs Cooksley, after all, we have met before.'

Martha frowned. So her impression that she had met him before was correct, but there was still no why or how attached to the who. 'It's strange that you should say that Mr Ingliss, for I've had the impression that I knew you from somewhere, but even now I can't say where.'

'At the doors of the Hall of Science the night of the Campfield riot. I was in ordinary clothes that night, but I am a member of the Manchester police force, and I'm assigned to Stockport to help the local force.'

'He's been very helpful to me,' interjected Richard. 'It's not an exaggeration to say that without Mr Ingliss' help I might now be facing possible bankruptcy.'

Ned Ingliss smiled, but it did not escape Martha that he looked quickly but carefully for the effect Richard's remark had made. Someone who thinks a bit too much of himself, she thought.

'Have there been any problems with getting the calico safely out of the dying vats?'

'None. The Committee of Public Safety was as good as its word. It took a day or so to get the men needed to save cloth out of the vats, and it took them no more than a couple of days to process the order. The works were shut again straight afterwards but at least when we open again we will be paid, and disaster averted.'

'That's a very satisfactory outcome all round,' added Rosemary. Solicitously, Ned gave her arm a gentle pat. Rosemary smiled to the extent that it might have been considered a simper.

'Well it's nice that he has swollen our congregation by one, at least for the time being,' said Mr Cooksley.

'Since you were there at the riot, did you encounter my son by any chance?' asked Martha, expecting the answer to be yes. She was disappointed.

'I'm sorry, no I haven't.'

The rest of the luncheon went off well. Ned was good company and especially appreciated by Rosemary. But the more charming he became, the more Martha started to suspect his sincerity. A quotation from Matthew's Gospel kept coming to mind, *I send you forth as sheep in the midst of wolves: be ye therefore wise as serpents, and harmless as doves.* Martha was a practical Christian, good and generous to those in need, forgiving to those who sinned, but fierce in defence of the integrity of the chapel and congregation.

She cross-questioned her husband about Ned on the way home. 'What do you think of Mr Ingliss, Thomas?'

'I haven't had a lot of contact with him, but he has done a considerable service to Richard. His presence in the congregation on Sundays has been noticed and it's clear that Rosemary is developing an affection for him. Some of the members more prone to gossip are talking of a wedding soon. Do I detect you have reservations, my dear?'

*

Over the next few days, Martha Cooksley tried very hard to suppress her reservations about Ned Ingliss, but she failed. There was something out of tune about him, in short, off-key. But there was nothing to be done. A feeling was no evidence of any sort, and any action, even words she might speak, even in private, would be wholly improper.

She was shopping in the market square when she was

approached by Sergeant Smith. He touched his top hat in salute. 'Good morning Mam, I don't often see you in the square.'

'It is very good to see you, Sergeant. How are the police faring in these troublesome times?

'Most of the mills are quiet and the centre of activity has moved to Manchester. If the general situation improves then I think mills will start going back to work. But I came over mostly to ask how Josiah is getting on.'

'Well, I don't see Josiah as a natural tipstaff, but then I never really saw him a likely constable either, and there I have to admit I was wrong. So I half-expect to be wrong again. But there is something you might help me with.'

'It would be an honour.'

'I have run into a Mr Ned Ingliss who is attached to the Stockport force. Do you know anything about him, Sergeant?'

Smith hesitated. 'I know of this officer and he is indeed stationed in Stockport at the moment. He is a Manchester man, but he is not attached to the Stockport force. Like Josiah, he has been taking orders from central authority through the Manchester force. That is all I know.'

'Would he know Josiah?'

'It's rumoured that have done some operations together. Best to ask Josiah directly. He will know what he can say and what he can't.'

'Thank you for your advice, Sergeant. I owe him a letter and today seems opportune. I'll broach the mater then.'

Tiviot Dale Methodist Manse

21ˢᵗ September 1842

Dear Josiah,

I hope this note finds you in good health. First, a bit of housekeeping. Mr O'Carroll has confirmed that the hampers I have been preparing for you have been going off to Crewe for you to collect, and empty ones have been returning for refilling. Thank you for the notes that you have sent in the empties. I think we can say we've got a working system. It seems to me that the rights and wrongs of the cases individuals face are a matter for the court, but I'm pleased to help you in your endeavour to be humane. Thomas and I are proud of you.

This is a bit of a longer note than I normally send, but I have a few questions that I'm advised by Sergeant Smith you might be able to answer. They concern one Mr Edward Ingliss, who, the good Sergeant tells me, is a Constable of the Manchester Force. Mr Ingliss has been attached to the Town Hall here but is not under the jurisdiction of the Stockport Force. He has been a very great help to Richard Hopgood over the matter of saving a large order of calico spoiling in Richard's dying vats. Mr Ingliss was successful, became a favourite of the Hopgood household, and, as a result, has become rather attached to Rosemary. In fact, he has been a regular on her arm at Chapel and there is talk, among the more gossip-prone members of the Congregation, that a marriage might not be far away. One aspect of this matter that had been bothering me is that I was convinced I had met him before, but I could not tell where or when.

We went to lunch at the Hopgoods on Sunday, and Mr Ingliss was present and was being very attentive to

Rosemary. You may not be surprised that she is as silly as she ever was, a state that is encouraged by her Father but deplored by her Mother. In short, it turns out that I have met him before, on the door of the Hall of Science on the night of the Campfield riot.

Sergeant Smith thinks you have had joint activities with Mr Ingliss. I hope I don't sound gratuitously inquisitive, but I cannot get the notion out of my head that there is something not quite right about Mr Ingliss. Can you set my mind at rest, within the proper limits of respectability?

My thoughts and prayers are always with you,
Your loving Mother

30ᵗʰ September 1842

Dear Mother,

Thank you for your note. The arrangement with the hampers is working well and the accused are very grateful to you for your concern.

I am most intrigued that Ned Ingliss has appeared in Stockport. Sergeant Smith is correct. I was partnered with Ned in observing the activities of the turn-outs before the Stockport Riot. Please show this note to Sergeant Smith and tell him I give him Cart Blanche to tell you details of what he knows of my activities at that time.

But now to Ned Ingliss. You are right to be suspicious of Ned; he is a very efficient officer, a member of Inspector Fidel's Chosen Men, who do difficult work, if not quite consistent with Mr Peel's rules for the guidance of police activities. Ned does those jobs well and has more than once helped me stay out of trouble and danger.

As much as Ned comes from a family not known for its legal probity, his main weakness of character is that he has a very wandering eye where pretty girls are concerned. I know that Rosemary Hopgood took his fancy at the Hall of Science. If he has got close to Rosemary, then she and her parents should be most cautious of taking him at face value.

Your affectionate,
Josiah

CHAPTER 42

The letters of Rosemary Hopgood

Wednesday 21ˢᵗ October 1842

Dear Cynthia,

Things are getting rather serious in my courtship with Mr Ingliss. He has been visiting regularly as his duties allow and was at Sunday luncheon when the Minister and his frightfully nosey wife were invited.

It is clear he is a policeman, but exactly what he does at Stockport Town Hall is something of a mystery. Whatever it is, it leaves him plenty of time to be around the house often, as well as walking out with Mamma when we go shopping.

There has been an increasing number of times when he and I have been left alone together. He has of course been the perfect gentleman on these occasions, though I have been longing for him to show more than simple civility. Affection is what I crave, and his affection in particular. As a result, I was taken aback the other evening by what happened.

I was playing the piano for him before supper. The candles were lighted. The early evenings at this time of year are so full of romance. Mother was with us, but something was on her mind. In the end, she put down her sewing and went off to the kitchen muttering that she wanted to talk to Cook. Mr Ingliss had been turning the pages of the music for me.

I finished the piece I was playing and asked him if he would like another. 'Will your mother be long?' he said.

'That is very likely, Ned,' I call him Ned in private, he gave me permission, 'When she goes to the kitchen at this time in the evening it's usually because she is suspicious Cook is not preparing the meal in the way Mamma wants it done.'

Ned had taken the music I had just played from the piano's music stand. He laid it down on the top of the piano and turned to me and knelt beside the piano stool. He took my hands in his.

'Rosemary, I think you must realise that my affection and respect for you has been growing over the last few weeks as we have spent more time with each other,' he said. As you might imagine, my heart skipped a beat at such an open admission of affection. I reassured him that my experience of his company had been the same.

He went on, 'But you must know that I find the strictness of your family rather irksome. I would like to take you out of an evening on my own account.' I was going to say that that might be possible in time, you see I was taking his good sense seriously when he cut me off.

'Rosemary, by chance I have been given two tickets for a symphony concert in Manchester next week. I have never been to such a concert, but you are such an accomplished musician, if you were with me I am sure that you would be able to introduce me to the music and help me obtain some understanding. I do so wish that you could come with me, but I know that you would not wish to upset your parents, by doing so in secret.'

He was so sweet that I said that I would try to think of a way we might go together but that he would have to give me a little time to consider the matter. He looked so happy that he pulled me to him a gave me the first proper kiss I have ever had. You can imagine how my head spun.

Your perpetual friend and cousin,
  Rosemary

Monday 24th October 1842

Dear Cynthia,

Mr Ingliss' attentions are growing in intensity. I had to tell him that the idea of my getting away so that we could have a pleasant evening attending the concert was delicious but impossible. I explained how adamant my parents were that I should not go out alone; so, it would be impossible for me to get away with him even for a stolen evening. He should continue to cultivate Pappa and Mamma's favour and hope an opportunity presents itself. The truth is that I do not think they will let me step out with anyone unless an official engagement has been forthcoming.

Oh, Cynthia, I do not know what he could make of this. I crave another of his kisses. My ardour is fully aflame, and I burn, yes, I burn. I dream Ingliss and awake in the depth of the night sweating and panting from the vision.

I mistake other men glanced in the street for Ingliss and my heart skips. If I am idle and my mind is not occupied when I sew, even sometimes when I read, a vision of his face floats into my mind and I sigh.

Cynthia, I will see him alone. I am not the puppet of my backward provincial parents! I am Rosemary Hopgood and I WILL find a way of being alone with him!

Your perpetual friend and cousin,
  Rosemary

Friday 28th October 1842

Dear Cynthia,

How quickly the affairs of frail human beings can change. A few days are sometimes all it takes, but I will not spoil the revelation. Only allow me to say that the despair and frustration of my last letter have been illuminated by a beam of radiance and sunlight.

On Tuesday night Pappa came in with a message that he announced over the supper table. The Association of Dyers and Cloth Printers, to which he and all the owners of manufactories in those trades belong, is to hold a soiree or a dinner party, or, perhaps, it's a ball, I don't know the correct term.

As with everything in the boring business of industry, it is not about fun or anything like that. Oh no, it's about contacts with people. The purpose, as Pappa so gleefully told us, is to invite the mill owners and others who have the responsibility for placing orders with businesses like his to

242

the occasion so they can better get to know those with whom they might wish to do trade. So it's business, business and more boring business, or so I thought to myself.

Then Pappa went on. He said that since the Association of Dyers and Cloth Printers is a relatively small association, without much money, they must cut their cloth to fit their purse. I must have looked puzzled. He looked at me and said that in short, they could not afford to pay for whole families to attend and that the event would be limited to owners and their wives.

Oh, bother I thought, Mamma will refuse to go and I must go instead as an alternative to her – but no! They must have already talked about the matter for she was astonishingly willing to go. I asked her what would happen to me? 'Well you can pick what you want for your evening meal and Cook will prepare it. I'm sure you'll do perfectly well on your own. Look on it as an opportunity to catch up with sewing those vests for the poor children at Christmas. You're behind with those.'

So, I thought, they'll go off galivanting and poor little me is to be left on her own. Then it occurred to me I will be alone for a whole evening, with no one to watch me. Gradually as plans were discussed it became clear that they would be out for many hours. They would need to go early to prepare for their guests, and stay to the very end, at least midnight so it seemed. With care, I might disappear from the house for a tryst with Mr Ingliss and back without anyone to notice I had been gone at all. The date for this occasion is fixed as Saturday 19th November.

Your perpetual friend and cousin,
  Rosemary

Monday 14ᵗʰ November 1842

Dear Cynthia,
  My plans are laid. All that must happen now is that they are executed without any problems or accidents.
  I had no difficulty in making it clear to Mamma that I was content that I was to be left on my own next Saturday. I took a good time thinking about what I would like for supper, which I graciously and gratefully simplified when I heard that Cook had asked permission to visit her sister on that day. Mamma commented that it was very generous of me to take such a kindly view of the matter. She confided that she was not all that happy at having to go to such a folderol, as she put it, but she would see my behaviour and attitude repaid with something pleasant for me in the future. What would she have said had she known what I planned?
  With Cook out of the way, I will only have to deal with the maid. But even here fate seems to have shone on me. I was coming out into the hall when I noticed the front door was open. I peeked down the steps and there she was, chatting with an overseer of the steeping sheds, one Pat Gaskell. I'd been thinking for some time that she was sweet on Mr Gaskell and a delicate piece of eavesdropping confirmed it.
  'What you doin' next Saturday evening,' I heard him say.
  'Not a lot. The family's out at an evening occasion or

some such.'

'That means you're on your own.'

'Nearly but not quite. Cook's off but Miss Nose-in-the-air is still around.'

'Sounds dull.'

'Dull is a very tame word for it.'

'Don't quite see why you got to be on duty? How about if I come around and keep you company?'

She giggled and while in other circumstances I'd have got her into hot water for that Miss Nose-in-the-air, it was as perfect an opportunity I was ever likely to get. Marie will be canoodling with her young man and she will never even notice I am gone. So, I wrote to Ned and said all was prepared. What was I to expect of the evening?

He replied that he had an especial treat in-store; he had hired a private room at one of the best hotels in Manchester. With it came a pianoforte and he had added a pianist to play for me. Supper would be served after our private concert. No expense would be spared. We meet at Heaton Norris station at half-past seven.

Wish me good fortune Cynthia, I could not be more excited.

Your perpetual friend and cousin,
Rosemary

CHAPTER 43

Supper

The room was comfortable, and in many circles would have been thought lavish. For others, it was perhaps slightly tawdry. Those who felt that would have included most of Tiviot Dale's chapelgoers.

The door opened, and a man entered. He carried a small leather bag. His priority was the piano. He went over to where it sat in an alcove with red velvet curtains. Without sitting, he played several scales, arpeggios and chords. A woman came in and he looked around.

'Piano seems in fine fettle, Teresa.'

'So, it should, I had it tuned especially. No expense spared for our Mr Ingliss.'

The man took off his overcoat. Underneath was a suit that looked tidy enough, but as with the room, closer inspection would have revealed its shabby side. He sat on the piano stool and looked around.

'How many occasions will this be?'

'Nine to my knowledge.'

'I wonder how he does it? Is it always the same?'

'Varies. The one this evening likes music, that's why you're here. But he's cut corners a bit on the food.'

'But not on the booze I'll be bound.'

'Oh no, never cuts corners on imbibing. Says it lubricates the whole process.' They chuckled. There was a noise on the stairs.

'Sounds like them now. You better start tinkling the ivories while I go down the backstairs. Music always impresses them when they first arrive.'

The man sat down, placed some music on the piano stand and started to play one of Chopin's simpler studies, one he knew by heart as it happened.

Rosemary was smartly dressed in her best silk dress, a colourfully embroidered shawl around her shoulders. Her hair was up and even an objective observer would have admitted that she was very attractive.

The same was true of her escort. Ned always looked reasonably smart, except when undercover, but his best, well only, evening suit made his animal attractiveness more obvious.

As she came in Rosemary gasped: the music and the plush setting working their magic. Those who have never seen real luxury cannot be expected to see through insincere imitation. Josiah might have thought vanity, vanity; Michael would have signed the cross and prayed for the girl; Martha Cooksley would have boxed her ears and taken her home. But she had no protector present, and her father and mother were a few miles away, attending to those who might place orders and help Hopgood's Dyeing and Bleaching recover profits lost in the strike, playing the game that every manufacturer is forced into within the thrall of business.

'Oh, this is divine,' Rosemary gasped.

'I'm glad you like it,' said Ned. 'Is the music to your taste?'

She smiled at him. 'Chopin? Yes, he is one of my favourites.'

Ned took her shawl and draped it over the back of the

Chesterfield that was close to the fire. There was a knock. 'Come,' called Ned.

The hostess came in. She was carrying a tray with two glasses, and a bottle wrapped in a wet, white cloth that was keeping it cold. She curtsied.

'I have come to say that we will be ready to serve supper in a few minutes, but in the meantime, I hope you will enjoy this champagne while we prepare.' She placed the wine and glasses on a side table and Ned ushered Rosemary to a Chesterfield and offered her a glass. She took it and he chinked his glass against hers.

'Here's to a delightful evening,' he said. Rosemary looked at the glass and took a draft. She started to cough.

'Oh, I'm so sorry,' he said, got up and came back with the bottle. 'Another sip will stop you coughing,' and he topped up her glass. She obediently took another sip and miraculously the coughing stopped, though the bubbles went up to her nose and she sneezed. 'Bless you!' a smiling Ned said.

Supper was served on a table in the corner of the room opposite the piano. There were three courses: soup, fish and a dessert. Rosemary tried very hard to keep track of the menu but found its detail escaped her. She made a much more determined effort to keep track of the amount of wine she was drinking, but she failed on that count as well. The fact was that Mr Ingliss was so attentive, it was hardly possible for her to concentrate on anything other than her companion. The only thing she noted was that, as much as she drank, Mr Ingliss seemed to drink less, though by the time the meal was finished she wasn't certain that even this observation was correct.

When they had finished, and the hostess, assisted by

another servant had cleared the table, they went back to the Chesterfield, though before seating himself, Mr Ingliss went over to the musician and paid him his fee. The man left and the couple were alone.

'I hope you have enjoyed yourself this evening,' he said.

Rosemary yawned, stretched and smiled at him, 'I have never experienced an evening like it.' She yawned again and moved closer to him. He put his arm around her shoulders and pulled her a little further than she had intended. He cupped her face in his hands and kissed her. She moved even further towards him and this time it was she who initiated another kiss.

After a few more exchanges Rosemary felt a gentle pressure on her breast. There was a curious dichotomy in her mind: she knew that she should object and physically push Mr Ingliss away, but this knowledge did not stop her from responding with more passion.

Exactly when it happened, she was not sure, but she felt lifted in his arms. They passed through a door at the end of the room which she had only been vaguely aware of before, and he placed her on a bed. The bedroom was very badly lit, perhaps only by a single candle. So, when the door shut behind them, they were in total seclusion.

CHAPTER 44

The letters of Rosemary Hopgood

20th November 1842

Dear Cynthia,

I do not know quite what to tell you about my encounter with Mr Ingliss yesterday evening. I had expected a concert, but what happened was more like an individual recital than a public concert.

The musician who played for us accompanied our supper. Ned told me much about his life, though now I find some of the details vague. How he had been brought up in a poor family, how he had been inspired to become a policeman and cut away from the rather dishonest lives of his family after his mother and father died.

The food came and went, each served with a glass of wine. Each had been selected specially to go with different parts of the meal. The tragedy is that I cannot remember as much as I would care to about the latter stages of what we ate. One thing I did notice was that Ned did not drink very much at all.

When the meal was over, we settled down and were soon canoodling. But good things never go on for as long as perhaps we would like them to, or perhaps sometimes for longer than is good for us. Ned had received a note from the Manchester Police Station and had to go to attend to something in the line of duty. A carriage came which took me home and I was safely in my room before Mamma and Pappa came back.

A successful evening, but not one I would be in haste to repeat often if ever. Now I must go and try to rest. My head is aching, and I feel more than somewhat bilious.

Your perpetual friend and cousin,
  Rosemary

P.S. Cynthia, if you are ever tempted to do as I have done, remember a man's unbridled passion is a very powerful thing and difficult to resist.

Thursday 29th December 1842

Dear Cynthia,

Thank you for your Christmas letter and my apologies for having been unable to send you one before the season of good cheer. Things have been very busy here, especially for Pappa, as he has got the manufactory going again after the terrible strike.

Things have gradually got back to normal. The troops who brought order back to the town are gone. Most of the turn-outs, as they styled themselves, were still very reluctant to go back to work but only a few mills held out. We new the dispute was over once Quarry Bank was reopened by the Greg family.

Mr Greg had treated his workers very leniently in closing his establishment at what had been the first sign of trouble. Many in the town here expected the mill to reopen quickly. But it was a good month after the soldiers arrived that the men returned to work at Quarry Bank.

However, the worst thing that I have had to face since my last letter to you is that every day since the middle of November I seem to have been sick or felt sick. It has been horrid. I've been hiding the matter from Mamma as much I have been able, but I think she suspects that something is wrong.

But the biggest shock came when I was out shopping with Maria. A woman who was selling herbs or the like came up to me near the Lancashire Bridge. "Good luck, missus," she said. I was puzzled and asked her pardon. "Good luck to you and the baby. Let me guess I'd say you were about 14 weeks." I was so shocked that I tried to pay her for her little posy. She laughed, "Thanks for the thought love. Give it to the baby when she comes."

Cynthia, you're the only person I can ask. Could I be pregnant after my encounter with Mr Ingliss? You have much more experience in this sort of thing than me, having a bigger family.

Your perpetual friend and cousin,
  Rosemary

Wednesday 6th January 1843

Dear Cynthia,

You are of course right. There is no point in my dwelling on things that have happened. You are also right when you say I need to face up to my predicament and make sure I know with certainty what has happened and how I must behave.

I was foolish and naïve in my dealings with Mr Ingliss. I put myself at his mercy, believing in my silliness that I would be able to outwit him or play him along for my own satisfaction: a puppet to dance for my amusement. It was daring and foolish. I ignored that I was a tyro in such matters, and like a moth, to a candle, I may have danced in the bright light for a time, but I was powerless against him after the same flame had touched my wings.

What a terrible choice now lies in front of me. If I am with child, then I must come to terms with marriage to a man I now despise and on terms, he will no doubt dictate. If I am not, then if my liaison with him is found out I shall be labelled as a hussy or worse, should the matter ever become public. My choice seems to be disgrace or servitude.

Your perpetual friend and cousin,
Rosemary

Wednesday 12th January 1843

Dear Cynthia,

I have seen Dr Kay, who is reputed to be the best and most reliable physician in the town. He has confirmed the worst. At least the sickness will abate, but he has said it will be unlikely that it will not be obvious that I am expectant for more than a few more weeks.

So, I have very little time to inform Mr Ingliss and ask him what his intentions might be.

Your perpetual friend and cousin,
  Rosemary

Wednesday 16th January 1843

Dear Cynthia,

I informed Mr Ingliss by letter the day before yesterday. A note from him was dropped round no more than two hours later. From the note, his intentions are very clear. Allow me to quote some of what he said.

"I am sorry of course to read about your predicament Miss Hopgood, but unless you can bring me proof other than your word, I am afraid I will be compelled to deny that this baby is mine."

He continues, "As you might understand, I have had many encounters of the sort we shared on the evening you refer to in your letter. It was I confess a very enjoyable and memorable evening from my point of view, for which I thank you, but I have come to understand those young women desperate to find a paternal defender for their errors of judgment are often very prone to suggesting that gentleman A is responsible for such a situation when in fact it has been gentleman B or even C or D."

He made the accusation even more shamelessly when he ground in his implication, "Young women who throw their favours about in the sort of way you have done with me, tend not to be faithful to one gentleman at a time. I do not believe that any more correspondence would be profitable to either of us."

I wept very hard indeed when I read his sentiments. I had never thought people could be so cold-blooded, so exploitative. I will have to think very hard about how to resolve this matter if indeed it can be resolved. I may not write to you for some time. Bless you, my friend. Had I taken heed of the good advice you gave me then it is probable that I would not be in this dreadful position.

Your perpetual friend and cousin,
  Rosemary

CHAPTER 45

Rogue male

'Well Mr Ainscough, it appears that you will be one of the lucky few,' said the chief clerk.

All Josiah could think to do was look expectant. 'Sir?'

The clerk looked at his face, and laughed, 'For such an intelligent young man you can be uncommonly obtuse.'

'Eh, sorry?' The clerk laughed again.

'You will know better than most how many of accused we are likely to find arraigned before any trial commences. You will also be in a very good position to judge the rate at which new accused will be added, depending on the level of questionable activity. You will also have worked out for yourself how many there are likely to be at the end of this affair, and even, I daresay, when the trial will take place.'

Indeed, Josiah had pondered just these issues and his estimate was early autumn, but he did not indicate this to the chief clerk.

'One thing is going to be clear, while we are in a bit of a lull now that situation is not going to last long. After that then not only will there be a rise in the number of new accused coming to Lancaster, but there will be more work for the tipstaffs to do as defence cases are considered and the list of accused finalised.'

Josiah began to see where this line of argument was leading.

'The result is that those who can be released for a short period now will be given some rest with their families, in preparation for the onslaught to come. That includes you Mr Ainscough, so I don't expect to see you for at least a fortnight unless there is an emergency, in which case I will have to recall you. Is that to your liking?'

'Most certainly, Sir.'

'Keep your lodging on, you'll need it again when you get back.'

On the train to Stockport, Josiah pondered a problem that had been on his mind since his mother had written to him about the situation between Ned Ingliss and Rosemary Hopgood.

Though on the face of it Josiah knew nothing definite to trouble him concerning Rosemary and Ned Ingliss, he found he could not escape worrying. Josiah had no certainty about Ned's appetites in affairs of the heart, strange phrase that, for *an affair of the heart* suggested moderation, and that was not a virtue Josiah easily associated with Ned. He adjusted his affections for young women as quickly and as often as many men adjusted their hats. But so far Josiah had no evidence of those affections going further than propriety might allow, though he could not rid himself of his suspicions. After all, he had his own example to remind him that he had been shamefully guilty of the sin of lust, so it was more than plausible, Ned might claim licence for in such matters more easily than he would.

Thanks to a good connection at Crewe he got home early in the afternoon. The lady who opened the door squealed with delight and hugged him.

'Your mother will be very glad to see you, Josiah,' she said as she showed him through to the scullery. Three chapel ladies were sorting washing for those in the area who couldn't manage it themselves: Martha Cooksley was one. She came straight over, hugged him and kissed his cheek. The wide smile on her face said all he needed to know.

'You're a sight for sore eyes as well as a very pleasant surprise. Give us a hand and then we'll be able to talk.'

When everything was organised into parcels, the ladies went off to get them delivered. Then Martha and Josiah sat down over a pot of tea.

'How are things?' he asked.

'Much the same as usual, though Thomas has had a touch of arthritis in his right knee. You know what it's like, a big Methodist church at the heart of town has to carry on no matter what happens. Our neighbours are our concern, prayer and praise, our strength. But your turning up like this is not only a happy chance, it's also very timely.'

Josiah looked at her, 'It's Rosemary isn't it?'

'I don't know how you do it, but you're right.'

'Inspector Fidel says I'm psychic as well. The truth is she's been on my mind since your letter. Is she all right?'

Martha took a steady sip from the cup, 'No I don't believe she is and though not many are aware I think she is in a great deal of trouble.'

'And am I to conclude that this has something to do with my colleague Ned Ingliss?'

As if it was too personal to voice even in the quiet of the manse, Martha nodded sadly.

'Does Elizabeth know?'

'She hasn't said as much but I think she does. But I don't think either of them has yet found a way to tell Richard. At least I have you to talk to about it.'

'I'm here for a fortnight before I must go back to Lancaster. So, I might be more useful than just helping you talk things through. If I may I'll stay here this evening, then tomorrow early I'll go and see what extra information about Mr Ingliss' record there might be from Inspector Fidel if I can catch him in his office.'

*

Josiah was lucky the following morning. He got a lift on an early coal train from Heaton Norris and was opening the doors of the Manchester station house in less than an hour-and-a-half. Even more luckily, inspector Fidel was in and happy to see him.

'Does this mean you've committed some dreadful crime in Lancaster and have come grovelling to me for your job back?'

'I would that it was that easy,' Josiah replied, 'It concerns the love life of Constable Ned Ingliss.'

'Nothing simple then. What's happened? Has he got another of his doxies with child, as it says in the Good Book? I see from the look on your face that's what it is.'

'Not the first time?'

'You surmise correctly. To my knowledge, there have been three others.'

'Three!'

'Three pregnant, but more than that ruined. You're shocked?' Josiah nodded.

'When you're an Inspector of Police you'll realise that the morals of the officers you command are only relevant to you, when and if their worst moral failings interfere with their performance. If you choose to run a personal group like my Chosen Men the difficulties can be even greater, since you rely on the ability of some of those officers to push the boundaries of legality in the interests of effective policing. Ned Ingliss' abilities in that direction are very useful, though they come with the overhead of his moral failings. This is a case of his repeated moral failing.'

'He never got near to marrying one?'

'No, it's almost a badge of honour. The girl you are concerned about, a member of your chapel I'll be bound.'

'Can he be bribed do you think?'

'I think you'll have to talk to him to find that out. Is there enough money in the family to make that an option?'

'Possibly.'

CHAPTER 46

Confrontation

'Who the fuck do you think you are, her brother!'
Up to the point that Josiah had made it clear why he had come to see Ned, things had gone well. But as soon as Josiah had mentioned Rosemary Hopgood, Ingliss had bridled, and his expletive was his response to Josiah asking a straight out if Ned had seduced her and if she was with his child.

'I'm her brother in Christ,' retaliated Josiah, regretting it as soon as he had said it. That was a lesson to leave God out of matters like this with any policeman.

Ned stood up and his chair fell over. The crash attracted the attention of all the people in the public bar of the Good Hope; they were expecting a fight. But a fight would not be good for either him or Ned. He remembered a proverb of Sergeant Smith's: *Never fight with a pig in the street: you get filthy, and the pig likes it.*

Josiah stood, turned his back on Ned, and walked out, wishing all the way he had taken a swing at his erstwhile friend. Discretion, he tried to think, was the better part of valour, and at least he'd not made a very bad matter worse. He could even look on the bright side, and he'd be able to tell Michael he had resisted the diktat of his temper. But the fact was he'd got nowhere near mentioning a marriage bribe.

*

Ned Ingliss strode purposefully across Stockport's market square towards the town hall. The swagger in his step was there that morning because the previous evening he had met a lady with a most fetching face and attractive deportment. He was unsure whether she would be another one who might need the advanced version of seduction. That would be clear as time went on, but with the money he had laid out on Rosemary Hopgood, it might be better for his purse if this one proved to be a less expensive matter. It was, in any case, a very good start, fully justifying the tune he was whistling.

His mood was somewhat dampened when he found Inspector Fidel at his desk, clearly awaiting Ned's appearance. The Inspector looked up.

'Is this the time you normally get to work? I've been here an age.'

'To what do I owe the pleasure, Inspector?'

'You see me here in the reduced capacity of Sir Grancester's message boy.' The Inspector looked at his pocket watch. 'It might be both pleasant and prudent if we took an early luncheon at the Good Hope Inn,' he lowered his voice. 'The matter is somewhat sensitive.'

Ingliss and Fidel walked over the Mersey bridge up the hill and over the Manchester border. They entered the Good Hope.

The landlady looked up. 'I've put you in the back room. Do you want the pot boy to come and take your orders?'

'That would be helpful,' said Fidel. He led the way to the room and opened the door. 'After you,' he said to Ingliss. Across the room from him were five chairs in which four people sat.

Then a powerful set of arms grappled him and pushed him to the floor. He heard the door close behind him.

'Thank you, Mr O'Carroll, you can let him up. I'm sure we can rely on you to keep him in this room.'

'A pleasure, Inspector. I'm at your disposal.'

Ingliss got up rubbing his arm. Mr O'Carroll placed a chair in front of the four others. Three occupants, he recognised: Josiah Ainscough, Inspector Fidel, Richard Hopgood and, he wracked his memory. Then he stiffened, the fourth person was Josiah's stepmother.

Josiah spoke. 'Clearly, all of us have an interest in your behaviour Ned, for different reasons, but it may be useful for you to know that it is through Martha Cooksley's perspicacious observations, that you have been brought here to meet us all. The matter before this meeting is the same as the one that I tried unsuccessfully to discuss with you a few days ago, that is the situation we believe that you have placed Rosemary Hopgood in by your seduction of her. Do you deny that she is pregnant and that you are the father of the child she carries?'

Ingliss remained silent.

Josiah continued, 'Very well, all of us here have an interest in Rosemary's wellbeing. Martha represents the Methodist community of which Rosemary is a part. Richard is her loving father and wishes her good name to be protected. Inspector Fidel has a less direct reason to be here, partly he is here to represent legal authority, you are after all on Manchester soil, and partly to guide us as to the legality of actions we might suggest or take. Lastly, he can bear witness that Rosemary is not the first young women you have seduced, left with child and abandoned.'

'And you think by bringing me here you're going to change my resolve in this one case?'

Richard Hopgood spoke, 'No, Mr Ingliss we are here to offer you certain incentives to save Rosemary from disgrace and improve your situation into the bargain. In my case, I can offer you money to wed my girl and give an honest name to her and your child. If that is not enough I have it on the testimony of Inspector Fidel that you are clever and resourceful. Those are good characteristics for a partnership in, shall we say, a dyeing business. I have no sons, indeed no other children, so you would inherit the company in due time. Come, say yes and change from being the villain of the piece to a valued son-in-law.'

'A good and fair offer, but where's the catch.'

'No catch Ned,' added Mr Hopgood.

'There's always a catch,' replied Ingliss.

'Well there is the law,' said Fidel. 'Rape isn't a capital offence anymore, but it does carry the sentence of transportation for life. Seduction in the style you favour, that involving intoxication and possibly other drugs, without any proof of permission from the other party could well be considered by a jury as rape.'

'That would be very messy and very uncertain. She would have to accuse me and there would be a public trial that would damage her reputation more than mine.'

'But you would not be able to continue your career as a policeman,' said Josiah, 'and with the cat out of this bag who knows whether parents of your other victims might not be prepared to take revenge, let alone fellow officers you have served with, who have many useful contacts if violence is required.'

An Irish voice was raised,' Don't forget how your family might feel. They like it quiet for their criminal stock in trade.'

Josiah had watched Ingliss' demeanour as he had sat in front of them. He had been truculent at first, but now there was just the hint of a crack in his façade.

He turned to Mr Hopgood,' Well we made a fair team against Monsieur Smith, so I think I could make a go at being your partner.' Ingliss got up and shook hands with Richard, whose face was one of resolution, neither satisfaction or even excessive relief.

The bargain was made but, wondered Josiah, at what price to Rosemary's future life and happiness.

CHAPTER 47

The disappointments of a revolutionary

Peoples do not judge in the same way as courts of law;
they do not hand down sentences, they throw thunderbolts

Maximilien Robespierre

The time for action ebbs away. The pace of this timid revolution slackens, and soon there will be no more use for me and no real change in this laggard country. My targets are now few and the orders are restrained. They would be easy for a milksop to perform.

The Lone Policeman is now a tipstaff and is banished to Lancaster. He dances to my master's tune but is not within my reach. I went to Lancaster for my master, and I glimpsed the constable there. He is not at ease, nor does he look challenged. It is rumoured he follows his love, but I saw no love between them. Dianne Burrell is there at the court attending to the needs of her father, whatever the naïve Policeman may believe.

When this court has finished its irrelevant considerations, then there may be work for me, but I doubt it.

CHAPTER 48

The last of the accused

The locomotives busied themselves at the junction shunting freight wagons, puffing up and down between the platforms, leaving a layer of smoke and steam collecting above the platforms which reduced the visibility up and down the line to that of a foggy morning. Occasionally, a passenger train would stop, and the passengers get off, some to stretch their legs and some to dash desperately to get some food in the ten minutes that they were allowed.

Josiah Ainscough had not warmed to Crewe station and was very glad that this would be the last time it would be his dubious honour to collect a prisoner coming from further south and convey him to the court at Lancaster. The general grime and coal dust played havoc with all the gold braid across the chest of his extravagant uniform. As a result, when he got back to Lancaster Castle, it would take him hours to bring it up to the sparkling perfection needed to satisfy Sir Grancester.

But this was the last of all the accused and for that small relief, he gave many sincere thanks to God. Those thanks were matched by those that he gave each week when a fireman on one of the express trains, a friend of Michael O'Carroll's, passed him a note confirming that no coded messages threatening Dianne Burrell had been issued in the press. He might be Sir

Grancester's lapdog, but his master was, for the present, keeping their bargain.

The Birmingham train came shuffling into the platform where he was standing. These locomotives were some of the filthiest on the system and left more than their fair share of sulphurous smoke and coal dust suspended in the air.

The train reached a squealing halt and the passengers jumped down. He could see Constable Bludgeon ambling back to the brake wagon at the rear of the train. Josiah thought Bludgeon was an apt name: Bludgeon by name, nature and looks. Every time Josiah had met the train from the south to collect a prisoner he had to remind himself that he should not call any human soul for whom Christ died vile, but if it had been allowed by his catechism, it would have been easy for him to make an exception for Constable Bludgeon of the Birmingham Constabulary.

Bludgeon had obtained his cargo from the brake wagon and was happily pushing the handcuffed man in front of him down the platform. Bludgeon did this with his truncheon which he twirled flamboyantly between prods. He whistled at the pleasure, between shouting out to anyone within touching distance of his captive, 'Stand aside there, dangerous felon in transit for trial.' Constable Bludgeon loved his work.

Some of the crowd caught Bludgeon's mood and hissed at the unfortunate as he passed them. Josiah had seen on a couple of occasions one or two ladies break free and belabour prisoners with umbrellas after Bludgeon's encouragement. Birmingham's finest gave the man one last push so that he nearly fell into Josiah's arms.

Then Bludgeon stopped and saluted. 'Prisoner Bryant, all

present and correct, Sir.'

Mr Bryant was present but not correct, as Josiah could see at a glance.

'Thank you, Constable here is my warrant,' he offered a small sheet of paper to Bludgeon. 'You may continue with your duties. I accept responsibility for the prisoner.'

Bludgeon removed his handcuffs and Josiah substituted his own. As usual, the man's wrists were badly chafed. Josiah was careful to make sure that he did not tighten his cuffs too zealously.

The man looked up. 'Sir, you look like a man of some responsibility. I should like you to please note that this officer has been excessive in his zeal and unnecessarily brutal.'

'Shut your mouth you Chartist gob-shite. You ought to get used to it, they'll not be as gentle as I've been on the transportation ships to Van Diemen's Land.'

'Well, he's my problem now, Constable. I believe some tea and breakfast is waiting for you on the other platform. Don't let it get cold.' Josiah shook the Constable's hand and Bludgeon went off whistling.

'Sir, did you hear what I said?'

Josiah looked at Mr Bryant and placed a forefinger on his lips. He watched as Bludgeon disappeared. Then he took the key for the handcuffs and released them from the prisoner's wrists.

'I must apologise for my colleague's zealous nature. No doubt he's had you cuffed to one of the handrails in the brake car for the whole journey.'

'Aren't you taking rather a risk, taking off the cuffs?'

'Hmm. It might seem that way. However, even if you wanted

to make a run for it, I'm a reasonably good runner and I have the advantage that I know the station very well, so I'd have the edge. Also, you staggered quite a lot coming down the platform, so I don't think you are recovered enough yet to be fit to run. But most importantly you're an important Chartist and most of you look on being indicted as a badge of honour, so you wouldn't run even if I left you here unattended.'

A broad smile crossed Mr Bryant's lips. 'You are a very knowing observer of humanity. He frowned, 'Bludgeon never actually said your name.'

'It's Josiah Ainscough,' Josiah offered Mr Bryant his hand. 'Your Christian name might be of help to me since we are to spend a little over four hours in the company.'

'It's Jonathan.'

'Well Jonathan, over there,' he pointed to a truck for loading luggage, 'is a hamper inside which you will find several things you may wish to make use of such as a towel, good soap and shaving materials. There's also food for the journey and some drink. The train to Lancaster will be here in about fifteen minutes. I would strongly advise you use the necessary on the platform, the journey will be a long one and though it stops at several stations there is no guarantee you will be able to make use of any facilities. I have arranged a compartment for us, so if you feel in need of sleep you will be welcome.'

Mr Bryant bowed, 'You are a most civil guard, Mr Ainscough.'

*

Mr Bryant had indeed been hungry and tired. He had a bottle or two of beer and some of Mrs Cooksley's best sandwiches. The new hamper had some cordial and Josiah's favourite potted meat for good measure. Mr Bryant had tried to talk but had finally put his feet up and given in to the arms of Morpheus.

Josiah curled himself up in the corner and got out his book. He could see the smoke rising on the outskirts of Manchester and Salford to the east, and in the west, there was a hint of the pall that hung-over Liverpool. The compartment they had been given was second class and towards the back of the train, well away from the engine, so having the advantage of not attracting much in the way of smuts or smoke inside.

Mr Bryant roused himself a little after they had crossed the Mersey and stopped at Warrington. He had swung his feet to the floor and rubbed his eyes.

Josiah had put down his book. 'There is more food, though I might suggest you keep off the beer, as good as it no doubt is. I may come from a household of total abstainers, but that does not stop my mother knowing about the best beer to put in a hamper when it comes to it.'

Again, the smile came readily. 'No, if you are willing, I would like to talk. What am I to expect when I get to Lancaster?'

'Well, you may be shocked to find that you are the last prisoner to be indicted. I think someone had the idea of making it up to a round 50. You will be held overnight in the castle itself; it acts as the town jail as well as the courthouse. The cells are not very cheerful but the whole of the area in front of them has been made into an effective common room for the accused. It's too small to cope with all the prisoners and so some are held outside in lodgings guarded by individual officers of the court. The most eagerly anticipated defendant is, of course, Feargus O'Connor. He has been given a small suite in another part of the castle.'

'Do we know when the trial will start?'

'Servants of the court such as me haven't been told officially, but when I left the day before yesterday the judge, Baron Rolfe, had arrived and the main prosecuting counsel, the Attorney General himself, Sir Fredrick Pollock was expected. I would surmise the trial will start next Monday, on the first of March. You'll know exactly what you'll be charged with when the indictment is finalized, which can't be later than Monday.'

'Thank you, that is helpful. It settles my mind. In my position, I cannot but think the worst.'

'Understandably, you are a very unusual case.'

'What do you mean?'

'You're one of the very few people who have been brought up from London. The others are all well-known members of the Chartist structures. You are also not the typical Chartist activist. As far as I am aware you are the only banker's clerk from an important city bank.'

'I suppose that could mean I'm indicted for the reason that someone may want me out of the way.'

'Odd way of putting it.'

'Possibly better to say I know too much. Mr Ainscough, may I tell you what I know? That way at least someone of fair mind will be able to tell my story while I am on my way to Australia.'

'If that helps you; we certainly have the time.'

'I have been thinking about in what particular way I may have offended. I was engaged in Chartist activity by personal conviction, but also because I was the protégé of one of Mr Cain at the bank, an important Chartist. He used me to help him organise the presentation of the second Great Petition to Parliament.'

'That must have been an uplifting day.'

'It should have been, but it was marred by a gruesome incident at the end of the day. Mr Ainscough, I witnessed the brutal, useless murder of a young child, all for the theft of a bugle from Peterloo.'

Josiah stiffened and sat forward on his seat.

'I hope this is not boring you,' said Mr Bryant.

'Not at all. I think I may have met the man involved. You mean George Blandford, don't you?'

'Yes, you know him?'

'Knew him. I was with him when he died.'

'I am sad to hear that he has passed on. We were returning to where we were staying, north of the river. By Waterloo Bridge, we were attacked by a man who appeared from out of the shadows. The little girl, Millie, was carrying the bugle. The man struck down George and me. Then he attacked Millie and seized the bugle. He killed her and kicked her body aside. He might well have thought I was unconscious, but I was not. I couldn't defend her, but I saw him and would recognise him anywhere.'

CHAPTER 49

The trial begins

There were three sharp bangs of staff on a wooden floor. 'Please be upstanding for His Lordship Justice Baron Rolfe.'

Everyone stood. The judge made his way to his chair at the centre of the ornate white canopy, all pinnacles and curlicues. Josiah sat in a discrete niche in the canopy, ready to relay messages from the judge to and from the court.

The clerk's desk lay in front but below the judge. It was oval and pushed forward into the body of the court. Around the outside of this tongue sat the lead lawyers, in prime position to catch Justice Rolfe's attention.

As Josiah watched, the Attorney General and two of his colleagues for the prosecution arrived and took up the most prestigious seats at the desk. Lesser grey wigs and black gowns had gathered in a few rows of ordinary seats just outside this charmed circle. The accused sat to the left of the judge, in a full box. Excess accused had to find seats where they could. Josiah noticed that Phillip Burrell had managed to sit with Dianne on one of the nearer public benches.

But the key accused was on his own in a small space containing a table and chair in front of the general box. Feargus O'Connor looked at his ease. His opponents might not be prepared, but he looked forward to the coming battle. O'Connor knew, as did everyone else in the court, that the defence of all the accused could hinge on his oratory and logic.

The jury sat opposite the accused and to the left of the witness box. The smart folk sat at the front of the remaining public benches, while the *hoi polloi* sat further back.

Josiah looked from the crowd to the ceiling. Plenty of light entered from high windows. A series of columns at the edge of the well of the court swept upwards to the full height of the ceiling. There each pillar supported a fan of converging ribs. The courtroom was elliptical, and the lightness of these columns created an airy feel.

Once the jury was sworn in, the charges on which the defendants were arraigned were read. These were multi-faceted with some indictments applying to one group of accused and others to another. Josiah had heard the accused call it the *Monster Indictment*, but it all came down to various charges of seditious conspiracy. At last, the Attorney General, Mr Pollock QC, rose to make his opening statement.

'If it may it please your Lordship and the Gentlemen of the Jury, let me from the outset of this trial make it clear to you all that the offence imputed to the defendants is that of endeavouring, by large assemblies of persons, accompanied by force, violence, menaces and intimidation, to produce such a degree of alarm and terror throughout the country, as to produce a change to fundamental points of the Constitution.'

The court was quiet and attentive. People sat on the edges of their seats. The jurymen lent forward, eager to hear Mr Pollock's next words.

'I shall not stop here to inquire, nor shall I detain you a

moment to discuss, the merits and demerits of the charge, nor to praise the constitution; I am here for the single purpose of indicating the law. This trial is not an appropriate proceeding to consider the validity of arguments for or against a change of any sort to the Constitution of our country. Gentlemen of the Jury, you have a simpler question before you. If you are satisfied that by evidence that the respective defendants have taken part in activities which had the objective of changing the Constitution by force, it will be your painful duty to find them guilty.'

Josiah saw many heads nod or whisper approval to their neighbours.

Justice Baron Rolfe interjected. 'Ladies and gentlemen, please restrain your comments. Proceed, Mr Pollock.'

'Thank you, your Lordship. I will, in general, allow the evidence you will hear to speak for itself, but I will at this point give you one example of the sort of events you will be called upon to consider. It concerns one of the defendants, Mr Phillip Burrell, who addressed the crowd in Stockport after the town's Union Workhouse had been ransacked and robbed by a group of turn-outs, led by Burrell's daughter, Dianne.

'In his speech to the turn-outs, before they marched down into Stockport's market square. You will hear evidence that Burrell made it clear to those at that meeting that the turn-outs would and should continue until the Charter was enacted and the Constitution of this country changed to comply to the Charter's principles. Everyone in this court knows that the confrontation in Stockport between the turn-outs with the civil and military authorities after the Riot Act had been legally read, led to the death of several people by gunfire.'

Mr Pollock sat down on this rhetorical flourish and there followed a babble of voices and even some cries of *shame* from parts of the public benches, as well as some people pointing at Dianne and shouting, *she's here, she's here*. The judge had to bang his gavel several times to restore order.

One of the court clerks from the well of the court held up a note for Josiah. It simply said a visitor was asking for him at the public entrance. Josiah made his way out, curious as to who could be asking for him by name. He was surprised when he found it was Michael O'Carroll.

'Michael, what are you doing here?'

'I'll tell you all about it this evening. Inspector Fidel sent me; he thinks you may be in danger, but we'll talk about it tonight, over food. Be on your guard.'

'What?' Josiah was incredulous.

'It's a long story lad. Now get back on duty before they miss you.'

*

Josiah paid attention to what was going on in the court as he could, provided he was not running errands. Though there was nothing to be done about what Michael had said, he couldn't help speculating. When Michael managed to get a seat at the back of the court, Josiah felt much more comforted. Whatever had happened, if Inspector Fidel had taken the trouble to send Michael to Lancaster, it must be critical.

The afternoon dragged. The only light relief was provided a few minutes before the end of the day's proceedings. Phillip Burrell, who was defending himself, took the opportunity to cross-examine a witness who had been testifying as to the behaviour of turn-outs in Hyde.

'Was the witness aware that I turned out a mill in Hyde?' Burrell asked.

'No,' came the reply.

'Was the witness aware that there had been subscriptions from the turn-outs for the poor in Hyde?'

'No.'

'Had there been the coupling of Jennies in Hyde?'

The witness said he didn't understand.

'Do you know anything of spinning with three-deckers, so that one man has to look after three machines and do three times his normal work for no extra pay than if he had only one machine to mind?'

'No, I've never been in a cotton mill more than three times in my life!'

Several people smiled.

'He has told you that he does not understand,' intervened the Judge.

'He has no notion of what he should know, my Lord.' There outright laughter at this and a slight smile crossed the Attorney General's lips.

CHAPTER 50

Chop logic

The chophouse Michael had found was not far from the court. As they had eaten they had talked about comforting things: how Michael's Mary was and about Josiah's family. When they had finished, the conversation turned to the serious matters for which Michael had come.

'Well lad, I have plenty of sombre news to tell.' Michael had a pint of best porter in front of him and was going through the ritual of packing his pipe with tobacco. He lit up.

'After the bargain with Ingliss was made and you returned here, everything seemed alright for a time. Preparations for the wedding started, until one morning Mr Cooksley received a letter from Ingliss. In short, the note said that Ingliss could not face marriage and was not about to lay himself open to a charge of rape and risk prison, and so he was flying the coop.

'As it fell out when your stepfather received the note, he was with Sergeant Smith. They sent a message to me, and the three of us got round quick to where Ingliss was supposed to be staying, but he had gone the previous evening, his landlady said. That would have been that, except for the Sergeant. He's a cunning old soldier. He dug around the lodgings and found these.'

Michael reached into the simple satchel he had with him

and brought out something rolled up in an oily cloth. He opened it on the table. It was some sort of pistol, but with six barrels. There were a couple of boxes with it, one of ready-made ammunition and the other of some small copper, top-hat shaped objects.

'There was a brace. This one is for you, with Inspector Fidel's compliments. I have the other. There's enough black powder to fire all the ammunition in the box. You preload the six barrels with powder and shot, then pop one of these caps onto each of little stubs on the barrels.' Michael picked up the pistol and aimed it straight at Josiah's head.

'When you pull the trigger, the hammer comes down.'

Josiah watched; the hammer clicked as it hit the post where the firing cap would be.

'If the trigger is released nothing else happens unless the hammer has been cocked again by hand. But if the trigger is held in after the first shot,' Michael pulled the trigger again, 'the next barrel comes around and fires and so on until the gun is empty. It's driven by clockwork which has to be rewound when the pistol is reloaded.' He placed the pistol back on the table.

'I thank Inspector Fidel for his thoughtfulness and I'm happy to see you, but you didn't come all this way to give me news about Rosemary. That could have come in a letter.'

'True lad, but the good inspector thinks there's more and I agree with him. He's got a sniff of a rumour that someone is asking around about you. Fidel thinks you are under some sort of new type of threat, but it's not clear from who or why. So, my assistance and these beauties come as part of a job lot, so to speak. If you are under threat and it's anyone at all like, let's say, the Sneaker, then at least we're forewarned and forearmed.'

Josiah looked sadly at the pistol; the threats were not going away, even when Sir Grancester was quiet in his malice.

'What has happened to Rosemary?'

'She was rapidly dispatched to London into the care of family they have down there. A safe place for her will be found for her confinement.'

'Will she come back to Stockport afterwards?'

'No one is prepared to say, though it must be the thought of all who know her real position.'

With grim realism, Josiah thought what others would not be able to think. It would be unlikely she would ever be able to return unless she was married, and the baby explained away.

CHAPTER 51

Accusations

The following morning, Josiah was back in his accustomed seat as the trial convened, paying a bit more than casual attention to the crowd of visitors than the day before.

As soon as the judge had sat Feargus O'Connor stood. 'I understand My Lord that several more witnesses have arrived since yesterday and I wish to repeat my application that all witnesses leave the court. I see that the Right Honourable Secretary of State for the Home Department, Sir James Graham is here, and I wish to make an exception in his favour.'

There was a ripple of muttered surprise and several people who thought they knew what Sir James looked like began pointing in different directions.

'Let all witnesses leave the court, except for Sir James Graham,' commanded His Lordship. 'Does any defendant wish that Sir James Graham leave the court?'

There was silence. 'I presume not My Lord,' added O'Connor.

Josiah wondered why was it so important to O'Connor that the witnesses were not present. Was it so that they might be inconsistent in their evidence, or even that they might be too similar in their given details? Either might undermine the credibility of what they told the court. Clearly, Sir James was different in O'Connor's eyes. Josiah assumed O'Connor wanted the Queen's most senior minister in this area of government policy to hear the arguments put and see the political lie of the land for himself.

Sir James Graham had now moved onto the bench with the judge. Who and where he was would no longer be a matter of conjecture. It was rather like a move in the early stages of chess: what seemed inconsequential but might well become an important gambit.

A man wearing a police uniform went into the witness box. After he was sworn in, the Attorney General began to question him.

'Who are you?'

'Joseph Sadler, Sir,'

'What are you?'

'A Stockport police officer.'

Josiah looked at Sadler carefully. He did not recognise him and was convinced that he had never seen him before.

'How long have you held that position?'

'Seven years.' That settled the matter, the man must be a member of the remnant of the county force. He might like to think of himself as a Stockport policeman, but he was no such thing.

'Were you on duty on the eleventh of August?'

'Yes, I was.'

'Did you see people coming into the town?'

'Yes Sir, a very large group from the direction of Manchester.'

'How many were there?'

'Ten to fifteen thousand.'

There was a gasp from the onlookers in the court. The Judge seemed as surprised as the people.

'Ten to fifteen thousand did you say? Are you sure?'

'Yes, Your Lordship.'

The Attorney General continued. 'Had they any arms?'

'Bludgeons and sticks were all I saw, Sir.'

'What about placards or similar?'

'Several. I made a note of what they said.' The Officer took out a notebook. 'One said *We will follow where danger points.* Another *They that perish by the sword are better than those who perish by hunger,* and a third *No more work until the Charter is Law.'*

'Were these placards written by hand?

'No Sir, they were all printed.'

'How many placards were carried?'

'Ten to twenty.'

'Where did this mob go?'

'To the Union Workhouse. There they overran the gatehouse, forced the main doors and ransacked the building carrying off as much bread as they could.'

'Where did you go after you witnessed this outrage against the poor?'

'I followed them as they made their way across to Thatcher's Plot, as it's known. There were some twenty thousand more people there.'

'Twenty thousand?' it was the judge again.

'It might have been more, perhaps thirty thousand.' Some of the public laughed.

'What happened then?'

'Mr Phillip Burrell got up on a wagon and started haranguing the crowd.'

'Do you have notes of what he said?'

'I was not in a position to take notes. I was in uniform and it was made very clear that my spying on the turn-outs was going to be resisted violently if I did not desist. But I remember that Burrell was very forthright.'

'Let us be clear that it is the Burrell who is on the indictment, that you saw. Do you see him here in this court?'

'Yes sir,' The officer pointed straight at Phillip. 'I clearly remember that he said that they should confront the masters in their castles and not stop in any action, even violence until the Charter was the Law of the Land and foundation of the Constitution.'

Josiah looked at Dianne and Phillip Burrell. Dianne was incandescent with rage, but Burrell looked calm. He patted his daughter's hand to comfort her. Josiah had witnessed what had happened at the workhouse and knew the Constable testimony was no more than a sackful of lies. He could not swear to what Burrell had said to the crowd, he had been at that time more concerned with catching the Sneaker, but everything he knew of Phillip would lead him to be very surprised if Burrell would have been anything like as intemperate as this upstart Sadler had testified.

Errands for the court interfered with Josiah's judicial observations for a good hour. When he got back to his seat it was clear that much of that time had been spent in considering the issue of the placards and whether they had been printed. Printing equalled planning, which equalled conspiracy.

There was a new witness in the box and Feargus O'Connor was cross-examining. 'Mr Sadler, I may be slow of wits this morning,' laughter round the court, 'but as I understand it you say that you saw a pile of printed placards to one side at

Thatcher's Plot.'

'I did.'

'They were there before Burrell spoke?'

'Yes.'

'But absent after the people started to march towards Castle Mill. Did you see who removed them?'

'No.'

'Did you see who placed them there?'

'How long have you had problems with your eyesight?' This time there were gales of laughter.

Baron Rolfe banged his gavel for order. 'Mr O'Connor, you know much better. You are an experienced attorney and I would expect you to show better manners to the witness. I will content myself this time in reminding you that there is such a thing as contempt of court and that it is the Gentlemen of the Jury who need to be convinced of your case, not the public gallery.'

'I am sorry My Lord, I will try to be more mannered in future.' O'Connor turned back to the witness.

'Would it be fair to say you can tell us that they were there and tell when they were not, but not who controlled them and arranged for them to be passed to the crowd?'

'Yes, Sir, that would be fair.'

'You may step down,' said the judge.

'I call Colonel Richard Wymes,' said the Attorney General. Josiah stiffened in his seat. Wymes came in from the door to outside the court. He was dressed in uniform, without sabre and spurs. Even so, he made a dramatic entrance and looked disdainfully at all the accused as he passed them, making his way to the witness box.

'Colonel, were you in command of the regular troops at Stockport on the eleventh of August?' asked Mr Pollock.

'Yes, Sir. I was also responsible for the organisation of the local infantry and advised the police on the deployment of special constables, and men from the Castle Mill who were willing to defend their place of employment.'

'For those not familiar with Stockport, where is Castle Mill?'

'It is at one end of the market square in Stockport.'

'That was quite a force to defend one mill, was it not?'

'It was not without cause Sir.'

'Could you elucidate, Colonel?'

'We had reason to believe that there would be a serious attempt by the Chartists to destroy Castle Mill.'

'That sounds like very specific information.'

'Yes, it was.'

'Why would they wish to take such an extreme action?'

'Castle Mill is the most visible mill in Stockport. It can be seen right across the town.'

'So it would be a symbolic target for anyone attempting to make a political point?'

'I will leave the jury to judge as to that matter.'

'How were your forces deployed?'

'There was a short line of infantry with muskets, in front of the town hall.'

'Any others?'

'Small detachments behind each barricade. Their orders were to keep out of sight.'

'Any other men?

'The special constables were held back in the mill yard as a reserve. I led a group of horsemen, mostly local dragoons. They were held out of sight from the mob.'

'What happened after the Riot Act was read?'

'A single shot killed the chairman of the Watch Committee who had read it. It came from the mob.'

'What happened then?'

'I heard that initial shot and brought my cavalry into the square at the double. The infantry in front of the town hall had been pushed back. More shots were fired by the infantry in self-defence.'

Josiah noted slight unrest in the onlookers. Someone was standing up and looking intently at Wymes. It was Jonathan Bryant.

He pointed at Wymes and began to shout, 'Murderer! Murderer! Murderer! Murderer!'

CHAPTER 52

A matter of honour

Jonathan Bryant was not in the state of self-control he had been in when Josiah had brought him from Crewe. Some other officers of the court dragged him away, still shouting murderer at the top of his voice, but Josiah could not leave his post in the court and could do nothing to help.

As ever, Michael was alive to his friend's perplexity. He packed his bag and ambled out.

The excitement caused a furore. Though Justice Rolfe tried to restore order, he declared a short recess and departed to his private rooms to the rear. A note came to Josiah summoning him to go to see the judge. When he got the door of the judge's private room, a secretary indicated he could enter.

The judge had removed his red gown and full wig. He lounged in a large chair smoking a cigar. He did not look very pleased, except for the opportunity for a smoke. With him was Sir James Graham.

Josiah walked forward and came to attention at a distance he hoped was appropriate.

Rolfe looked at him. 'Now we may find out what all that uproar was about, Sir James. I believe you are the tipstaff who brought Mr Bryant to the court, is that the case?'

'Yes Sir.'

'I am also led to believe if anyone here knows anything about his situation it will be you.'

'I may know something, My Lordship.'

'The talk is that you are a rather independent and humane man. Treating those whom you have had the duty to deliver here with more than common civility and kindness.'

'I simply try to see them as my neighbours, Sir James.'

'Would that government and the law allowed us that leeway, Rolfe.'

'Indeed. What do you know of his outburst in the court just now? He seemed to be much moved by Colonel Wymes' testimony about the scenes at Stockport. Does he have connections with the town?'

'I do not think so, Your Lordship. He was the last person to be placed on the indictment, and as far as I know, his only connection between Stockport and himself is that he had the responsibility to act as a guide to an older man at the presentation of the second Chartist petition in London last year. I told him that that man had died, and he was saddened by the matter.'

Josiah wondered if it was what Bryant had told him about the killing of Millie that day that was at the bottom of Bryant's outburst.

'You come from Stockport?'

'Yes, Sir James.'

'You know of the killing of the girl Millie in pursuance of the theft of what was called the Peterloo Bugle, do you not?'

Josiah was impressed by Sir James command of such detail. 'Yes Sir, exactly. Millie Blandford, the girl's grandfather, George Blandford, was killed at the Stockport riot. I was with him when he died.'

'So this outburst of accusation could be a matter of distemper of the mind because of the general position Bryant finds himself in, or it could have a specific cause?'

'May I ask an impertinent question, Sir.'

'That is exactly what they said he was like,' said Rolfe to Sir James. 'Yes, Mr Ainscough you may.'

'Why do you gentlemen care so much about this matter? Whatever the reasons for his outburst, he is surely in contempt?'

'So far this trial has been relatively civilised and courteous. We wish it to stay that way. It will not do any good to have too much emotion running in the court. If the finding is guilty of any or all of the indictments, then fair and orderly proceedings make it less likely that large scale disturbances will erupt again.'

'Perhaps if I spoke with Mr Bryant, I might find out why he made the outburst?'

The eminent gentlemen looked at each other. 'Very well Mr Ainscough. But be warned, this is a private matter; this conversation never took place. If there is even a whisper of it in public you will be in Botany Bay before you know it, either as policeman or convict, it matters little.'

Jonathan Bryant was pacing up and down his cell when Josiah opened the door. When he saw him, Jonathan smiled and sat down on the bed, transferring his tension to into wringing his hands with a panicked intensity.

Josiah entered and the solid metal door slammed shut. With the light from the open door extinguished, all that was left was a thin beam of the sun shining from a high window with a stout grill. Josiah did not suffer from claustrophobia, but even so, he felt a *frisson* of panic.

'How are you feeling?' he said.

'I've been better.'

'I've been sent to find out why you shouted what you did.'

'I thought you might understand.'

'I think I may, but I'd like you to tell me, nonetheless. Was it to do with the evidence about the Stockport riot?'

Bryant looked at him, 'Not the evidence, just the man.'

'You mean Colonel Wymes?'

'Yes, Colonel Wymes. He was the man I saw kill Millie.'

Josiah sat down next to Jonathan. 'Thank you, I had thought as much. Have they explained your position?'

'I'll be held in contempt and probably not let to return to the court.'

'The gentlemen who allowed me to come to see you can prevent that outcome. I think they will be happy enough if you return to the court so the judge can make it clear that such interference with the due process of this trial will not be tolerated from you or anyone else in future. That will be an end to the matter.'

Jonathan looked astonished. 'Thank you, Josiah.'

'You may not thank me when you have to hold your tongue as you hear things said that are arrant lies, as I have to. But there is another issue: are you representing yourself at present?'

'Yes, I wanted to stand shoulder to shoulder with my fellow Chartists.'

'A laudable intention but one that I think maybe imprudent. Would you mind if I see someone who might be able to ensure that you become represented by legal counsel?'

'How can you do that?'

'Let us just say that there is one in this court who might be able to arrange it. Have I your authority to try?'

'Yes.'

'Good. The judge will deal with this matter as soon as the court reconvenes.'

On his way back to the court, Josiah had to pass through the circulation area that had been allowed for those on the indictment to gather and talk. He noticed Feargus O'Connor talking to some of the accused and went over and stood where the Irishman could see him, but where he was not interfering with O'Connor's conversations. When he had finished, O'Connor turned to him.

'Well if it isn't that turncoat lickspittle policeman I see before me.'

'Well I suppose that is an improvement on what you called me the first time we spoke: then I was a scalpeen. I do not expect you to think on me with any favour, but I have just seen Jonathan Bryant and I think he would welcome some help in his defence. Can you arrange it? He is, after all, the most obscure and latest arrival on the indictment, and not at all experienced in such matters as this.'

'You still might very well be a scalpeen, but I've heard how humane you've been in the discharge of your duties. I think it can be arranged.'

Josiah made to go but turned and came back to O'Connor. 'I was at the Stockport riot and witnessed much of the fighting. There was a sniper there who shot several people, including the Chair of the Watch Committee before the troops fired. It was the same assassin who nearly killed you. His purpose was to induce violence. The turn-outs did not have firearms, as far as I saw, and I was with a goodly group of them, most of the day before they got to Stockport.'

The court reconvened. The first matter of business was the issue of Jonathan Bryant's contempt. As Josiah had predicted Jonathan had been allowed to return to the court. Mr Justice Rolfe made a harsh but clear condemnation of Jonathan's behaviour. Before Jonathan could make any reply, the Attorney General stood.

'I understand that Mr Bryant is not only the last of the accused on the indictment but also the most remote from the matter of this trial, coming as he does from London. I have been informed that Mr Dundas QC has said that he will speak to Mr Bryant's defence. Is that so, Mr Dundas?'

'It is My Lord. Mr Bryant regrets his outburst and wishes for me to say on his behalf that he did not intend it to be any reflection on the conduct of this trial nor his respect for Your Lordship.'

'Make sure that is the case in future Mr Dundas.'

The Judge glanced down at his papers and then directed his attention elsewhere. 'Mr O'Connor, I believe when we left matters you were about to cross-examine Colonel Wymes.'

It was clear that as far as the judge was concerned the matter was at an end. There was nothing left for Jonathan but to go back to his seat, where there was a note from Mr Dundas' junior attorney, Mr Atherton, saying that he would come to see Mr Bryant that evening to talk over his future defence. The note added that as far as he could see, Mr Bryant's position was very strong and Mr Atherton had hopes that a good outcome might be obtained.

Feargus O'Connor shuffled his papers and stood and Colonel Wymes went back towards the witness box. As he passed Josiah,

Wymes gave him a malevolent stare.

*

For the rest of the day, Josiah considered what had happened. He had been drawn in by the judge and a member of her majesty's government to ensure that the trial proceeded in a civilized manner. He had obtained much needed legal help for Mr Bryant, with the help of Feargus O'Connor. But more chillingly, he had been given the eye by Colonel Wymes.

Jonathan Bryant would be a very convincing witness against Wymes, provided he was not spooked by the unfamiliarity of such a monster trial. But in the end, Josiah felt it very unlikely that Sir James Graham would think, given the current situation, that a trial of such a prominent officer involved in the management of the troubles in the Manchester area would be politically helpful. Even if a case for murder was brought against Wymes, it could be seen to boil down to the word of the Chartist Mr Bryant against the word of the distinguished and gallant cavalry officer who had helped saved Manchester from the worst excesses of the mob. There was a need for something that linked Wymes more definitively to the murder. There was only one thing that Josiah could think of, the Peterloo Bugle. Later that evening he put his reasoning to Michael over another chop.

'You have absolute confidence that Bryant did see what he says he saw?'

'Yes, if for no better reason than that his emotional outburst in the court was sincere and heartfelt. He was not dissembling.'

'I agree. Then you do have to find the Bugle in Wymes possession to make sure of a plausible case.'

They had finished the meal and Michael took out his pipe to start his usual ritual. 'If Wymes murdered a child to get an old bugle there must have been an intensely personal reason for such a disproportionate attack.'

The picture of Wymes driving his charger into the crowd at Stockport came into Josiah's head: how Wymes had slashed repeatedly with his sabre without any restraint or discrimination. That was the way Wymes had always seemed to him. Intense, a man of action who saw himself as a hero but who could easily be overtaken by passionate desire, but for what: revenge? Who was Wymes revenging himself upon?

'He is a proud man, that's clear.'

Michael took out his old fob watch and placed it on the table. 'It's not much of a watch is it lad?'

'No Michael it isn't, but it's part of who you are, like that awful pipe of yours. You wouldn't be you without either of them.'

'After we ate my Da's prize pig at his wake, it was the only thing I had left of him. Whenever I touch it, I'm reminded of him. I could afford a more expensive one but not one that would be more precious to me. If the bugle is the same for the proud colonel, then he'll keep it with him. Sounds like the only way we will be able to find it is by resorting to a bit of burglary.'

CHAPTER 53

Burglary with good cause

The clock on the parish church struck two as Josiah slipped down from his room in the lodging house and out into the night streets. He was on his way to meet Michael at the corner of Castle Hill and Market Street.

They had slept on the notion of housebreaking to find the Peterloo Bugle. In the end, they concluded that while the risks were substantial, even if they had no direct evidence that Wymes had the bugle with him, the need for evidence in the cause of justice for Millie and her grandfather tipped the balance.

It had taken Michael most of Saturday to find and reconnoitre Wymes' lodgings. Josiah sat in court listening to evidence with only half-an-ear, thinking about what Michael was getting up to, jealous of the possibility of action, fearful of its risks. 'If he's in barracks this is going to be impossible from the start,' Michael had observed. Josiah hoped that was not been the case, but at the end of the day, the news was good.

'The good colonel has taken a small suite of rooms near the centre of the town. They belong to the Kings Arms Hotel and connect with the hotel, but they can be rented out to people with the money to burn. He's got three reception rooms on the ground floor. There's a smart front entrance off Fenton Street for any fine people who might visit.'

'That doesn't sound encouraging.'

'It's not the front that will interest us. Our way in is round the back.'

Josiah had looked quizzical.

'You'll see lad, you'll see.'

Michael led the way into Market Street and then sharp right into Fenton Street. Past the front of Wymes' rented house, Michael turned left into a ginnel. This sloped down and opened out into a small courtyard at the back of the buildings.

'There,' he whispered to Josiah, nodding towards a set of stairs that ended in a small balcony and a door. 'That's his kitchen door.'

'Cook, maid, batman?'

'Don't fret, they all sleep with the servants in the hotel. He's the only one who sleeps here and with a bit of luck we'll be in and away before he even turns over.'

They walked carefully from shadow to shadow across the courtyard and then up the stairs. Everything was still, not a sound disturbed the night. The clock on the church chimed the half-hour.

Michael stooped, there was a rattle of a couple of lockpicks and the door opened. Their course was now set. There was no chance that Josiah or Michael would have any hope of explaining themselves if accosted at this point. They might not be breaking, but this was burglary.

Michael crept into the gloom beyond the door. They had brought two firefly lanterns with them, but Michael felt his way forward, not risking any light at this stage. A rat scuttled across the floor, making Josiah start. A second door was opened, and they entered the kitchen. The range glowed dully, not much

298

heat but enough red light to outline the room.

They pressed on into the hallway. Michael opened his lantern. The hallway was in front of them with a solid inner door beyond a glazed porch. Michael tapped Josiah on his shoulder. The door to the first of the reception rooms was to their left. It seemed a pleasant enough room in the thin light of the lanterns. They looked in all the cupboards and inside a writing desk, but there was nothing of interest.

The next room was no more informative than the first, though it was much more untidy as if the Colonel was using it as a place to work. Uncharitably, Josiah expected Wymes would not attempt to tidy his own mess. After he'd made it a wreck, a single order to his batman would be enough.

There was something that revolted Josiah about Wymes, something he might never really know or understand. It was not even a dislike based on the crime of which Wymes was accused, as repellent as that was. It was nothing but a prejudice, acquired from the first-time Josiah had seen Wymes. He looked just the sort of arrogant and cruel officer who would have charged the crowd at Peterloo, and for Josiah, the proof of that perception was when he saw Wymes assault the crowd in front of the town hall at Stockport and fought George Blandford.

All that was left to be searched was the largest of the rooms at the front of the house. It was bigger, more comfortable and well furnished. This was seemingly going to be much more difficult to search, that was until Michael pointed to something over the mantelpiece. In the dim light, Josiah could see a bugle. It had faded favours tied to it, which would once have identified the detachment of militia to which it belonged. The knocks it had received over the years were visible even in the faint light.

'The arrogant bastard,' said Michael.

'Not as arrogant as you two rogues.' Wymes was standing in the doorway holding a pistol. 'Now which of you should I kill, and which keep?'

Straight away Josiah sensed Michael began inching to the right, spreading the target they offered, giving himself a better angle for an attack. If Michael was going to tackle Wymes Josiah needed to play for time.

'You have caught a police officer in pursuance of his duty. No more than that. I am investigating the murder of Millie Bamford. I take it this is the Peterloo Bugle?' He reached out and took it off the wall, glanced at Michael then threw it at Wymes' head. Michael launched himself at Wymes and knocked the pistol out of his hand and the colonel to the floor.

There was a lot of scrabbling and fighting but though Wymes was a fit soldier, he was not a match for Josiah and Michael combined. While Wymes was face down on the floor Josiah handcuffed his hands behind his back. Then they hauled him to his feet and half-threw, half-pushed him into an easy chair.

Michael picked up the pistol and pointed it at Wymes's head. Josiah put the Peterloo Bugle on a small table and lit a candle on a silver candlestick so that the instrument shone dully in a pool of light.

Josiah pulled up a chair and sat opposite Wymes. 'Colonel, when we leave, we will take the Bugle with us, but before that happens, I want to know more about what it means to you.'

'Why bother, it is of no significance.'

'I do not believe you.'

'You mistake yourself, Constable, it has no particular importance to me. I picked it from a local market stall for a few pence.'

Michael snorted, 'Officers and gentlemen do not hang souvenirs bought for a few pence above the mantles of their homes, even a temporary one.'

'There is no point in lying to us. We have an eyewitness to the crime.'

'Who?'

Josiah had to give Wymes his due, he was pugnacious, but Josiah held the trump cards in his hand.

'Jonathan Bryant. You were so keen to get the bugle that when you pushed Mr Blandford aside and had incapacitated Mr Bryant, you did not realise that Mr Bryant was still conscious and saw you kill Millie and take the bugle.' Wymes' look of insolent confidence slipped slightly. 'Perhaps you are not as clever as you think you are?' The expression of confident insolence immediately returned.

Josiah paused: there was something he had missed. 'I don't think you knew he had seen you, but were you concerned about him in any case?' The doubt in Wymes face returned. 'Did you persuade Sir Grancester to involve Mr Bryant in this trial? It would be to your advantage if the only possible witness was safely in Van Diemen's Land. Then you would be completely clear of any future accusation. You were very unlucky. Not only did I accompany Bryant to Lancaster, but he also told me he had seen who killed Millie. I was with George Blandford in Stockport when he died and was told the story of the Peterloo Bugle afterwards, so I could connect the two. Bryant did not know your name until it was given in court. I might have doubted that he knew you, had it not been for his outburst aimed at you in the court.'

301

'This is all conjecture, Mr Ainscough. Bryant is a Chartist conspirator and therefore not a reliable witness. There's not enough proper evidence to hang a cat for murder in the course of the theft of an object so poor and tawdry, let alone a colonel in the Queen's Cavalry.'

Poor and tawdry; the bugle was poor and tawdry. But there was something else at stake here, something of great importance to this vain man. Something which was not poor and tawdry, at least in his eyes. What did Wymes prize above all other things? Perhaps it was reputation, what he might call his honour.

Josiah looked carefully at Wymes. 'Where were you born?'

'Powderham, since you ask.'

'What year?'

'What has this got to do with anything?'

'Humour me.'

'1804.'

'Was your father a cavalryman by any chance?'

Wymes paled.

'Yes, he served at Waterloo.'

'So, it was natural for you to join the dragoons when you were old enough. He must have been proud of you. Even at twelve, you could have been a bugler, ready to sound the charge for a troop your father headed. Were you at Peterloo?'

Wymes looked aghast but was silent.

'I think you were, and George Blandford pulled your bugle from your hand and took it away as a prize from that terrible day. George dishonoured you and your family name. You could not expunge that dishonour except by getting the bugle back. You saw your chance in London and you took it. It was Millie's bad luck to be in the way, but then when ordinary people die, like those at Peterloo, it is always a matter of bad luck. In any case, they are of no importance to great men like you.'

Wymes exploded, 'They were worthless, nothing but straw under the hooves of my father's charger. He swung his sabre to cut them down and, on my pony, I blew my bugle. It was glorious and honourable until that oaf Blamford grabbed hold of the bugle and tore it from my grip. The conspirators and the turn-outs and all the hateful people Sir Grancester and I have been fighting in these past months are the same. You are the same.

'I will ride you down! I will ride you down! I will ride you down!'

Then Wymes started to sob, rolling about as best he could within the confines of the cuffs. After a little Josiah took off the restraints. Colonel Wymes made no attempt at resistance, something inside him had given way.

A wave of pity flooded over Josiah. He picked up the pistol and exchanged it on the table for the bugle, then he found some writing material to keep the pistol company.

He crouched down and looked Wymes in the face. 'Colonel I will give you a choice. We can take you now to the local police to have you arrested.'

'No not that, the shame, the shame of it.'

'There is an alternative for you. Your pistol and writing material are on the table. A note and a single shot will put an end to all this. That is what I believe is called by men like you, an honourable alternative.'

Josiah got up, and he and Michael left the way they had come in. Josiah tried to keep his mind off what Wymes alone in the house was doing and what he must be feeling.

CHAPTER 54

Tipping point

Josiah and Michael had spent Sunday keeping their counsels. Josiah felt very heavy of conscience. To give Wymes the way that he did had been intended to be an act of mercy. He now felt that he had failed in his duty. Wymes should have felt the full weight of the law. Josiah could no longer understand what should have been the proper choice.

He went to chapel, but he longed to see his father, discuss the whole matter and hopefully find some peace. He envied the solace that Michael would have found in the confession and restitution of the Mass. But Monday came and he must be back at his post.

As soon as Baron Rolfe sat, the debate between the Judge and Feargus O'Connor about the exclusion of witnesses from the court began again.

'My Lord, you made a rule that witnesses should leave the court, and I take it that that was for the protection of the parties involved and so that nothing could be done to interfere with them. My Lord, I am prepared to show that invariably half-an-hour, before the witnesses are brought into court, one Irwin, has access to them and instructs them as to how they are to proceed when giving their evidence.'

'Mr O'Connor you have raised points like this several times

in my court. I do not know about the jury, but I am beginning to become somewhat bored with the repetition. Is this question really necessary?'

'My Lord it is my intention, in due time, to bring a case of subornation of perjury against one or other of these parties.'

'Mr O'Connor let me make my view plain. My main reasons for not being in favour of turning witnesses out of court is that it is seldom productive of any good. In any case, we have ample enough on our hands in this case without trying a collateral case as to subornation of perjury.'

Josiah wondered what the jury made of these arguments about perjury and interference with witnesses. If inch by inch, drop by drop, while O'Connor made no real advance on getting his accusations considered by the court, the jury might well be losing confidence in the veracity of the prosecution's evidence. Perhaps that was O'Connor's real aim?

A note was passed up to Josiah. It came not from the judge or the attorneys, but another of the officers of the court. It simply said *Colonel Wymes is dead by his own hand.* Josiah looked around the court. He could see other small notes being passed and small groups of people were whispering together. He saw a note pass along one of the benches where sat some of the accused. When it reached Jonathan Bryant, Josiah saw peace spread over the young man's face. One, at least, was certain that Josiah's choice had been a good one.

The effect on the order in the court was that whilst no one said much the general hubbub in the room grew. Finally, the judge stopped the proceedings. 'What is the matter?'

The clerk of the court rose. 'My Lord, I gather that there is news that Colonel Wymes has been found dead.'

The Judge sighed. 'That news is correct, but tragic though it might be, it is not a matter that should delay this case.' He turned to Sir James Graham, who was sitting with him on the bench. After a few words, the Home Secretary rose, bowed to the judge and left the court.

It took no more than five minutes before another note was passed to Josiah, this time from Sir James Graham himself asking him to attend on him. Outside Baron Rolfe's rooms was Sir Grancester The door opened and Sir James's Graham secretary showed them in.

'Thank you for attending on me,' said the Home Secretary. 'As you will know, the news that Colonel Wymes was found dead yesterday has just been made public. That was inevitable. He was found dead by his own hand. He left a note as to his reasons for killing himself.' He handed a piece of paper to Sir Grancester, who read it and passed it on to Josiah.

My conscience does not allow me any longer to carry the burden of guilt concerning my part in the Peterloo Massacre and subsequently in my dealings with matters in the disturbances last year.

As Peterloo I acted as a boy-bugler to a detachment of dragoons commanded by my father. During a charge into the crowd, one of the rioters seized my bugle and took it from me. The loss of that bugle led me to feel that I had lost my honour which became an obsession.

When the 2nd National Chartist petition was delivered to parliament I saw the bugle again, and I resolved to take it back by force. When I caught up with people who had the bugle it was in the hands of a small girl. I killed

her in an act of thoughtless manslaughter simple to regain
something which was no more than an object of my vanity.
I cannot live with that guilt anymore and, so you find me
as I now am.

In clearing my conscience, I want to also confess to my
acquiescence to the use of an assassin to ferment the shoot-
ing in Stockport. I believe that the use of that person was
procured by Sir Grancester Smythe. I do not know the
details. If anyone does know it may well be Constable
Josiah Ainscough.

Josiah handed the paper back to Sir James. 'Can either of you cast light on the matters Wymes raises?'

Sir Grancester spoke. 'It appears to me that the balance of the mind of my old friend must have been disturbed. Certainly, his suicide is an indicator of such disturbance. But his idea that I procured an assassin in some way is preposterous, a fantasy worthy of Mr Dickens.'

'And you Constable Ainscough, can you give me any information?'

In some parts of the natural world, there are moments of balance. The moment a tree remains standing before fall-ing because of the work of the axe of the woodsman, or the moment a wave near a beach curls over before it crashes down. These are moments of stillness before things change. Josiah was at such a point. Tell the truth and shame the devil or walk away and with a shrug of his shoulders and fail to give his testimony.

'There was a sniper at Stockport,' he said quietly.

'I'm sorry young man; what did you say?'

'There was a sniper at Stockport,' Josiah said more firmly.

'Ridiculous,' dismissed Sir Grantchester. 'I was there, I saw nothing but the mob attacking our brave red coats.'

'Do you have any proof, young man?'

'I have the proof of my own eyes. I chased him. He was in the tower of the parish church that overlooks the market square. I saw the smoke from his gun's barrel at the top of the tower, heard the reports and saw people fall. He shot Mr Prestbury, the Chair of the Stockport Watch Committee, through the head, just as he finished reading the Riot Act.'

'I do not know what your aim is in telling the Home Secretary these malicious falsehoods. Sir Graham, I give you my word of honour this is all fantasy.'

Sir Graham held up his hand.

'These are very serious accusations. To believe you I need more detail. For instance, what was the distance of the shot?'

'Allowing for the height of the tower, about two to three hundred yards.'

Sir Graham frowned. 'That is a long shot even for an expert, doubly so if it was, as you say, Mr Prestbury was hit by the assassin's first shot.'

Sir Graham asked for more information, but there was little Josiah could offer. 'I am no marksman Sir, so could not say, but there were several of these found in people's bodies that day.'

There was only one last thing he could offer. He had kept the conical rounds he had found on the flat iron building. After the carnage of the riot he had always kept one with him, a sort of grisly keepsake. He fumbled in his pocket and his fingers found it. 'This ball I found complete with an unused cartridge on another rooftop across the main road in Stockport.' Josiah placed the ball on the table in front of Sir James. I believe that is was this sort of ball that killed Mr Prestbury.

Sir James picked it up and weighed it in his hand. Then he put it down again. 'Completely through a man's head at three hundred yards. The Royal Arsenal will be interested in that small fact, and probably any other of your observations on the effects of these small horrors.'

'Have you seen such things before, Sir?'

'I have had that misfortune. Projectiles like this are intended to increase the range, accuracy and potency of the Army's standard Baker rifles, though we did not invent them, it was the French who had the original idea. At firing the cone at the bottom of the projectile expands and forces the bands to grip the helical rifling in the bore of the gun. Being smaller they are quicker to load and so increase the rate of fire of the rifle. Being conical they not only spin but they travel further having lower wind resistance. You were correct, there was a sniper in Stockport that day.'

Sir James turned to Sir Grancester. 'You and I Sir must have a long talk about Colonel Wymes' other *fantasies*. But that must wait for the present. I have another matter to deal with. I bid you both good day.'

Sir James left and Sir Grancester looked at Josiah. 'You realise, young man, that you have now ended our arrangement? That my tolerance of your knowledge about how the messages to my assassin work are at an end, and that I will now place your doxy back to the top of my list of targets? Have you nothing to say?'

'You are too predictable, Sir. The trial is coming to an end. Whether Phillip Burrell is free afterwards is down to the jury, but in any case, Dianne Burrell will be free. At that point I always expected you to threaten her again.'

Sir Grancester stepped close to Josiah. His voice was low but full of controlled hatred. 'In which case you will not be disappointed.'

CHAPTER 55

Defence statements

A ll witnesses had been called, heard and cross-examined. There was nothing left but for each defendant to make their final statements or have them made by their attorneys, the judge to sum up the case and the jury to pass its verdicts.

The public benches were as filled as they had been on the first day, with people who knew one or other of the accused, people who hoped their champions would be victorious, professional gossips of the press, and the persons of the court from the lowest to the apex of Justice Baron Rolfe.

Josiah was most interested in the statement of Phillip Burrell. Phillip was expected to be called just after midday, but before then there was a surprise. Mr Dundas asked that Jonathan Bryant be acquitted by consent. What Wymes had written in his death note had cast a shadow over the validity of Jonathan's involvement in the trial at all. The judge agreed, and Mr Bryant was added to the list of those who had already, for various reasons, been acquitted.

At the recess, Josiah was delivering messages to various of the attorneys when he felt a light touch on his shoulder. It was Jonathan, complete with an irrepressible smile. He took Josiah's hand and shook it most warmly.

'I could not leave without thanking you, Mr Ainscough,'

he said.

'I have done only what many would do,' said Josiah.

'I would that was true, but in these times we live in, too few find it in their hearts to act with the integrity you have shown. If there is anything I can do for you, please tell me and I will do it.'

Josiah thought for a moment. 'I surmise that you will be getting away from this depressing place as fast as you can?'

'You surmise correctly. I have a through ticket to London and enough money for a room in a hotel near the station at Birmingham. I will break my journey there this evening.'

'Would you take an object I have with you to London for safe keeping?'

'It would be an honour.'

They walked together to Josiah's lodgings and went up to his room. From a cupboard,

Josiah took an object wrapped in a velvet cloth that he had bought for the purpose.

'I think you should see what I am asking you to carry.' He laid it on the narrow bed and opened the cloth.

'The Peterloo Bugle,' said Jonathan. 'I will guard it with my life, and faithfully to deliver it to my protector there. He will make sure it remains safe in the vaults of his bank.'

In the street outside they embraced, and Josiah watched Mr Jonathan Bryant set off on his way home a free man. Then Josiah walked briskly back to the court in case he had been missed. None of the court servants or attorneys had been in need of his services, but Michael had been looking for him.

'Some good news lad, at last. I was approached by Feargus O'Connor with message for you. Sir Grancester is in disgrace with the Home Secretary and has had his Queen's Warrant revoked. Sir James Graham has summarily sent him packing to London, allowing him only to stop off in Manchester to collect any personal possessions. It seems that his days of ruling the roost are over.'

'I am happy his wings have been clipped, but it is not yet the end to his potential mischief. He will have time to have coded messages against Dianne Burrell placed in Thursday's Manchester newspapers, regardless of tomorrow's verdict on her father. He is a vicious man Michael, and his viciousness is not yet contained.'

*

It was a-quarter-after-ten when Phillip entered the witness box. He looked drawn but determined. The court became quiet.

'Gentlemen I am about forty-six. I was asked last night if I were not sixty, but if I had as good usage as others, I should look like a man of thirty-six.' The poorer people in the court chuckled and heads nodded.

'I was gone to be a handloom weaver when I was ten years of age. The first week I ever worked in my life I earned sixteen shillings. I was a hand-loom operator until 1840. I was married with a family: a wife and a daughter. In 1840 as a hand-loom operator I could only earn six shillings and sixpence a week, no matter how hard I worked. Yet sooner than become a pauper, although I detested the factory system, I became a power-loom operator in Stockport.'

A quietness fell over the court. There was something about this man that demanded attention.

'But the longer I worked in the factory, a reduction in my

pay crept in on one side, and then another. Some masters always want to give less wages than others. But I see this to be an evil, as injurious to the master or the owner of cottage-property or the publican, as it is to a man like me; all of those people depended on the wages of the working man. As a result, I became an opponent of the reduction of wages to the bottom of my soul; as long as I live, I will continue to keep up the wages of labour to the utmost of my power.

'In 1840 there was a great turn-out in Stockport, in which I played a conspicuous part. We were out for eight weeks. Six thousand power-loom weavers were engaged in that turn-out. We were up every morning from five to six o'clock to march in procession in Ashton, Hyde, Duckinfield or elsewhere. We had our processions in Manchester, and all over the country, and we never had interference from anyone. No one meddled with us, no one insulted us. We were never told that we were doing that which was wrong. Parliament had repealed the Combination Acts in 1824, something in which I believed; that as an Englishman and factory operative, I had a right to do all that lay in my power to maintain my wages.'

Men listening nodded in acquiescence. The attorneys stopped looking at their notes and sat back in their chairs.

'Peace, law and order was our motto and we acted upon it. In Ashton-under-Lyne, not one pennyworth of damage was done to property although we were out for six weeks. My Lord and Gentlemen of the Jury, it was a hard case for me to support myself and my family, but not as hard as for some. A friend had two sons. The eldest, who was sixteen, had fallen into consumption and left his work. As a result, that family's earnings were brought down by sixteen shillings a week. My friend told me that he had gone home some days and seen that son lying on a sickbed and dying pillow, having nothing to eat but potatoes and salt.'

There was a gasp from those listening and a woman's voice could be heard, 'The poor boy!'

'Now, Gentlemen of the Jury, just put yourselves in this situation, and ask yourselves whether seeing a sick son who worked twelve hours a day for six years in a factory – a good and industrious lad – I ask you, gentlemen, how would you feel if you saw your son lying on a sickbed and dying pillow, with neither medical aid nor any of the common necessities of life?

'My friend told me that if there were more reductions in his wages, rather than submit to them he was determined to terminate his own existence. In his condition, I might well have felt the same. It was with my friend's situation as well as those of many other good men pressing on my mind that I spoke at public meetings. I spoke from the heart and I always tried to make peace where I could and to obey the law if peace was not to be had.

'Gentlemen of the Jury, it is stated by one of the witnesses that I was the father of this great movement; father of this outbreak. If that is so, then punish me, and let all the rest of my co-accused go free. But I say it is not me that was the father of this movement. I say that the masters with their proposal of a reduction in wages in all of the mills have made a conspiracy to kill me, but I have combined to stay alive.' Burrell's fist hammered into his left palm.

There was a second of stillness. Then people started to applaud. Voices were raised, and *Well said Sir*, was one cry that was repeated by many people. Attorneys spoke to each other and nodded their heads. The judge himself looked moved.

CHAPTER 56

Summation and verdict

Unless the jury were badly divided about their verdicts and so took much longer than expected, this would be the last day of the trial. There remained forty-two still to be balanced in the scales of justice, including Feargus O'Connor.

He had been his mighty best in his final defence statement and crossed swords several times with the Attorney General. It seemed to Josiah that O'Connor had captured the feeling of the court most perceptively when he had admitted that he did not expect the jury would be able to set aside any opinions they might have about him gained from newspapers and rumour. That had been a bold move, it might gain him sympathy, but it might well put him on the wrong side of the law after the judge had summed up.

The fact was that everyone involved in the trial was tired. As Josiah returned to the court his own ennui was reflected in how he walked, slowly taking in the sounds of the morning. Passing through the gate he came up the hill towards the entrance to the prison area. People nodded and shook his hand; they too were seized with this sense of it all being at an end. Inside he was hailed by several of the men he'd brought to Lancaster, who thanked him for his kindness and sense of duty.

Phillip was there with Dianne. To Josiah's surprise, they

approached him. Phillip greeted him. 'A day of judgment, a day of fire?' Phillip said.

'Well let us hope not for you, Phillip.'

'I am content. I have done what I should do and been what I should. I have no regrets. Like Martin Luther, all I can say is *here I stand I can do no other*. But Dianne has something she wants to say to you. I'll leave you two alone. Walk well in the world Josiah.'

Dianne was not at her ease. She stood tall but her hands plucked at her dress. 'Josiah, my father has made me see over the days of the trial that perhaps my attitude, indeed my condemnation of you, has been unfair. He has pointed out to me often that you are as trapped as any man forced to dance to a tune a master sets, be it the rhythmic tyranny of the power loom or the whim of a powerful official. The word is among the accused that you have been true to yourself, and as a result, one oppressor, Sir Grancester Smythe, is now gone from these proceedings. It would be churlish of me not to thank you myself.'

She made to go then turned back took a step forward, reached up and kissed him on the cheek. 'Josiah, I wish we could go back to the day on the way back from Ashton when you suggested we should be friends. Then there was nothing between us but hope.'

Bewildered, all Josiah could do was to stand on his own as she withdrew. Michael must have been watching for he came over to him.

'You know, though that looked like parting I think there's more to be said between you and Miss Burrell.'

Josiah sighed, 'In any case, when the court closes this evening

I will be out of a job and will want to go home as soon as I can. How about you?'

'Ah yes hearth and home, it seems much too long since I had Mary in my arms. Post haste to Stockport it will be.'

Everyone inside the court seemed to be in the grip of much the same mood as Josiah and Michael. From his customary niche at the front of the court, he could see people shaking hands or saying farewells while they had time. The greetings extended everywhere between attorneys and their legal colleagues, the clerks and other servants of the court. When Justice Rolfe took his seat, it took some time for people to get to their feet, emphasizing their longing for the conclusion of the proceedings.

The judge began his summing up.

'Gentlemen you have been told over and over again that what these defendants stand charged with is the crime of conspiracy and that alone. It has been said that there is great difficulty in explaining what constitutes conspiracy. I do not see those difficulties to the same extent as has been suggested by others. Doubtless cases may arise where it is difficult to say why certain acts constitute conspiracy, but in the present case it is sufficient to say that acts constitute conspiracy when two or more people combine together to do or cause others to commit an illegal act.

'I give you an example. Any of you may choose not to deal with John Smith the baker, but if all of you combine together not to deal with him, whilst that would not be an illegal act, it would be a conspiracy. The indictments define the sorts of illegal actions that have been incited by the accused, and therefore the bases for the charges of conspiracy, and why they might be guilty of such.

'In the first indictment, the charge is that the conspiracy was, by seditious and incendiary speeches, placards and other publications, to unlawfully bring about tumults that would change the constitution of the realm. But you will remember the point that Mr Burrell made in his evidence that simply placing the heading of a placard before you as evidence might be very misleading as to the placard's larger purpose or contents. The Attorney General argued that the heading of the placard was enough to substantiate an attempt to incite conspiracy. In general, the difference between Mr Burrell and Mr Pollock is that for Mr Burrell there is no act of conspiracy if there is no act of combination. Mr Burrell forgets, however, to point out that the abolition of combination as an offence in itself, was abolished by the 1824 Combinations Act. However, Mr Burrell failed to remember that in the next parliamentary session that had to be corrected by the 1825 Conspiracy Act, so that combination of workmen against masters, of masters against workmen, and even the combination of workmen against workmen were to be considered as conspiracies. You will have to make up your minds between the views of Mr Burrell and Mr Pollock as to which of these laws applies to the first type of indictment.

'The second indictment is very much the same as the first, except that it does not enumerate the methods but talks in terms of a general conspiracy by force and violence to create alarm. Here Mr Burrell was again at odds with the Attorney General. Mr Burrell remembers 1824, when the Combination Acts, that then regulated strikes and turn-outs, were repealed. As a result as the law then stood, and still stands, that turn-outs

320

must follow the common law of peaceful assembly. So, meeting in support of a strike could not be considered illegal as such, yet the Attorney General disagrees relying on the definition of conspiracy. Again, this is a point you will have to consider before giving your verdicts for individuals.

'The third indictment says very much the same as a concatenation of the previous two, except that it is not specific about it being a matter of the Charter, but a much looser manner of insurrection.

'In the case of the fourth indictment, there is a possibility of a conspiracy by people who intend the actions of turn-outs to go beyond the situation envisaged by the repeal of 1824, but that must be clear for each individual defendant.

'In short gentlemen, the first four of the indictments are very similar but the fifth charge varies the nature of the charges significantly. In one view of the case, this last charge is very important and requires your particular attention, since it asserts that the accused sought to incite the Queen's subjects to disaffection and hatred of her laws. How could this be done?

'This view of the case interprets events as being motivated to persuade people engaged in trade or in labour to leave their employments to produce a widespread cessation of labour in a wide section of the realm until the laws were changed as proposed by the Charter.'

It was clear to Josiah that the judge did not agree with much of the argument that the Attorney General had made at the start of the trial. It seemed that Justice Rolfe had allowed individual verdicts in some individual cases though not in others. He seemed to have widened the ground for innocent verdict guilt under the fourth indictment so that only the fifth stood on a firm footing as a basis of a general verdict of conspiracy.

The judge moved on to consider the evidence heard during the trial. Messages flew fast and furiously as lawyers checked details and consulted, which resulted in Josiah being more out of the court than in. The judge's summation came to a close a little before a-quarter-passed-midday. The jury were released to consider their verdict and there was little anyone could do but wait.

Josiah's duty to the court was done but there was the possibility that there might be messages from the jury to the judge to convey, and he was set to that task. He was sitting outside the door to the jury room when Feargus O'Connor came to him. The Irishman looked very pleased with himself.

'Well my young scalpeen you have heard as much of the case as anyone from that high seat of yours. What do you think will be the jury's verdict?

Josiah considered his answer. 'I think, Mr O'Connor, that it will be very difficult to find many if any guilty under the first three indictments. Perhaps there will be a minority who will be found guilty under indictment four, if they were intemperate in public statements and the prosecution witnesses are believed. The majority of guilty verdicts will be reserved for those who clearly advocated the strike as a means to the end of the Charter and hence to the constitution. I suspect this puts the more senior members of the Chartist movement, such as yourself, under the most threat.'

'It is a pity you did not turn that brain of yours to the law, you would have made an excellent advocate. I agree with you my chances of not being found guilty are but slim, but I suspect your friend Burrell will have made such an impression on the jury that he will be acquitted. I do not think our paths are likely to cross again, but it has been a pleasure to make your acquaintance, Sir.'

They shook hands, and as O'Connor walked away a note was passed through the door to Josiah. It read, *Please tell the Judge we are ready to give our verdict.*

The court reconvened and His Lordship took his seat.

'Who speaks for you?' said the clerk to the jury.

'I do,' said a tall jury man who had been near the front of the jury box for much of the trial.

'Please read the name of each of the accused in turn, followed by your verdict.'

The list began. When it was finished, of the original forty-two remaining, twenty-nine had been found guilty, of which one was indeed O'Connor. All the rest were acquitted, including Phillip Burrell.

When his name was read out Josiah watched as Phillip caught Dianne in his arms and there was a ripple of applause from the gallery of onlookers.

CHAPTER 57

Crewe

The show was over, and Josiah and Michael were for the high road home. Josiah went back to his lodgings to change into his clothes. He packed the few belongings he had in his room and took his uniform back to the court clerk, who thanked him for his work and said that he would always be welcome to continue to act as a tipstaff at any crown court in the land and offered his services to give Josiah a reference, if he could not integrate back into the police.

Michael was waiting at the Castle Gate, and soon they were striding out towards the station, determined to take the fastest route that would get them back to Stockport. Michael was singing at the top of his lungs and Josiah decided to join in. People they passed stared and shook their heads, but it did nothing to temper the spirits of the friends: they were free of the court's tyranny.

'Did you see Dianne and Phillip leave?' Josiah asked after they had calmed down a little.

'They were among the first out through the door. I think they were even happier than us to be free.'

'God's speed to them and all those who were acquitted.'

'And so say I, lad.'

The station was busy but not choked with people. Michael

got them two through tickets and they were soon running down the steps onto the platform where their train was waiting.

'Seemed easier to go through Crewe,' Michael said as they settled themselves down in an empty compartment. 'It may be longer but from there are plentiful trains to Stockport.'

As the train pulled out of the station, they relaxed. Michael set to his pipe but Josiah contented himself to gaze at the passing countryside. By the time they got to Warrington, cloud from the west was coming in steadily. Rain would catch them before they got to Stockport, but so what, they were free.

At Warrington, Michael had managed to beg a couple of newspapers from a countryman of his who had come from Manchester. He had been reading them when something caught his attention in a copy of the *Stockport Express*. He folded it back and laid it out on the seat next to him. Then he leafed through the other paper, folded it back on itself and placed it next to the other.

'You know you said Sir Grancester was a vicious man?' he pointed down at the papers.

Both had the same message in them, in the now-familiar pattern of the code.

'Pity we can't read them,' said Josiah.

'I think we both know what they will say, I would expect that phrase *all force* would be mentioned, along with the name of Burrell.'

'Let's hope we get to Dianne and Phillip before the Sneaker gets to them,' said Josiah.

When the train pulled into Crewe station they got down.

'It will be about half-an-hour before the Manchester train is ready, let's get something to drink,' said Josiah.

They had to cross over to another platform by way of a metal bridge. As it happened, Josiah looked down and his blood ran cold. A powerful man was pulling Phillip Burrell towards the far end of the platform. Phillip was struggling but his attacker was much too strong for him.

Josiah pointed and yelled, 'There Michael, there!' Travelling bags were dropped on the spot, and they ran pell-mell down the steps towards where Josiah had seen Phillip.

They pushed their way through the passengers who were crowding onto a train that had just pulled in. But when they got to the end of the platform Phillip and his attacker were gone. Worse, in front of them was a maze of sidings filled with goods trucks.

Josiah stopped and stared, then from behind one of the trucks appeared Phillip. Somehow, he'd broken free and was running as fast as he could. Michael and Josiah ran towards him trying to protect him and got between Phillip and the man. The attacker stopped.

'In the name of the Queen I command you to give yourself up,' shouted Josiah.

The man's face was full of hatred. On he came, but all that fury made him careless. The sidings were a complex of lines, trucks and carriages, with engines running about getting trains ready for the mainline. As the man charged at them, he failed to look behind him. An engine was shunting trucks. It had appeared on the big man's blindside. The driver blew three sharps blasts on the engine's whistle, but by the time the man turned it was too late and the engine took him full in the face. His body flew through the air and caught a second blow that spat him out between the lines. Josiah, Michael and Phillip might have suffered the same fate, but they managed to find safety by flattening themselves against a stationary truck.

The man's injuries were fatal, but he was not yet dead. Blood rattled in his throat as he tried to speak. Josiah stooped down to listen. The man's lips moved then he breathed his last. Josiah stood up.

'What did he say?' asked Michael.

'Races into the river.'

'Odd final words.'

Josiah looked hard at the dead man's face. 'I've seen him before,' he said. 'He was the strongman at the penny-gaff where I went with Dianne. They put on a pantomime about the riot at the Hall of Science where I was featured. He must have been able to recognise me, and he was the man who wanted the cryptograph and was willing to throttle me to get it.'

Phillip was leaning on his knees gasping for breath. 'He wasn't alone. Another one grabbed Dianne.' He coughed and gasped again. 'But I think I know what he might have meant. There are tunnelled water races that feed the wheels of the mills at Portwood in Stockport. Those tunnels sound the sort of place where information could be extracted without calling attention to any noise.' Phillip and Josiah shivered at the through of Dianne being tortured.

A whistle sounded from the direction of the platforms. 'That will be the Stockport train,' said Phillip.

Josiah saw a group of men running towards them. It was go now, or run the risk of delay.

'Phillip, tell them who I am and that I'm pursuing a man who has abducted your daughter.' Then he and Michael turned and ran as fast as they could back to towards the platforms.

They arrived just in time to see the Stockport train moving out of the station. Josiah got a glimpse of a face at a window, it was Dianne.

Josiah ran down the platform in the hope he might be able to get on the back, but he ran into a porter and they both went flying. By the time he got up, the train was gone.

He went over to the porter and helped him to his feet. 'Bloody hell lad, what's so important about getting to Stockport!'

When he'd heard Josiah's explanation he grinned. 'There no passenger service for a while, but there's a train that collects urgent mail to be delivered in Manchester that calls at several places along the line, including Stockport. As it happens it's that one over there. Tell the guard what you're trying to do and I'm sure he'll help.'

CHAPTER 58

The brink

The lake that fed the Portwood races looked peaceful in the golden light of the sunset, but it did nothing to show anything but the dark outline of the gates, sluices and other waterside paraphernalia. Josiah and Michael had followed the path through parkland and now they stood looking into the two featureless blacknesses of the mouths of the race tunnels. They were listening. Water cascaded down the sluice gates, a blackbird gave a warning call as it went to its roost, there was the murmuring of machinery from the mills at Portwood which were working through the night. But what Josiah and Michael were straining their ears for was anything that might indicate which way the Sneaker had taken Dianne.

'You're certain they came this way?' Determination had got Josiah this far but now doubt was creeping upon him.

'They must have got to here at least, but there's no way to say which of the tunnels they went into.'

'And in a system like this, there will be a lot of side tunnels and junctions.'

'At least this is the place Phillip told us to come. The only thing that might help us is you can be sure of is that sound travels a long way in a tunnel system. If there's noise, we'll hear it clear enough.'

They waited a little longer. 'I think we'll just have to try it. Which tunnel will you take?' asked Josiah.

'The right one's nearer, I'll take that one,' Michael said.

They ducked down onto a sill in front of the tunnels and entered the gloom beyond.

*

As Josiah's eyes got used to the inside of the tunnel, he found there was enough light from the entrance to see the water lapping around his feet and to make out a dry raised path to his right. He clambered up and moved forward. The tunnel roof was low, and he rapidly found that the best way of keeping his bearings was to run his hand along the tunnel wall.

There were places where the water came in from drainage pipes. The further he got in the less light came from the entrance. At length, the tunnel turned gently to the right and he lost any light from the outside.

He stopped to allow his eyes to adjust. He could still see a pattern of reflections from ripples in the water, but they would fade as he progressed. The air was cold and still. Water dripped from the roof and he shivered. Then out of the darkness came a woman's scream. It reverberated back and forth, fading away as a dull roar; but it was unmistakable.

As quiet returned he could hear mumbling, then there was another terrible scream which seemed to completely envelop him. He must go forward. His right hand lost the wall. He was on the very edge of the path and had nearly pitched forward headlong, heaven knew where.

Another drainage pipe. But the gap was bigger, and he could hear much more water flowing into the tunnel than could be accommodated by any pipe. He stooped and felt the edge with his hands. Then he lowered himself down into the water, hoping it was not too deep. The water came up to his knees. A strong flow pulled at his legs. He went on downstream. Surely water had to flow towards the river, where the mills with wheels to be driven would be most likely to be sited.

The cold was eating at his nerve along with fear of the dark and a growing sense of claustrophobia. He hoped there would be a way out at the end of this tunnel, but that was more a matter of faith than reason.

He pushed on, the water level rising to his armpits; the cold was making it hard to breathe so that he had to stop and force himself to inhale and then exhale deeply. At one point his hair brushed against the ceiling of the tunnel; there was only a foot of headroom left. Then there was an unexpected relief as the tunnel turned sharp right and he saw a light. It flickered, a flame of some sort, accompanied by the low voices he had heard earlier, now discernible as speech.

'Why are you doing this!' It was Dianne's voice. She was clearly in pain.

'Because I can,' said a second voice.

There was a sharp slap, not of a hand on flesh, more like a blow with an object, a whip perhaps. It was followed by another scream.

Josiah tried to hurry on but he couldn't move any faster. Slow and steady, he thought, slow and steady.

In a few more steps he realised that the light was coming from a roughly semi-circular outline of something on his side of the tunnel. There were pinpoints of light in that grey shape and the sound of a large cascade of water.

The grasp of the water on his body was stronger. To his left there was another sound, a water wheel idly turning over, disengaged from any drive to a mill; beyond that wheel would be a cascade into the Mersey. The grey outline to his right was higher than the main tunnel. Was it a maintenance platform of some sort? Would it have steps down to the water?

'You know at other times and in other places, you and I could easily have been comrades.' The voice was deep. It carried a lisp.

'Strange sort of comrades when you're going to kill me when you've had your pleasure!'

'You are of course right, but I do not kill without orders. I have been ordered to kill you today, but I could have killed you the night of the meeting at the Hall of Science; instead, I spared you.'

Josiah moved towards the lights and the voices. Then his hands, which he'd been holding in front of him touched brick, a set of brick steps leading upwards.

He still could not see the flame, except that there was a flickering glow illuminating a brick-lined arch. Below this was a wooden platform, the end of which was over the main tunnel. The light must be coming from a couple of oil lamps or something similar, and the platform must be something to do with maintaining the waterwheel.

The brick steps emerged from the water and led up towards the platform. He hauled himself out of the water, his legs cold and cramped. Before going any further, he would have to get the life back into them so they could carry his weight. But now, from where he sat, the conversation between Dianne and her captor was quite clear.

'So, was Feargus O'Connor your target?'

'No that was a whim on my part. I couldn't resist it. The main target was your father, I was ordered to kill him.' There was no humanity in the voice, no empathy.

'You are a champion of the poor; you seek to improve their lot in life. You take risks and lead them. You are an honest revolutionary in your heart as I am myself.' There was another of those dreadful slaps and another scream from Dianne. Josiah gritted his teeth, but he must wait until some strength returned to his legs.

The Sneaker was speaking again. 'I escaped death. I took to the life of a circus performer, found a lover here and joined a troupe of players in this country. An acrobat can work anywhere, and I am a very good acrobat, almost as good as I am a shot with a rifle.'

'You were the acrobat at the Promenade of Wonders, weren't you!' Dianne was near hysteria.

'Yes, I did perform at a penny gaff in these parts. The strongman was my lover, but since he has not found us, I presume he is dead. So, I will take your life in revenge as well as in obedience. Are you ready to die?'

Now was the time, whether Josiah's legs were willing or not. He got to his feet and tottered up the steps to the platform.

What he saw was like a scene out of a medieval painting of hell. Halfway down the platform, Dianne was tied by her wrists to a hook in the ceiling. She was facing towards Josiah. The Sneaker was behind her and had in one had a small cat-of-nine-tails and in the other a long-bladed knife ready to cut Dianne's throat.

CHAPTER 59

Reckoning

For the first time, Josiah saw the Sneaker clearly and completely. The figure looking at him with such baleful intent was naked to the waist. Until that moment he had never imagined that the Sneaker was anything other than male. But the figure before him had small breasts, though somehow, they did not carry the conviction of femininity. Much more striking was the pure white hair, cut very short, suggesting that the Sneaker could use a wig as well as female or male dress to give any chosen impression. The colour of the hair mirrored the whiteness of the skin. The features were somewhat pinched, and the body short, but not out of proportion it was rather graceful as if carved by a classical Grecian sculptor. She was also familiar; this was the acrobat at the penny gaff.

As he looked and marvelled, he realised that the features with the greatest impact were her eyes. They were intensely coloured, colours pure enough to be visible in the uncertain light from the oil lamps. What was unusual was that the eye on the left of the face was pure blue, whereas the eye on the right was pure yellow. The cap that the Sneaker had worn at the Hall of Science was not simply to shade her features, but to disguise the striking skin colour and those mesmeric eyes. Josiah gasped.

The Sneaker moved towards him, stepping between him and Dianne. 'You. I was about to take my revenge on this poor substitute, but here you appear, so I have my opportunity for true revenge.'

'Then why not take that revenge on me but let Miss Burrell go. The cause your loyalty was purchased for is over. Your master was Sir Grancester Smythe. He hid from you using the cyphers made with the coding machine. I found that machine in the river near where the water in this race drains. I placed false messages for you to find so that his intent could be foiled. But all that is over. Sir Grancester is in disgrace, the messages you are acting on now was his last. He is using you now as a private weapon of petty, personal revenge because I have thwarted him. Leave her safe, take me if you can and if you dare.'

As Josiah had been speaking the warmth on the platform had started to make him feel better physically. Life was returning to his legs and he might be able to get a few blows in on the Sneaker if he could grapple closely.

The Sneaker spoke calmly. 'I took you for a fool at The Hall of Science, a meddler, nothing more. I was wrong. You have principle and are brave, but I do not think that will save you, and then I will be able to act as my whim takes me. You see, I started with principles, but after what I saw on the field at Waterloo, how war destroyed my grand-père, honourable and brave as he was. I have no honour, I have no ideals, only the desire to make the world I touch as empty as my own heart.'

'How can you live without ideals?'

'More easily than with. There are no decisions, changing mood means nothing. No dealing with right and wrong. Before

I killed for ideals. Now, I have none. Is my lover dead?'

Josiah paused but there was only truth, 'Yes. He was run down by a train in the Crewe marshalling yards.'

The Sneaker's face relaxed. Then came a smile, but Josiah saw the preceding flash of sadness. His adversary was not entirely without feeling.

'You loved him?'

'That can mean nothing to you.'

'I love the woman you will kill,' Josiah glanced at Dianne. She was not struggling but concentrated on his face. 'Love is something no one can hide from. It opens the most closed parts of us. No matter how we try to avoid it or shield ourselves from it, we are changed.'

The Sneaker looked passive and unmoved. He smiled softly. For a fraction of a second Josiah thought his opponent would give in. Then her expression hardened, 'It is too late for me to hope, too late for more love.'

She came at Josiah with her knife at the ready. Josiah had nowhere to go. Backing up would gain him some time but that was all, he would not be able to get down brick steps backwards and if he tried; the Sneaker would simply turn and kill Dianne. Josiah stood his ground, hoping for an opportunity to grapple the Sneaker closely.

Two strides forward with the knife raised. Josiah remembered how the Sneaker had struck down on Constable Tyler in Castlefield before she had made her escape across the canal wharf. Josiah waited, and as the knife got to its apogee, stepped forward and enclosed the Sneaker with both his arms, lifting her clear of the floor. He expected to be stabbed in the back or worse, the neck, but the Sneaker was taken by surprise. Twisting and turning, she tried to find purchase, either to break Josiah's grip or to finish the blow with the knife. All she succeeded in doing was to lose her grip on the knife, which dropped to the floor.

Now it was a case of grappling and clawing: Josiah's superior weight and strength against the Sneaker's agility and suppleness. In the back of Josiah's mind was the question as to how long he might keep his superiority, in short, how much had cold water and darkness taken out of him.

The Sneaker's hand struck at Josiah's eyes. He dropped his head and hid as well as could from a storm of sharp swift blows. Then fingers were pushed in gaps between muscle and bone to find painful nerves.

At last, the Sneaker threw her body weight to the right and then left, a manoeuvre that succeeded. Josiah's grip began to slacken, the Sneaker broke free. They scrabbled towards the knife. The Sneaker had a hand on it, but Josiah kicked it passed Dianne's feet, but not far enough to put it into the stream. This time Sneaker had the edge. Cat-like, the knife was collected, and the Sneaker assumed an organised defensive posture.

This time the Sneaker was prepared but Josiah was exhausted. There was nothing he had that could or would protect him. Michael and he had taken a pepper-pot pistol each, primed and charged, but no pistol could withstand the soaking the one in his pocket had received. Pulling at and pointing it at the Sneaker would be a useless gesture, but he did it, nonetheless.

The Sneaker laughed in his face. 'Fool, a pistol will be of no use, it is wet beyond even your hope.'

Josiah pulled the trigger. The barrel revolved into position, the hammer came down on the percussion cap and the pistol's explosion reverberated around the arched roof above the platform. Blood streamed down the Sneaker's shoulder, but the astonishment on her face was more encouraging. 'Please give yourself up. I do not wish to kill you.'

In reply, the Sneaker uttered a stream of abusive French. Josiah waited until she moved forward then pulled and held the trigger in, emptying as many barrels that would fire at his adversary. When the ringing in his ears and the smoke had cleared the body of the Sneaker was nowhere to be seen; she had fallen into the weir and was gone.

Josiah fell to his knees and put his head in his hands. He had never killed another human being. Gradually, he pulled himself together, found another knife in the clutter on the floor, and cut Dianne down.

Not surprisingly, she was in a dead faint. He searched around the platform. Near the back wall, there was a pile of bedding. He looked for a blanket to warm her. Underneath the bedding, there was a box about the size of the encryption device. He opened it. In the bottom of the empty box were a few letters that fitted into the inner ring. The encryption device had been here.

He went back to Dianne. Blood was flowing down her arms from the whiplashes to her back. But she was becoming conscious. She clung to him.

CHAPTER 60

The leaving of Liverpool

The Liverpool docks on the edge of the Mersey were a forest of masts. Ships loading or waiting to do so were moored hugger-mugger, with smaller vessels lashed to each other or at anchor a little way off the quays near the fairway. It was said that you could walk the length of the dock without coming ashore at all.

Now the evening high tide beckoned and the urgency of getting everything necessary onboard for a multitude of voyages was obvious in the pulling, pushing and dragging of goods onto the ships, and in the swinging of loaded nets over the sides to be stowed away in dozens of holds.

Josiah picked his way through the confusion, looking for the *Boothbay*, an emigrant ship bound for Boston, on which Dianne and Phillip Burrell were to take passage. All he had to guide him was a note that said Landing J, Eastfront Lane, which hardly sounded nautical.

Josiah smiled—he was still getting used to being back in his Stockport uniform, but at least this time it attracted help, for which he was grateful. 'I'm looking for the *Boothbay*, somewhere on Eastfront Lane.'

The officer laughed. 'The road that runs behind all these warehouses is Eastfront Lane, but you're not far off. At least you were going in the right direction.'

He pointed further down the dock. 'See those three East Indiamen down there? The big ships with the fancy paintwork? The *Boothbay's* about four cables this side of them.'

Josiah thanked the officer and walked on. Even while at sea he'd never got the hang of nautical measurement and a 'cable' escaped him. At least if he got to the Indiaman he'd know he'd missed the *Boothbay* and could backtrack, but when he got close to the ship, he had no difficulty recognising it.

All around people swarmed. As well as luggage, everyone had some sort of object or victuals essential for their journey, from cabbages and loaves to butter and cheese. There were also many new tin cans, each of the right size and shape to collect a day's ration of water while onboard. They were so bright Josiah guessed that the water drunk from them was likely to taste of tin for at least the first few days.

In this cacophony, the Burrells stood appearing stoical. He went up and embraced them both. As he held Dianne there was the familiar scent of water of violets, which he had first smelt over the ledgers at Leavington's eighteen months before.

'It was good of you to come, Josiah,' said Phillip. 'Hepzi was not fit enough.'

'We said goodbye to them all a couple of days ago,' added Dianne.

A man came up. 'Mr Burrell? Could you come and see where we've put your bags and pick out somewhere to stow your victuals?'

'I better go and see,' said Phillip. 'I'll come straight back.'

It has always been something that struck Josiah, that even in the busiest of crowds there were occasions when you could feel alone with another person as if there was no hubbub around you.

'Are your wounds healed?'

'Yes, they healed well.' It was as awkward as if they were strangers. Then Dianne placed one hand on his chest and ran her fingers across two of his bright buttons.

'The dreams were worse,' she paused, 'I would that things were different.'

Josiah longed to respond but knew he must not. He felt her hand on his tunic again but took a firm hold of a fold of cloth.

'Josiah, I want to ask you something? Will you marry me?'

He swallowed hard. There was nothing to say. All he could do was fall back on the familiar excuse.

'Dianne, Sir Grancester is still free to act against you and your father. With the Sneaker and her partner dead, he has no accomplices to hand, but I believe he will try to harm you so long as you and your father are within reach. You will be safe in America.'

Her eyes pleaded. 'You can protect me! You have done it before! We have shared so much!' Her other hand had joined the first. She started to gently shake him. He took her by those hands to calm her.

'I cannot protect you. We would have to move somewhere we were not known. The trial has made you and your father conspicuous everywhere in the manufacturing regions. Sir Grancester would find us and revenge himself for Wymes, for his disgrace, or in pure hatred.'

He heard Phillip's voice — he was talking to someone on the deck of the ship. The moment was about to be broken.

'Yes — if things were different,' he said, knowing he had already chosen between her wellbeing and the security of her father, rather than his inclination. 'We cannot marry Dianne; you must leave, and I have to stay. That is the truth.'

Phillip was back and the moment was passed.

'Dianne, they want you to look at where I've said the victuals should go. They apparently don't trust a man of my reputation.'

She looked at Josiah, drew him to her, kissed him passionately full on the mouth. As she pulled away she looked at him hard. He had not responded. Their relationship was at an end. She turned and was gone.

They both watched her go up the gangplank. 'I gather you must have turned her down?' said Phillip after a long pause. 'I wondered if you would. Many men would have taken her, but if you do not love her then you have done the right thing. You are a very upright young man and I admire you for it.'

Josiah felt a great pressure rising within him, anger mixed with excruciating regret.

'You are wrong Phillip. I do love her, and I would have taken any risk to be with her. I could keep the secret of my love from her, but I would never have been able to keep your secret about Fred's death. Why did you kill him?'

Phillip's face was passive, reflecting no reaction, but there was another long pause before he answered.

'How could you think that? I didn't kill him.'

'I think you did Phillip; I think I know how and why.'

'Well, why don't you enlighten me?' His voice carried the hint of a sneer, or was it fear?

'Very well, I will lay out my case. At first, when I helped take Fred's body from the Mersey, I wasn't sure he had been murdered, even though there was a wound to the back of his head.'

'It might well be something he got after he fell in the water.'

'Exactly, no real proof. The only thing that seemed odd to me was where he was found. Why was he there? After all, there was no reason that he should be in Stockport after dark, especially in a particularly bad storm; at least as far as I could see.'

'So, what? Fred didn't go often to Stockport, but he did on occasion.'

'I argued the same to myself, but I couldn't get it out of my mind. Then soon after, on my way back home, someone put a bag over my head, dragged me into a lock-up and more than half-throttled me while talking about a silver watch. That was no accidental ruffian, and as soon as I was up and about, I went to see if my attacker might have seen me help recover Fred's body.

'I went to find Charlie McGuiness, the knocker-up in those parts for the mills, who had seen Fred's body in the river. He put me on to Billy Scraff, the scavenger, and it turned out he had found the silver watch in the Mersey. Well, it looked like a silver watch, but wasn't one.'

'Come again. I don't see what this's got to do with me.'

'You might if I tell you the man who scragged me was the man who died in the sidings at Crewe, the one who was chasing you. It was his lover who abducted Dianne. All you need to know is that you and Dianne were the target of a murderous conspiracy to cause violence and insurrection by inciting Chartist violence. It was led by Colonel Wymes and Sir Grancester Smythe.'

'The Wymes who committed suicide? You became a tipstaff to protect us?'

Josiah nodded.

'Specifically, Dianne, but here and now I am concerned about you and Fred Sowerby. I don't know for sure, but I think at some point you thought you were being followed and you asked Fred to guard your back. You were right; from time to time they probably were following you.

'One night when Fred was helping you, he saw the Sneaker and tracked him. You probably got wind of it and decided, on the off chance, to follow Fred. The scent took both of you to the tunnel races at Portwood. The Sneaker went in, Fred followed, and you followed Fred. Am I right?'

Phillip didn't reply.

'You and Fred were much savvier than I was about how to navigate the tunnel system, so you didn't need to go swimming. But in that maze of tunnels, I think Fred lost the Sneaker but found the platform above the water near to the outfall from the tunnel. They must have been using it as their headquarters even then. He also found the silver watch and pocketed it, realising it was both something unusual and possibly important. But he left the box behind, inside which were some of the letters needed to set it up. You caught him unawares, hit him or pushed him, and into the water he went.'

'You've no evidence that I knew anything about where they found you and Dianne.'

'I have what you said at Crewe, and I have a witness in Michael O'Carroll. You were so quick to tell me about the tunnels. You had seen the Sneaker before, and you were so desperate to protect Dianne you had no choice but to be clear.'

'You said you thought you knew why I did it?'

'There's the irony. The loss of the watch unravelled a political plot of national importance which cost innocent lives. But at its heart was a simple crime of passion. When I went to see Hepzibah, Caddy suggested I read her favourite poem. I read and Hepzi she fell asleep. I thought it a strange poem to be her favourite. I thought it pointed to passion in her marriage to Fred. But then I began to see it differently. It was her favourite poem because it evoked her first passion.'

'Yes, but once she met Fred, he was the love of her life,' said Phillip.

'Yet first loves are always the most heartfelt,' said Josiah.

'You're right there, lad.'

'And Fred wasn't her first love. You were Phillip, and that love was consummated, steady and sure until she met Fred and your ambition to be a leader of working men overtook your love for her. I saw that affection between you and Hepzi when she dried you off, after the turn-out meeting. Her bond to you was a memory, but your bond to her still lived. That, combined with the solitary nature of your work for the causes you espouse, meant that you were desperately lonely.'

'Have you never loved and lost?'

'Yes, I have. But Fred saw you with her and he knew what the looks and smiles meant. Did he confront you when you caught up with you in the tunnels? Did you kill Fred in the hope that Hepzi would turn to you and heal your loneliness?'

Phillip was silent. Josiah could hear the sounds of the docks, the creak of the ropes holding the furled sails, the chatter of the other emigrants, even the screaming of the gulls as they wheeled between the quay and the decks of the ships, squabbling and fighting over scraps.

'You are near enough right Josiah. He was there looking at the water in the race. There was a lantern-lit and I could see him clearly. I was jealous and, in that spasm, I pushed him in. God forgive me; I regretted it as soon as I had done it, but by the time I looked over the edge and called after him he had already gone.' He paused. 'Will you turn me in?'

Josiah paused, 'No. Unless you were to confess, there is not enough evidence.'

'Then you could still marry Dianne; I will go alone. Call her back Josiah, make her happy.'

Josiah thought of how seconds were making minutes and those minutes would take away the woman he loved. 'It would not work. I might keep your secret when you are gone, but she would sense it and wheedle it out of me and then our marriage would be over. She must go with you. In any case, there's a third person involved.'

Phillip frowned. 'Who?'

'Caddy.'

'Hepzibah's daughter?' He sounded incredulous.

'Hepzibah and Fred's very intelligent daughter. She is now the cornerstone of that household, despite her youth. Either Hepzibah will say something because I think she senses what you have done, or Caddy will work it out for herself. When that happens, I think she will come after you for revenge. Better that you and Caddy are separated by an ocean. Better I let Dianne go.'

Whistles were being blown from the deck of the *Boothbay*. Men came up from the boat and started to usher passengers onto the gangplanks. 'Go now Phillip, I give you your freedom. Let time heal Dianne's heart of my love without her realising anything of what you have done. Never return.'

There was nothing left to say. Phillip turned and went aboard. The wind was offshore and once the passengers were

346

aboard the gangplanks were shipped and a small amount of sail unfurled.

With the aid of a couple of rowing boats, the prow of the *Boothbay* turned towards the fairway, and as the wind caught the sail she started to make way. Phillip and Dianne waved from the deck. As the ship moved out, more sail was hoisted. Soon Josiah could see no individuals, not even high on the masts.

That was the end. The quickest way home was by rail. He walked towards the centre of the city with as much determination as he could muster. His path led him past one of the Indiamen. There was a large squad of soldiers lined up on the quay, ready to board. Their uniforms were like the normal British redcoats, but their trousers were light blue: soldiers of the East India Company's private army.

'Slope-*arms*,' shouted their Lieutenant as Josiah passed. The men put their weapons on their shoulders. One was shorter than the rest. He didn't carry a musket but a rifle; a musket would probably have been too long for him. The soldier caught Josiah's eye and winked. His right eye was pure blue, the left pure yellow.

'Right-*turn*,' was the next order, and the squad turned as a man. 'Prepare for boarding. Orderly now and patient. There's room for all.'

They moved off. The small soldier's movements were familiar to Josiah.

He glanced up at the poop deck of the Indiaman. Leaning on the rail was Sir Grancester Smythe. He was being exiled but his assassin was alive, still loyal to him and was going with him to an exotic country on the other side of the world.

ACKNOWLEDGEMENTS

I have many people to thank for their help in writing *Circles of Deceit*.

Firstly, my thanks go to Eve Seymour for helping me as my structural editor, for hammering into me the idea that just because this is a Victorian murder mystery, it still needs the pace of a present-day thriller.

To my friends who formed my beta-readers panel: Barbara and John Balaam, Wendy Foulger, John Owens, Maggie Willetts and Stephen Williams.

James Stanley for his construction of a working Wheatstone Cryptograph using computer 3D printing. This allowed the resolution of some of the ambiguities in how such a machine worked. He and I may well have the only two fully working cryptographs in existence at this moment.

To Gary Dalkin for copyediting the final draft, who also pointed out the need to resolve some important plotting issues.

Historical notes

The geographical arena of the book is the whole of the northwest of England. Its context is the course of the national General Strike of 1842 and its conclusion in 1843.

The "Jubilee" Primitive Methodist Chapel is just off the road from Marple to Romiley and is as described. Some Methodist chapels housed Chartist branches at the time and it's most likely that individual chapel members would have been politically active, though the general principle of the Methodism of the day was that they did not condone direct political action as an organisation.

The Hall of Science existed much as described. In 1842 it was the largest meeting hall in Manchester. The account of the fighting in the book between the Chartists and Anti-Corn Law League members on the 7th March, follows much of the account in the Chartist newspaper The Northern Star published a few days later. There was no assassination attempt on Feargus O'Connor, the speaker on that evening.

The second Chartist National Petition was presented to Parliament on 2nd May 1842, the main text of which was written by Feargus O'Connor. It was signed by 3,315,752 people from all over the UK, though the majority of signatures came from Lancashire and Yorkshire. The full terms of the petition can be found in Hansard, Vol. 62 (1842) columns 1373-1381, though the contents of the petition were not debated by Parliament. The details follow several contemporary sources of the event.

The description of the "Penny Gaff" visited by Josiah and Dianne is an elaboration by me on the source referenced by Anthony Horowitz in *The House of Silk*, Little and Brown Company, 2011.

The assault on Quarry Bank Mill follows an account from the mill archives, for access to which I must thank Quarry Bank's National Trust staff.

The pillaging of the bread from the Stockport Union Workhouse took place and is commemorated in a well-known engraving from the Illustrated London News as well as in contemporary reports in Stockport and Manchester newspapers.

The Stockport Riot never took place. The law that governed strikes resulted in the strikers having to collect contributions of food or money from other potential turnouts in other factories or industries. This led to an ebb and flow of turnouts entering and then leaving a given town or area for several days until some sort of event came to a head. This process is not reflected in *Circles of Deceit* since a modern reader would not put up with it. The violence referred to in the description of the Stockport Riot is consistent with the riot at Preston and some other places.

The assassin, called the Sneaker in the book, uses a rifle from the top of St Mary's Church to kill Mr Prestbury with a single shot. The bullets the Sneaker uses are of a type that expanded in the barrel of the rifle, engaging with the helical tracks in the barrel before exiting at the muzzle. This type of bullet revolved faster, was more stable in flight and so had greater accuracy and range than a spherical ball fired from the same gun. They could also be reloaded more quickly. They were used in the American Civil War and by the French in the Crimean War. However,

Henri-Gustave Delvigne was producing similar bullets as early as the mid-1830s and assisted Minié in making the versions used in both wars.

The circle of deceit itself, called in the book the "silver watch", is modelled on the Wheatstone Cryptograph presented at the Paris Exhibition of 1867. But there was a prior invention of the machine with very similar principles, by Decius Wadsworth in 1817. There was a great deal of invention and reinvention of cryptographs of this sort in the period, some of which, including the Wheatstone Cryptograph, were pre-cursors of the German "Enigma" machine.

Believe it or not, there was a "Committee of Public Safety" in Marple Bridge reported in a single line in a contemporary edition of the Stockport Times. What it did or what it was is unknown, but I just could not resist applying a little revolutionary imagination.

Much of the argument used at the *nisi prius* court at Lancaster follows the verbatim account in the Northern Star made after the trial. The defence offered by Philip Burrell follows the way Richard Pilling, a chartist from Ashton-under-Lyne, defended himself. The summation presented in the book closely follows that of the judge, Justice Baron Rolf.

The underground water races for the mills on the Portwood in Stockport existed at the time and were shown on several maps. Some of the tunnels may still exist and there is a bricked up tunnel mouth in a place above the Mersey that could be part of the old system.

Go to https://www.paulcwbeattyauthor.co.uk/ for more information and Notes for Reading Groups.